Magician First Class

Kate Healey

For Erin, Rebecca, and Mads, who made Thirteenth Avenue
real.

Content note

This novel is an urban fantasy, which means it contains a grab bag of occult, folklore, and magical elements, and may present them in ways the reader does not care for. It also contains physical violence, attempted murder, vandalism, theft, day drinking, vigilantism, public making out, unsubtle parallels to contemporary politics, and unsanctioned expansion of the New York City subway system. Caveat emptor!

Contents

Chapter One

It was the fourteenth of May when I first stepped into the Thirteenth Avenue Community Recreation Center. I was less worried about the date—sixty years since the Cataclysm had brought magic roaring back to the world—and much more worried that I was missing my graduation ceremony so that I could go to an interview for a job I didn't think I was going to get.

As a newly-minted History graduate with a specialization in post-Cataclysm urban America, I had naturally *noticed* the date. I just hadn't paid it much mind.

Later, I wondered if that might have been my first mistake.

It was a gorgeous spring morning, with the kind of warm breeze that softens the air and breathes gently over your skin. I left my dorm, walked through Riverside Park to the top of Thirteenth Avenue, and walked south towards 97th Street. I should have been mentally revising interview questions, but instead I was leaning into some heavy self-pity that I couldn't walk across the stage and throw my cap into the air with the rest of my graduating class.

It would have been really nice. But getting a job wasn't just nice. Unless I wanted to move back in with my mom in the suburbs, it was an absolute necessity.

Unfortunately, we were in a recession. Half of my class had taken one look at the job market and gone straight to grad school applications. I'd sent out my resume to museums and cultural centers, applied for positions at public and private library archives, and trawled through the website of what felt like every non-profit organization in the five boroughs, looking for leads. I wanted to work on Museum Mile, but I wasn't foolish enough to think I'd get into one of those august institutions right away. But I'd been an excellent student, I had sterling references, and I'd expected *some* interest from *somewhere*.

In two months of searching, the Thirteenth Avenue rec center had been the only place to even offer me an interview. I wouldn't say I was desperate, because my mother didn't raise women who gave in to despair, but yesterday I'd spent my last thirty bucks on a manicure to fix my stress-chewed nails.

I made way for a werewolf walking his goldendoodle, then sped past a walking bus of mostly-human kids, who were too cute not to smile at. A little imp girl smiled back at me, flashing a half-grown fang in her gap-toothed grin.

I caught a glimpse of myself in the window of the store behind her, and stepped out of the pedestrian flow to do a quick self-assessment. Nails, looking good. Dark red hair, mostly behaving. Pale skin, mostly blemish-free. Make-up, subtle and professional. Clothes, likewise. The black slacks, white button-up and dark grey blazer weren't exactly my favorite outfit, but the message I was trying to portray was "punctual, reliable, learns quickly, and a good fit for your office culture" not "super fun at the club."

I focused hard on my reflection and cast a quick look-see spell to see if my back looked as acceptable as my front.

At least, I tried. I pronounced the words correctly, and the gesture was just a quick flick of the fingers. The problem came when I reached inside myself, seeking my other-else, the tiny spark that made me what I was, and threw it at the glass. My other-else was eager to please, but anxious. It threw itself at the spell and ran out of juice two-thirds of the way through.

My mirror self should have obediently turned around so that I could see my butt. Instead, she rolled her eyes at me.

"Okay, fine," I muttered, and walked away.

The problem was, I was still glaring at my reflection, and I walked straight into the chest of a man who'd stopped to watch me.

It was an impressive chest, wrapped in a tight black T-shirt, and I bounced right off. He grabbed my hand to steady me as I stumbled, and I got the ping of not-human. This time my other-else worked fine. I'm a crappy magician, but the one thing I can reliably do is identify when someone isn't baseline human, and usually what flavor of not-baseline they are.

This guy was pinging *demon*. Not full demon, and not very strong, but a parent or grandparent definitely wasn't human.

"Sorry," he said, looking abashed.

"No, I should watch where I'm going." I pulled a bit at the grip he had on my hand and he let go at once. He had thick, dark hair, long enough to brush the nape of his neck and flop into his eyes, tan skin, and deep brown eyes.

And muscles. I mean, not that I was looking, but his biceps were swelling from the cuffs of his T-shirt, and I bet that if he'd lifted the hem I would have seen a perfectly defined six-pack.

"I'm Anton," he offered. His smile was kind of shy, which is not something you see every day on a half-demon.

"Well, sorry again," I said, and ignored the opening to give him my own name. Not just because I had to get to my job interview, but because exchanging names with a demon can be seen as a contractual exchange, and that gives them a hold on you. Not a big deal, just a little hold, but demons are famous for turning a little into a lot.

I gave him an acknowledging nod instead, and kept walking. I could feel his attention on my back—which I was now *really* hoping looked okay—and after a second I heard his footsteps. Okay, so we were traveling in the same direction. A perfectly normal thing for someone to do. Half the people on this sidewalk were doing that.

My hand was tingling where he'd held it. And he'd let it go the second I tugged. *You need a job*, I reminded myself, and tried not to think about how long it had been since I'd had a date.

I walked past an empty lot that was fenced off with plastic sheeting behind high wire fences, signs on the fence reading "AUTHORIZED PERSONS ONLY", "SIGN IN WITH SAFETY OFFICER", and "NEW PARK OPENING FEBRUARY!!" The last one made me blink, but with construction in this city, who knew if they were three months late, or planning for next year? Either way, there was a lot of shouting and machinery noise from the hidden lot.

I hadn't looked behind me, and I couldn't hear any footsteps over the engines' grind, but my other-else had decided to pay attention to Anton. I noticed when he hesitated, pausing outside the wire fences, and when he sped his steps to catch up with me.

Too bad, because that was 97th Street coming up, and across the road was the Thirteenth Avenue Community Recreation Center. It was a largish two-story building constructed from unappealing concrete slabs, although there were some attempts to prettify the path to the front door with a couple of columns and some roses in pots.

The roses were pretty spectacular, actually. I admired the scent as I stepped up to the automatic glass doors.

Anton was right behind me. I turned around.

"I'm not stalking you," he said immediately.

"We're just going to the same place?" I said, raising my eyebrows. I wasn't scared; it was broad daylight, and there was a building full of community-minded people right through the door. But four years in the city had taught me to be alert.

"I guess so," he said, giving me a look from under the swoop of his hair. I thought he was trying for smoldering, but he still looked kind of shy. "I have a job interview."

"Oh," I said, and then took another look at his clothes. Tight black T-shirt, ripped jeans, black sneakers... "You're interviewing for the administrative assistant position?"

"Yeah," he said, looking more alarmed than I thought the question demanded. "You too?"

"Yes," I said, and took the three steps it took to get me across the boundary and under the protection of the building's wards. My other-else registered their presence, a kind of faded welcome. Anton followed me with no problem, so he probably didn't have malign intent. But either he had no idea how to dress for a job interview, or I was wildly overestimating the formality required.

The glass door opened automatically, and I stepped into a reception area with buff vinyl floors and cream walls. It was clean and welcoming, but as faded as the wards. Two chairs with worn leather upholstery were set around a battered coffee table in a little seating area. The reception desk was tall, with one of those shelves you had to peer over at the front. Down a wide corridor came the steady thump of balls on wood, and the poppy, frenetically fun kind of music that suggested a Zumba class.

The rec center was run by a non-profit organization, not the city or state, but it had the same kind of institutional vibe as a public school—people trying to do the best they could with limited resources.

The receptionist was busy on the phone, so I looked at the wall placards telling the history of the center, trying my best to ignore Anton's presence. Probably none of the information would come up in the interview, but after a bookish childhood and four years of rigorous academic training, I pretty much read anything my eyes fell on.

Besides, the history of Thirteenth Avenue was really interesting, particularly because sixty years ago, it hadn't existed at all.

No one seems to know how or why the Cataclysm began, or even if it was, as popularly believed, a response to the gradual decline of magic from our world. It's true that according to what we can piece together, magic had almost completely disappeared by the Age of Enlightenment. Certainly by the 1960s, most Americans didn't believe magic had ever existed; the gates to the Fae and Demon Realms had closed centuries ago and their inhabitants were just stories. The last credible eyewitness account of a werewolf transformation was from the late 1600s, though there are questions about the Beast of Gévaudan. There were still a few vampires lurking about, on account of the not-dying thing, but they were keeping very quiet, and there's a persistent rumor that they'd lost the ability to turn humans sometime in the Victorian era. I don't know if it's true, and it's not like an elder vampire will ever admit to a weakness, but my other-else sometimes gives me a vague impression of vampire age. It does seem as if they're all either centuries old, or they've been vampires for just a few decades.

Various immortals, including the vampires, had been working on the dying magic problem for a while. Some theorists say the magical decline and the Cataclysm after could have been something like magnetic pole reversal or supervolcano eruptions—something natural, massive, inevitable, and thankfully rare. More than one faith claims it was an act of god, or gods. One theory—and it's not supported by much, but I think it's the most plausible idea—is that some person or group of people found out what had been draining magic out of the world and reversed it. Then they either died immediately in the ensuing chaos, or have been keeping their mouths firmly shut for the last sixty years.

But whatever caused the Cataclysm, on that fourteenth of May, magic came back to the world, and it wasn't fucking around. Dragons roared through the sky, spitting fire at airplanes. Basilisks resurfaced in the Greek Isles. Stonehenge disappeared, which must have scared the hell out of the tourists who were visiting it. The Fae and Demon Realms started reconnecting to the world, immortals casually announced themselves on evening radio shows, and the vampires came out of the shadows.

Humans reacted to change, uncertainty, and perceived threat the same way they always have; with violence, fear, and civil unrest. It didn't help that a lot of calls were coming from *inside* the house, as humans all over the world suddenly realized they had supernatural abilities they'd never suspected. Magicians discovered they had another sense that eventually came to be called the other-else. The werewolf gene reactivated with the massive surge in ambient environmental magic, and a lot of people started turning furry once a month. People who might have had a fae ancestor eight or nine generations back got very glamorous overnight, pardon the pun.

The world got kind of messy, for a while. Things have calmed down a lot since the Faerie Accords were signed, but having a scar instead of an open wound doesn't mean you were never bleeding.

One of the smaller, almost insignificant changes on that first day of the Cataclysm was that a narrow piece of land humped up from the Hudson river, right beside Riverside Park, from 91st Street to 110th. In Manhattan, that much undeveloped land was a goldmine, and under the circumstances everyone was too distracted to think too hard about zoning laws or city planning. Real estate developers rushed in where angels feared to tread, and that's how we got Thirteenth Avenue, New York City's one and only entirely post-Cataclysm neighborhood.

And, I hoped, the location of my new gainful employment.

The receptionist put her phone back in the cradle—a lot of places still prefer landlines, which can be reliably warded—and looked over to me. She was a short, slender woman with dark bangs that actually looked good on her, and big green eyes that seemed to look right through me. I got an other-else pulse off her too, but the category wasn't clear. Sort of wizard, sort of not.

"Hello!" she said brightly. "Are you here for the administrative assistant interviews?"

"That's right."

"Oh, great!" she said, and flashed a dimpled smile to my left. "Hi, Anton!"

Anton grinned at her. I was probably just imagining the conspiratorial look that accompanied the smile. "How's it going, Oona?"

"Awesome! Thanks for coming in. Here, put this on." She handed him a sticker with his name on, and then turned to me, "And you must be... Charlie, right? Charlie Cross?"

"That's me," I said, and Oona handed me my own sticker with a flourish.

"Well, you're the last candidates to arrive!" she said brightly. "Let me take you upstairs." She put a sign on the desk which said "back in ten minutes" and led us through the building.

The public spaces of the center were in better repair than the staff zones. Oona took us through a staff-only door to a narrow set of chipped concrete stairs and a stainless steel railing that wobbled alarmingly when I put my hand on it. The rec center obviously saved the cleaning and repairs budget for the spaces their patrons used, which I thought was a good sign of their priorities, if not of their financial health.

Oona and Anton chatted as they went up the stairs. I was trying to fight the sinking feeling in my chest as I followed. They were obviously friendly, and that meant he was a local boy, or maybe an internal candidate. My chances of getting this job looked lower by the second.

Anton went through the door first, and held it open for Oona and myself. He might have been a ringer, but at least he had nice manners.

"Thank you," I said.

He smiled at me, and took a seat in one of the battered chairs in the little sitting area. The admin space was just a big room with four desks, and a bunch of filing cabinets and bookshelves. Towards the back were two doors—one led into a little kitchenette and the other probably led further back into the working space. Oona sat behind one of the desks.

"We're running late, sorry," she said.

I took a look at the rest of my competition as I sat down, and my heart sank right through the floor. I should have gone to my graduation ceremony.

As well as Anton, there were another three candidates for the position. Seated to my right was a girl who looked about my age, tall and blonde, with a salon-perfect blowout and the kind of spectacular charisma that often comes with a touch of fae blood. Next to her was a human woman in maybe her late thirties. She was wearing almost exactly the same thing I was: crisp white button-up, black slacks, and a light grey blazer, but hers looked like the real deal, bought sensibly on sale at Saks, and not from a clearance rack at Target. Opposite her was the only other man in the room, a guy in his late twenties with a sharp suit and the kind of haircut I associated with Columbia's business school guys.

Business bro sneered at Anton, dismissed me without even thinking about it, smiled at the blonde, and eyed the woman in her thirties with an air of competition. She was very obviously the only person he considered a serious contender.

He absolutely reeked of wizardry.

I am, technically, a magician. I have the other-else that's the official defining trait, but I have very little raw power and even less aptitude for spellcraft. My mom had encouraged me to apply for the magic academies, but I hadn't been surprised when they all turned me down. They were used to freshmen losing control and setting their lab partners on fire, but who wants a student who can't even light the flame? My only real skill was a knack for guessing what kind and how much power someone was packing, and that wasn't going to get me through Invocation A.

Business School Wizard was packing a *lot* of power—I was guessing he was Eighth Class. And I was guessing he *was* a wizard. People use the terms interchangeably, but a magician is just anyone with the other-else. A wizard is someone who has trained the use of their other-else, and actually *works* with magic, not the half-hearted stuff I do to try and check out my own butt or turn on a light without getting off the couch.

The job market was even worse than I thought, if someone with that much power was applying for low-paying admin positions. One thing was clear; I was totally out of the running. I didn't have the charisma and looks, the obvious experience, the raw power, *or* the hometown advantage. I'd been brought in to make up the numbers, or perhaps so someone else would look even better in comparison.

I wondered if I could get away with claiming a forgotten appointment and running uptown. I was too late to walk the stage, but at least I could applaud my classmates.

Anton nudged my shoulder with his. "Hey," he said under his breath. "Everything okay?"

I was going to have to move back to *New Rochelle* to live with my *mother*. I wanted to glare at him, but it wasn't his fault I was doomed.

"I'm fine," I muttered.

He tilted his head at me, then grinned, shifting his chin towards Oona. "Watch this," he murmured, and another woman walked through the wall behind her.

I jumped. It wasn't that I'd never met ghosts before—there'd been that whole incident with the journalist in the library, which I was still pretty proud of—but it was still unusual to see one holding down a day job, and this one was wearing a name badge that read "Hannah" pinned to her wide lapel.

"Hi," she said. "The director's running a few minutes late. Can I get anyone a cup of coffee or some water?" She sounded mostly like a New Yorker, but that "water" was pure Philly.

"I'd love a caramel latte, half-skim, half-whip," the spectacular blonde said promptly.

Hannah blinked behind her large wire-rimmed glasses. "We have drip or instant."

"Oh! No problem! Drip is fine."

"Drip, please," the older woman said. The wizard bro shook his head, not even bothering to conceal the curl of his lip at the thought.

Hannah turned to me. "And you?" she asked. "Charlie, isn't it? Can I get you something?"

"Um," I said, startled by her interest. "Just water, please."

"You got it!" She headed through the kitchenette door at the back, this time obeying the laws of physics. A moment later, a little white dog with tight curls trotted out and curled up under her desk.

"Oh my gosh!" the blonde cooed. "Who's this little guy?"

"That's Mr. Scruffles, Hannah's dog," Oona said. "He's the cutest, right?"

"*So* cute!"

Oona sat beside the blonde and beamed at her. "Just as well, because he pees *everywhere*," she said. "Totally *ruined* my new pair of Jimmy Choos."

Mr. Scruffles whuffled indignantly.

The blonde's forehead creased, just a little. "Oh... really?"

"Honestly, though, that's nothing, compared to all the body fluids you have to deal with here." Oona gave a tinkling little laugh. "Oh my gosh, the last time we ran a Credentials for Creatures drop-in session, someone forgot to label the juice boxes. One poor vampire drank cranberry juice by mistake, and the next minute she was power-vomiting *everywhere*."

What the hell was she doing? The professional-looking woman was eyeing Oona with an air that suggested she wouldn't be allowing such gossip in her office once she was in charge, and the wizard was looking bored. I snuck a look at Anton, and saw that his eyes were narrowed with amusement.

"Does that happen often?" the blonde asked.

"It's always *something*, you know? Werewolf kids who haven't mastered the urge to mark their territory, people insisting that they should be able to house their mounts in the bike lock-up—do you have any *idea* how bad pegasus poop smells?"

The blonde's tan skin was getting a greenish tinge. "Um..."

"And then there are the *hours*," Oona said. "We're technically open 10am to 8pm, with a nine-hour working day, but if we're catering to the nocturnal crowd we get called in for later, and if we're working on crepuscular time that's a split shift, working pre-dawn *and* evenings." She sighed, just a little too theatrically. "It's the *worst* for your social life."

"But you like working here?" the blonde asked.

"Yes," Oona said, and then wrinkled her nose. "I mean, obviously, if I didn't have to work here, I wouldn't. Like, you're so pretty, you obviously don't need to. You could totally be a model."

She was laying it on pretty thick, but the blonde perked up.

"Do you really think so?"

"Yes!"

"I thought about it," the blonde confided shyly. "But my dad thought it would be good for me to get, like, an office job, just to try it out?" She gave Oona an anxious look. "I didn't know about the, like, *fluids*."

The professional woman had caught on by that stage, and she was giving Oona a level stare. Anton was shaking silently beside me, trying to suppress his laughter. I wasn't nearly as amused. Why was Oona trying to push this poor girl away from the job? Was she trying to make room for Anton, or did she not want to work with another beautiful woman, or what?

I was trying to decide if I should say something, and if so, what that could possibly be, when Hannah came back with the coffees and deliberately spilled them all over the wizard.

I was distracted by Oona's psychological warfare, but I was looking right at Hannah when she did it, so there was no chance that it was a mistake. One moment, she was perfectly tangible, a mug held steadily in each hand. Then she passed by the wizard, her hands shifting to hover over him, and stuttered momentarily out of existence.

The mugs spun and dropped, and the wizard jumped up with a disgusted noise as he got doused from neck to knees.

I was on my feet in an instant—a girl in my dorm had gotten seriously scalded from hot coffee in sophomore year.

"Are you burnt?" I said, my hands going for his shirt. I touched cool, wet fabric, and then he recoiled.

"I'm fine!" he snapped, and Hannah rematerialized, looking believably distraught.

"I'm so sorry!" she said, wringing her hands.

"You should be," he said, glaring at her. "This shirt is *ruined*."

But he wasn't hurt. His hands had been hit directly, but when he wiped them dry with the box of Kleenex Hannah meekly held out for him, they weren't even pink.

"Would you like me to reschedule?" Oona asked, her enormous eyes wide and innocent as she went back to her desk.

The wizard scowled at her, then grudgingly admitted he would be free on Wednesday afternoon. At which point, of course, he'd only be getting the job if the previous candidates had failed to impress.

He didn't seem too worried about that, though he left muttering about the cost of dry-cleaning.

"Guess they didn't teach him any clean-up spells," Anton said in my ear.

I snorted before I could stop myself—laundry spells should have been easy for an Eighth Class, but I somehow wasn't surprised this guy hadn't bothered to learn them. Then I caught

Hannah bending to pat Mr. Scruffles under her desk, the corner of her mouth quirking in satisfaction.

I supposed it was reassuring that she'd only soaked the guy instead of scalding him, but the fact that she'd had cold coffee ready to go argued for a psychotic level of forethought. Meanwhile, Oona sat down with the blonde again, telling her a story about a werewolf pack that counted the rec center as part of their territory. I wasn't surprised when the gorgeous woman left a few minutes later, citing a vague "appointment I have to get to."

"And then there were three," Anton said, nearly under his breath. He sounded satisfied, and I was annoyed that I'd ever thought he was even a little bit hot. He hadn't done anything to the other candidates himself, but why would he need to? He had two henchwomen pulling the strings for him.

I locked eyes with the woman sitting across from me, and saw the same grim realization in her eyes.

She stood up. "I'm afraid I can't wait any longer," she said crisply.

Oona and Hannah exchanged glances. "Would you like me to arrange another interview?" Oona asked.

"No," the woman said flatly. "I don't think I'm a good fit for this workplace culture. I prefer an open and honest environment."

Damn. Oona winced as the woman swept out, and Hannah looked at her uncertainly.

"I need to get back to reception," Oona said, making some sort of gesture at Hannah I couldn't interpret. "Um, Charlie, it won't be long now..."

I gave her my best death glare, trying to come up with an equally good line to make my own grand exit. Out of the corner of my eye, I caught Anton frowning at her, and then his gaze rested on me.

"Listen," he began, his tone oddly earnest, and then an older woman walked into the office and I stopped paying him any attention at all.

She didn't look that impressive. Short, stocky, late sixties, blonde hair fading to white and styled in a tight perm. She wore a navy skirt, sensible, low-heeled shoes with tan pantyhose, and a frilly blouse that tied in a fussy bow under her chin. She limped, just a little, as she walked through the seating area—ignoring me completely—and seated herself at a desk in the back corner.

She wasn't wearing a name badge, but that didn't matter. I knew who she was.

I took one look at her impassive face, and felt the world shift. I *had* to get this job.

Chapter Two

Historians, contrary to popular belief, spend at least as much time in the present as they do in the past.

When the Cataclysm hit, every historian, anthropologist, and archaeologist, no matter their specialty periods or areas of expertise, knew they were living through something incredible. Perhaps even more importantly, they were watching future research funding opportunities materialize right in front of them. It's amazing to think about how *young* some of them were. Big names like Thandiwe Scott and Simon de Platt weren't even graduates yet. They could have chosen to nail horseshoes over the door and hide under their beds, but instead they hit the streets, gathering as much raw data as possible.

It's true that they didn't do a lot of analysis back then. That got left to the next generation, who started making headway in the late 80s, when things had calmed down. Real historians in the 60s and 70s went gonzo, with a mania for documenting everything that was happening, as fast as it was happening. They couldn't be objective, so they didn't even try. Columbia's History department alone holds so many first-person accounts and personal observations that it's going to take at least a century to trawl through them.

Most of the historians even survived, which is kind of a miracle when you consider how unsettled things were back then. It didn't hurt that the Faculty Chair of History at NYU came out as a 3000-year-old immortal, who not-so-casually declared that every historian linked to an institution was under his personal protection.

My senior thesis was an oral history of post-Cataclysm City Hall, concentrating on 1978-1984, the years leading up to and right after the North American Faerie Accords Act. Manhattan had been acting as a kind of sanctuary city for fae exiles—we still had a much higher population of fae than most other urban centers—so there was a lot of juicy detail about how the city had influenced the Accords, whenever I could get anyone to talk about it. The great and frustrating thing about oral histories is that people get off track—they don't always want to talk about what you want them to talk about, but what they do end up saying is nearly always interesting.

That was when I'd first encountered the stories about Bev Thornton.

She'd started work straight out of high school in 1979, doing unspecified things with a non-profit called Populi that did "community engagement and youth outreach". When Populi closed its doors, she'd bounced through a few non-profits and government jobs, and then eventually became a truancy officer with the Board of Education. It didn't take much digging to discover that Bev had been much more than your usual bureaucrat. She'd never been a capital-H Hunter, deliberately staking out killer vampire nests or taking out wizards gone dark, but in her mission to get kids back to school and make sure they stayed there, she'd faced down some of the worst threats the city had to offer.

She was, as far as anyone could tell, entirely human. That hadn't stopped her from busting up a gnome child labor ring in the Garment District, punching a demon lord in the nose when he'd lured some of her cases into a cigarette-shoplifting scheme, or persuading a fangxiangshi to exorcise the hungry ghosts of Bloody Angle from a kid everyone else had written off as a dangerous waste of oxygen.

Fascinated, I'd followed Bev through the decades, prompting tidbits out of my sources, and chasing down city documentation and the occasional news piece. There were few pictures of her, but what I could find showed a short, stocky white woman with a level gaze, permed hair, and fussy blouses. She was one of those people who'd found her look and stuck with it through the decades.

The last big story about Bev started in 2013, when Councilman Aloysius Jacobs proposed a city ordinance lowering the age of consent for vampirism to fifteen years old.

A lot of people thought this was a joke. Being fifteen was bad enough. Being fifteen *forever* was so evidently a terrible idea that it couldn't possibly get any traction. It wasn't just humans saying it, either, even though only humans can get turned. Magicians already have the other-else, which stops us from going vampire, but almost all of us have human relatives, and we didn't want their teenagers going toothy. Werewolves tend to be protective of children, whatever their species, and every vampire who is even halfway normal would rather have their fangs snapped off than be responsible for a flock of baby bats for eternity.

But then it became clear that Jacobs had been working on this for a while, and he had some serious backing—and the support of other council members. The evidence at the subsequent trials was mostly sealed to the court, but there was enough to hint at a huge mess of blackmail, mauvais magic, a couple of forsworn fae, and some good old-fashioned bribery.

At the time, all people could see was that it looked like he might have the votes, and that vampires might be able to legally transform teenagers—the demographic who are most likely to think vampirism sounds like an amazing deal, instead of a life-altering trauma. And since only the worst kind of vampire would do that to a kid, we were going to have a lot of new vamps raised by the worst kind of vampire; i.e., Aloysius Jacobs.

That was when Bev stepped in. As far as I could tell, she didn't have much history of organization or activism, but what became rapidly obvious was that she had a *network*. A lot of people knew and liked Bev. A lot of people owed her favors. She probably knew a lot of things that some people really didn't want her telling anyone else.

And she'd dedicated her working life to protecting kids.

Three of Councilman Jacobs's most loyal supporters fronted the media and said they'd changed their minds. One accused him of hiring mauvais wizards to hex her family; the other two said they'd been threatened and blackmailed. None of them publicly revealed how the pressure had been lifted, but more than one of my sources pointed to Bev, pulling strings and making deals that Jacobs couldn't anticipate or counter.

Jacobs went from imminent triumph to catastrophic defeat in two days. He was going to lose the vote, obviously, but also his job, and almost certainly his freedom. The DA's office had received a lot of information from a "credible source".

Aloysius Jacobs and two other vampires visited Bev in her City Hall office, under the assumption that if they couldn't get what they wanted, they could at least murder the woman who'd made it impossible. City Hall was a public place; they could walk right in.

They never walked out.

Bev, who was by that time in her mid-fifties, killed three centuries-old vampires with the contents of her purse in just under a minute, under the eyes of a dozen startled witnesses who were all prepared to testify it was self-defense. The D.A. declined to press charges. Bev ignored all requests for interviews, and kept doing her job until she took a severance buyout in a City Hall restructuring the year before I started college.

And after that, there were no more stories about Bev Thornton.

From the moment I'd first heard about Bev, I'd wanted to write about her. Her time period was ready for more analysis, and she'd be the perfect subject to anchor a dissertation. How had she built that network? What else had she done that no one knew about? What secrets could she lead me to?

The problem was finding her. All I knew for sure was that she didn't turn up in any death indexes or obituary archives, and that everyone in the Education Department stopped talking to me the second I brought up her name. The most anyone would pass on was a vague rumor she'd retired to Florida.

And now we were in the same room. She *hadn't* died or retired. The legend herself was sitting at the back of this community center office, parked in front of a supply closet, pulling her glasses case out of a brown leather purse. It could have been *the* purse. It definitely looked old enough.

Anton frowned at me, and I realized I'd sat up straight and still, my face pointed at Bev like a hunting dog who'd found the scent. Oh, God. I had to get this job.

Hannah was looking back and forth between us, fading in and out of view with a puzzled expression. Her phone rang.

"Oh, great," she said into it, nodding at me. "I'll bring her right in."

I stood up, mentally scanning through my resume. There wasn't much of it, that was the problem, and I was already working against the odds.

Hannah escorted me down a narrow corridor. "IT is down there, conference room over to the side, staff bathroom here," she said, weirdly chatty for someone who didn't want me to succeed. "Okay, now, Felantheril is a little... unusual, but I happen to know she wants a wizard, so that's a great start." She knocked on the door that read "Director" before I could tell her I *wasn't* a wizard.

"Enter and be welcome!" a female voice called, and Hannah pushed the door open.

"She's a dryad," Hannah whispered, and winked at me. "Compliment the plants."

I walked in, saw the woman behind the desk, and realized why Hannah had been pretending to be friendly. There *were* a lot of plants in this room, lush and green, but my other-else went into high alert, all metaphorical sirens and red flashing lights going off in my head.

I'd encountered full-blooded fae before. My favorite middle school teacher had been a brownie, and one of the bouncers at my favorite club in Tribeca was a redcap. They were wildly different people, but their magic had the same feel.

But Mrs Serinisa and Erik were both what the fae themselves call members of "lesser Faerie". Feudalism, still alive and well in the Fae Realms, wasn't magically neutral, which was one of the reasons so many *non*-High Fae had come to Manhattan. To my other-else, pixies, sprites, naiads and so on all felt like they were *connected* to something, a kind of grounded magic. High Fae aristocrats, terrifying and glamorous, were the magical equivalents of bringing a bomb to a knife fight. That gorgeous blonde job applicant had only had a tiny touch of High Fae magic, like maybe an ancestor had a brief liaison with a Daoine Sidhe noble before the portals all closed.

The Thirteenth Avenue Rec Center director wasn't a mere dryad, and she didn't have a smidgeon of High Fae glamor from a great-great-great-grandmother. I'd never been in the presence of true High Fae before, but my other-else knew that this woman was magic down to the bone. I could feel it simmering off her like heatwaves from summer sidewalks.

I had no idea what the hell she was doing here. High Fae rarely bothered with the mortal world at all; they might drop into the UN for an important session on magical rights, or occasionally grant political asylum to a rogue wizard for opaque reasons of their own, but they had no real reason to leave their magical courts and seats of power.

Why was this one managing a small non-profit operation in the Upper West Side?

Still, stunned as I was, I was also smug that I'd worked out Hannah's trap. If I treated this woman like a lowly dryad by complimenting her plants, I'd be dead in the water.

"Hello," I said. "I'm Charlie Cross."

She pushed a wave of greenish-brown hair out of her face and made a lazy attempt to focus on me. She was beautiful, of course, with leaf-green eyes in a light brown face, her skin smooth and unmarked. Her delicate bone structure was the kind of thing enthralled poets wrote odes to, at least until the Faerie Accords had banned enchanting mortals for entertainment purposes.

"You may call me Felantheril," she replied, and I really should have expected her voice to sound like a brook burbling through a sunlit forest glade.

I didn't think she was trying to enthrall me. She looked as if she was having difficulty just staying awake.

"I'm really interested in the administrator position," I said. "I was so happy to see it advertised."

I was being careful with my wording here—you don't want to lie to any fae, much less a High Fae—but thanks to Bev, I *was* interested in the position, and I *had* been happy to see it advertised, because the prospect of moving back in with Mom meant I would grasp at any straw.

"Hm?" Felantheril said, blinking at me.

"Do you want to know about my qualifications?" I prompted her.

She blinked again. "I suppose you should tell me."

"I have a BA, with a major in History and a minor in English Literature. I specialized in post-Cataclysmic history, so of course I'm familiar with the history of Thirteenth Avenue, and I think that background would be an asset."

Her eyes might have shown a glimmer of interest at that. Or perhaps it was just the light.

"I was on the Dean's List every semester, and I'm graduating *summa cum laude*," I added.

"With highest glory?" she said.

"Um, that's the literal translation, but it means more like, with distinction."

"And what does that mean?"

I looked sharply at her, not sure if she was being sarcastic, but she seemed genuinely curious.

"It means I'm smart," I said. "I learn quickly, I notice patterns, I'm good at finding things out, and I can recognize and analyze cause and effect."

"Being clever can be a double-edged blade," she said, as if she was remarking on the weather.

What the hell? "I also have experience working with the public," I said, thinking back to my stint in Butler Library. "I'm accustomed to meeting the diverse needs of a broad cross-section of stakeholders."

This was a near quote from the job listing, but Felantheril's eyes had glazed over again.

"All right, well," she said. "Thank you?"

"Did you have any further questions for me?" I pressed.

Her nose wrinkled, and she looked vaguely around her desk. "I suppose... There was a list." She picked up a piece of paper and squinted at it. "Where do you see yourself in five years?"

"I—" I said, and then stopped. The real answer was "*halfway through grad school*", but I couldn't say that. Neither could I lie.

"Do you consider yourself a team player?" she went on, without any indication she'd noticed my hesitation. "How could you best contribute to this organization? Describe a problem you have solved in workplace environment. Describe a bad experience in workplace environment and what you learned from it."

"Could I please see that list?" I said, fighting to keep my voice level.

"Oh, sure," she said readily, and passed it to me. Yep, there it was: "[workplace environment]" in a fill-in-the-blanks list of job interview questions.

"I see," I said, and stood up. She had no interest in the questions, and even less in my answers, and I'd never had a shot. I bitterly wished Anton back to the realm that had spawned his demonic ancestor, and looked Felantheril square in the face.

At this point, she deserved the insult.

"I like your plants," I said, my voice clear and deliberate.

The transformation was immediate, and totally unexpected.

Felantheril sat up straight, sweeping her hair fully out of her face for the first time, and beamed at me, showing even white teeth that a human Hollywood star would kill for. "That's so kind of you to say!" she said, her voice gaining some animation. "Which is your favorite?"

She could have been making fun of me, but she *sounded* totally sincere.

"Well, I like that monstera," I said cautiously. "And I've never seen a snake plant that tall."

"He started out a little shy, but I had a good chat with him," she confided.

"And the first thing I noticed when I got here was the roses outside," I added. "Are those yours too?"

"Yes!"

"They're beautiful," I said. "Are they an Alba variety?"

"Alba/Gallica cross," Felantheril said, looking delighted. "How sweet of you to notice!"

Being forced to attend my Grandmother Cross's garden club meetings as a kid had been pure torture. If it got me this job, though, I owed her a box of bougie chocolates from my first paycheck.

And had I totally misread Hannah? Maybe Felantheril *was* a dryad after all? Even framing the thought got me a metaphorical head shake from my other-else, but if *this* part of Hannah's advice had been reliable, then maybe I should just go for broke.

"I don't know if I mentioned this, but I'm a magician," I said.

"Oh! That's good! I want a wizard."

That was definitely the kind of statement that got you in trouble with employment lawyers, but since this prejudice was in my favor...

"I'm not a wizard, exactly. But I am a magician."

"What class?" she asked, her eyes innocently wide.

I couldn't avoid it. She'd just assume the worst if I declined to reply anyway. "First Class," I said, as confidently as possible.

She pursed her perfect lips.

"And I've got administrative experience with booking systems and customer service, and I know I can pick up anything else I need for the position super fast, and I really need this job." I could hear the desperation in my voice. "Please. I can do it. I'll work really hard, I *swear*."

The last two words left my mouth before I could stop them.

I could feel the blood draining from my face. I dropped back into the chair before my knees gave out.

"You swear," Felantheril said, her voice very soft.

"I didn't—" I started, and she cut me off with a sharp gesture before I could complete the thought. I'd been going to say *I didn't mean it*, but the worst thing was that I *had*. I had just sworn a sincere oath to a High Fae, and I was completely, utterly screwed. I was miserably grateful that she hadn't let me compound the mistake by lying about it.

Felantheril no longer looked sleepy. She tapped her nails against the wood of her desk, her sharp green eyes never leaving my face. "It's not so bad," she said. "Generally speaking, managers like their employees to work hard."

She was trying to be kind. But I hadn't placed any limits around the oath, and I'd promised to work *really* hard. If she wanted to, she could make me work around the clock, until sleep deprivation killed me. She could make me do any kind of work, no matter how degrading or dangerous. It was the kind of oath stupid people made in the old stories, where a prince promised to dance with a lovely lady *forever*, and his bones are dancing still.

"You could release me from the oath," I said tentatively. Catch a faerie in a good mood, and maybe...

She shook her head. "As it happens, I cannot," she said, and her voice was full of soft regret. "Really, the best thing would be for you to leave."

I swallowed, but yeah, I'd definitely ruined my chances at this job. "Thank you for your time," I said, and gathered my strength to stand.

"Leave the state, I mean," she added.

"Leave *New York*?"

"Possibly the continent," she said, frowning faintly. "I wouldn't say the mortal realm, I don't think you'd have to go that far, but you really ought to put an ocean between us."

"May I ask why?" I said, my throat tight. I was only starting to comprehend the magnitude of the disaster. She'd said she *couldn't* release me, not that she *wouldn't,* which meant... what? That her magic wouldn't allow it?

Her eyes glimmered with warning. "You may. But I cannot answer." She frowned. "Or... I could offer you the job."

I blinked.

"I can't promise safety," she said. "I believe you would be safer if you left. But if you were working here, some of the oath's force might dissipate. An employment contract is a mortal thing. It would ease the bond, perhaps make it easier to slip." She gave me a direct look. "On the other hand, perhaps I shouldn't consider it. Someone who'd make such an error might not be the best candidate for the position, in a community like ours."

"I've never done anything like this before," I said, stung. "I'm usually pretty careful. And I really am familiar with magically diverse communities. I went to public schools, not wizarding academies. I've been living in the Columbia dorms for the last four years, and my classmates come from all over. Last year I assisted a ghost on an important research project, and we worked well together."

This was *not* the time to say that my best friend was a werewolf. It's true, but it's one of those things you can't just pull out when it's convenient.

Someone rapped on the door, and Felantheril's eyes instantly glazed over. It was eerie. I'd been talking to a bored idiot, then an enthusiastic plant-lover, then an intelligent, serious woman, all in the last twenty minutes. Now she was back to being a ditz.

Bev Thornton poked her head through the door without waiting for an invitation to enter. In the midst of my self-imposed disaster, I'd almost forgotten why I wanted the job in the first place, but now her severe expression and total self-confidence reminded me.

"Felantheril, Tiffany Chang is here," she announced. Her voice was husky, softer than I'd expected, but the twang of her accent was pure New York.

Felantheril winced. "Why?"

"She wants to know what happened to the booking for her niece's birthday party."

"Oh," Felantheril said, and inspected a strand of hair for non-existent split ends.

Bev's expression suggested divine forbearance. "Did you log into the booking system again?"

Felantheril shrugged.

"Sam asked you not to do that anymore."

"Oh, Sam," Felantheril said, with a doting smile. "He's always asking me not to do things. The other day he saw the notebook where I keep my passwords in my laptop bag and he was so upset. Poor lamb."

Bev closed her eyes and opened them again.

Felantheril looked at me invitingly. "The job, Charlie Cross? Do you still want it?"

"Yes," I said. Given the dark hints Felantheril had been throwing out, I wasn't sure I *should*. But I didn't want to leave the city, much less the country. My friends, my mom, everything and everyone I loved was here. My future was here.

And so was Bev Thornton, who was looking at me for the first time, her face absolutely impassive. I had no idea of how to take that.

"Excellent. Three-week paid trial period, and we'll see how you go before confirmation." Felantheril's teeth flashed as she smiled. "You can start by dealing with Tiffany Chang."

Chapter Three

When I followed Bev back to the main admin office, Hannah and Oona were nowhere to be seen. Anton was standing on Bev's desk, doing something to the lighting fixture above it with a small screwdriver.

With his arms above his head, the black T-shirt rode up a little, exposing a strip of tanned skin. The tight sleeves strained to contain his biceps.

"Get down from there," Bev said, and he jumped clean off the desk, landing in front of me.

"How'd it go?" he asked eagerly.

"*Amazing*," I said. You can lie to part-demons as much as you like. "She offered me the job on the spot."

"Congratulations," he said cheerfully, and turned to Bev. "I fixed that flicker."

I blinked at him. I'd expected some chagrin, maybe even indignation at the news. After all, he'd expected to be a shoo-in.

Hadn't he?

"We don't need a handyman," Bev said.

"Uh-huh," Anton said. "So I just imagined that loose stair railing?"

Bev shot him an icy glare. "You should be studying."

"Um," I said. "Should we keep this Tiffany Chang waiting?"

Now Anton looked chagrined. "Tiffany's here? Do you want me to—"

Bev rolled her eyes. "We've got it. Go back to school, Anton. And stay out of trouble." She walked out, and I followed her down the stairs, conscious of Anton's eyes on my back.

It was pretty easy to pick out Tiffany Chang. She was the one haranguing Oona and Hannah at the reception desk.

From the way everyone had been talking about her, I'd expected Tiffany to be at least six feet tall, and muscles from shoulders to wrists. Actually, the young woman waving her phone in Oona's face was tiny. She might have just hit five feet, and that was with a boost from the thick soles of her combat boots. She'd probably shopped for her ragged denim vest and slim-fit cargo pants in the kids section, but the patch on the back of her vest, with the crescent moon dripping blood over a cityscape, was definitely custom-made.

Werewolf, my other-else said, and when she turned to glare at Bev and I, it amended that to *alpha*. Her yellow-gold eyes nearly drove me back a step, but I could feel Bev's appraisal and stiffened my spine instead.

"Greetings, Alpha Chang," I said. "I'm Charlie Cross. How can I assist you today?"

The *power* coming off this woman. I was pretty sure I was facing off with the local pack leader. If I hadn't already met that Eighth Class wizard, and then Felantheril this morning, I might have freaked out more completely, but as it was, it felt like my other-else was giving in with a metaphorical shrug.

Instead, I thought about my best friend Laurence, and the time he'd first explained werewolf dynamics. We'd met when his family had moved in next door, and bonded as two nerdy weirdos at our suburban middle school, where our supernatural status was way less important than our total disinterest in sports. Hiding under the bleachers from a PE lesson, he'd told me how the word *werewolf* came from Old English *wer*, which meant "man", and *wulf*, which was obvious. Man-wolf.

"My dad says it's the man part that's scary," he'd said gloomily, scratching at his freckled knees. "Or the woman. Or whatever gender the werewolf is, I guess."

"How come?" I had asked, innocently naive about the detailed wildlife lecture I was letting myself in for. It turns out that wolves are pretty peaceable, on the whole, unless you're a deer or a rabbit. In the wild, there's no such thing as an alpha wolf, and fighting for dominance is incredibly rare.

But people can be vicious. People will absolutely fight to assert their status, and they don't like being disrespected.

It's the *wer* part that's dangerous.

Tiffany Chang didn't need height or muscles. She could throw me through a wall without a second thought. She'd do jail time for that, but that wasn't always top of mind for an enraged werewolf, and she was looking pretty steamed.

I shifted my gaze so I was looking at her left ear, pierced with three stainless steel studs and a thin bar going right through the cartilage. Now I wasn't showing fear, but I wasn't offering a challenge, either.

"Who the hell are you?" she snarled. Literally. I could nearly feel the words vibrating in her throat. "Where's your fucking boss?"

"As I said, I'm Charlie. Felantheril is unfortunately busy, but she's directed me to assist."

In my peripheral vision, I could see her attention shift to Bev, then come back to me. I could only hope that the prospect of picking a fight with Bev Thornton was giving her pause.

I crossed the floor to the reception desk, where Oona and Hannah were exchanging glances. "I understand there's a problem with a booking?"

"My niece's birthday party. My sister called to check what time she could come in to set up, and her reservation for the gymnasium had mysteriously disappeared." Every word was drenched in sarcasm, but at least she was talking. "Just like the inter-pack basketball league and the Blood Moon stall at the food festival."

"The missing stall was a clerical error, and we found you a table anyway!" Hannah said, sounding outraged. I winced. She could go intangible if Tiffany attacked, but the rest of us couldn't just wisp out of the way of a claw swipe.

"And the basketball league?" Tiffany demanded.

"Budget issues," Oona said, her voice wobbly. "It wasn't an easy decision, Tiffany. We had to cut a number of programs."

"Not the park project. How many months has that dragged out for?"

"The park has dedicated funding we can't shift to—"

"Let's focus on getting your niece a great birthday party," I said. There was history here, and I couldn't risk wading into it, but werewolves and kids... "How old is she going to be?"

Tiffany's face didn't soften, but her voice was a little less aggressive as she turned to me. "Eight."

"Aw, that's a cute age. She must be really excited." I walked around the reception desk, gesturing for Tiffany to follow me. Hannah backed up, giving us space.

Now Tiffany had been invited into our territory, instead of snarling at Oona across a boundary line.

"Could you open the calendar for me, please, Oona?" I said, as firmly as I dared. If she tried to sabotage me now, I was going to kick her. But she didn't show the least reluctance in opening the software, and to my relief I could see it was the same system we'd used in the Butler library.

"Okay, let's see," I said, and got the date. The multi-use gymnasium had indeed been booked, for something called the Committee for the Improvement of Avenue Thirteen.

Behind me, Tiffany made a noise in her throat that wasn't quite a growl.

"The conference room upstairs is available," I said. "How many guests should we be planning for?"

"Her entire class is coming, plus most of the Blood Moon pack," Tiffany said. "My sister made the reservation and paid the deposit a month ago, over two months in advance. She forwarded me the emails. The invitations have gone out, my niece has the dress, my sister is about to lose her mind. Get me the *gym*."

"Right," I said, and turned to Oona again. "How many people come to these committee meetings?"

"Up to thirty."

And the conference room seated twenty at most, so a straight swap wouldn't work. "What's this Credentials for Creatures thing happening in the dance studio?"

Oona perked up. "That's a drop-in session. We get lawyers and notaries to come and help people out with documentation and stuff. Like, if you're a ghost and it took a while for you to materialize, your will might have gone through probate, and now you want to get your house back, or if you arrived from one of the other realms and need ID—"

"Okay, got it. So if it's drop-in, people can come and go if it gets crowded, right? Could *that* go upstairs to the conference room?"

"I guess," Oona said doubtfully.

"Yes," Bev said, speaking for the first time since we'd left the office. "Any overflow can use the admin area."

"Great," I said. "So we put Credentials for Creatures in the conference room upstairs, we put the Committee in the studio, and your niece gets the basketball court, Alpha Chang. Is that acceptable?"

Tiffany grunted.

Hannah squinted over Oona's shoulder. "Wait, that's a Thursday night? Magic for Beginners always gets the conference room."

Tiffany made a restless movement out of the corner of my eye.

"I don't see a booking here," I said.

"Well, no, it's just the conference room is always free on Thursday nights, so..."

"We'll cancel the class," Bev said.

"But—"

"We'll cancel," Bev said again, firmer this time, and nodded at me. I entered the new bookings with a distinct sense of triumph.

"If you give me your sister's email address, I'll send her the details," I said, and risked meeting Tiffany's eyes.

The yellow-gold had faded to an amber brown. "What time do we get the space?"

"5:30 p.m. There's a bridge club tournament in there until five."

"We booked for five. We told the guests to come at 5:30pm."

"I'm afraid that's the best we can do," I said. Her eyes flashed briefly golden, but I stood my ground. There were social currents roiling around me, unspoken understandings and frustrations. "I'm sorry," I added, on impulse. "This shouldn't have happened. Maybe I can talk to the bridge club and see if they wouldn't mind packing up a little early, or I can help you with the set-up, so it goes faster."

Tiffany looked surprised. With the aggression wiped clean from her face, she was startlingly pretty, and younger than I'd first thought, maybe only a year or two older than me. Then she settled back into what I was beginning to think was her habitual scowl.

"I want a meeting with Felantheril," she said. "To discuss these *coincidental* clerical errors."

"I'm sure Oona would be happy to set that up," I said, throwing both of them to the wolves. Oona deserved it, and I was sure Felantheril could handle Tiffany.

I helpfully pulled up Felantheril's calendar for the next week before stepping away from the computer. Felantheril had a meeting with someone named Raphael scheduled for tomorrow afternoon, and a big all-hands meeting scheduled for Wednesday. And that was it. It was a weirdly empty schedule for the manager of a busy community center.

"Looks like she's wide open," Tiffany said, a grim smile tugging at the corner of her mouth. "How about tomorrow morning?"

"Sure thing," Oona said, with more enthusiasm than I'd expected. She tapped. "There."

"Good," Tiffany said, and eyed me curiously. "You're new, aren't you?"

"I was offered the job ten minutes ago," I said, and snuck a glance at Oona. She looked... thrilled. What the *hell*?

"Not bad, new girl," Tiffany said. "See you round."

She sauntered out of the building, pausing to sniff the roses on her way down the path, and I exhaled. My lungs felt tight, and I was fighting not to look at Bev, who went back upstairs to the admin area without saying a word. She passed Anton on the way. He must have been lingering in the doorway, watching me work.

My skin tingled again as he came towards me.

"That was a lot better than not bad," Anton said. His eyes were warm with admiration. "And congratulations again on getting the job. Welcome to Thirteenth Avenue." He pointed at Oona. "You owe me one."

"You didn't even do anything," she protested.

"Not my fault." He nodded at me and left.

I turned to Oona, who had clasped her hands together at her chest and was beaming at me. Hannah had disappeared again, either not here or just invisible.

"I'm so glad it all worked out!" Oona said. "This is going to be great!" Her eyes were sparkling. Not a figure of speech; there was actually something glittering in her irises, and once again I felt that spike of not-magician-but-close from my other-else.

It probably wasn't a good idea to pick a fight with a brand-new co-worker, but I hadn't understood more than half of what had been happening around me that morning, and I was sick of it. "Why are you being nice to me now?" I demanded. "You and Hannah were doing your best to push me out before I even walked into my interview!"

She blinked at me. "What? No, I wasn't—"

"You were chasing away everyone but Anton! You talked to that poor girl about fluids, and Hannah threw coffee all over that wizard guy. *Cold* coffee, which meant you *planned* this. What were you going to do to that human lady if she hadn't decided to leave?"

"Anton was going to flirt with her," Oona said, blinking rapidly.

Her honesty took some of the wind out of my sails. "Okay," I said, and settled back on my heels. "Look, I know that the job market's tough, and we all want our friends to find work, but

I need this job, and I want to do it well. I hope we can work together anyway..."

Oona held her palms up. "Charlie! Charlie, no. Anton wasn't here for the *job*. He was here in case Hannah and I needed backup. We were chasing away everyone but *you*."

I gaped at her. "What? *Why*? You've never met me."

"I'm an oracle," she said, her voice matter-of-fact. "I had a vision. If you don't work here, Bev's going to die."

Chapter Four

Oona declared it our lunch break, called Hannah down to cover reception, and dragged me to the local dive bar.

"We shouldn't be drinking on the job," I protested weakly, as she pushed me into a booth and signaled the guy behind the bar.

"They do great burgers," she said. "That'll soak up one beer. Unless you don't drink?"

"I do, I just—"

She shook her head, looking determined. "It'll help, I promise. It's not every day you learn you're the subject of prophecy."

I wasn't sure my credit card could take the hit, but I shut up and let her order for us. She kept up a running stream of chatter while we waited, talking about the rec center's regular events, the funding deficits that had led to program cuts, the relief she'd felt when Felantheril had finally approved hiring another assistant—"I wasn't kidding about the hours, you know, they can be really tough"—and let me make vague noises of agreement or concern, without having to form any kind of complex thought.

The food was delivered by a werewolf, considerably less powerful than Tiffany Chang, with the same bloody crescent moon emblem on his T-shirt.

"Thanks, Baz," Oona said. "Try the fries, Charlie, they're amazing."

I bit into one. The crisp hot exterior gave way to a pillowy carb center, and I relaxed a little. Fries were so normal. Nothing very strange could happen while you were eating fries.

"So, you're an oracle, huh?" I said, keeping my voice down. Seers weren't nearly as common as wizards or werewolves, and they didn't always want it widely known, in case people started asking them for prophecies. It was the same thing that stopped nurses from telling people their profession, on the grounds that no one wanted to deal with some guy they'd just met pulling off his shirt to show them a suspicious mole.

Oona looked bashful. "Not a very good one. I hardly ever get firm visions. Just impressions and feelings. Even when I get images, I can't tell if they're literal."

"I'm not sure what that means..."

She bit into her cheeseburger and swallowed before she answered. "Well, okay. I get this recurring one where I'm drowning and my boyfriend pulls me out. So does that mean I should avoid water, or that he's going to get me out of a dangerous situation in general, or maybe just that one day he's going to take me on holiday when I'm drowning in work?" She sighed. "Believe me, I'd love to be one of those seers who predict market trends or work with emergency response teams, but I don't get anything that reliable."

I winced. "But for me and Bev...?" I was sure that Bev had been the subject of prophecies before; she'd actually done important things. But I wasn't anyone.

"Hannah asked me to screen the applicants. I picked out three candidates, Felantheril approved, and I was writing rejection emails to everyone else. When I started writing yours, I got the vision, and knew we needed you instead."

"Saved from the reject bin," I said. "Thanks."

"I did read your application again afterwards. You're totally qualified! It's just that the others…"

"I get it." I ate another fry, and took my first sip of beer. It was delicious; ice-cold and just the right amount of sour. "So you added me to the interview list, and enlisted Hannah and Anton to help sabotage the others? Why not just tell Felantheril to hire me?"

"She's… unpredictable. I thought she might tell Bev."

I put my glass down. "Bev doesn't *know* about this prophecy?"

Oona grimaced. "Bev's stubborn. I wanted to tell her, but Hannah was worried she might not let you do what you're going to do."

"And that is?"

"Um," Oona said, and avoided my eyes. "I'm not sure."

"Seriously?"

"I told you I wasn't very good! I didn't even get a vision, like, not with my eyes. I got the smell of water, but there was something wrong with it, and someone was yelling, and there was dirt under my fingernails. And you were there. I mean, I didn't know who you were exactly, but the sense of you was there." She waved vaguely at me, and I chalked that up to 'seer stuff'. "And I could taste blood. It wasn't mine, but someone was bleeding."

"That's not great."

Oona shrugged. "Sure, but right after that, I had a vision where nearly everything was the same, but you weren't there, and I knew Bev was dead. I know it doesn't sound like much, but—"

"No, I get it. It sounds like my knack, where it doesn't really translate into human language." I pointed at the bartender with my chin. "To my other-else, he feels like, uh… wild lemon glitter.

That doesn't make any sense, but it's the closest I can get to in words. It *means* that he's a werewolf, not powerful, and the same pack as Tiffany."

Oona looked intrigued again. "You can identify the pack?"

"Only because I've met Tiffany. She's the pack leader, right? For the whole territory, not just the alpha for her family?"

"For the whole neighborhood," Oona said. She sighed. "I'm sorry you thought we didn't want you."

"I was going to give up and walk out," I admitted.

Oona looked appalled. "But then—"

"What was I supposed to think? I mean, Hannah told me Felantheril was a dryad, right before I stepped into the interview."

"She is a dryad," Oona said. She saw my face and straightened. "Isn't she?"

Had my other-else messed up? "Did she ever say she was a dryad? In those words?"

Oona frowned. "I don't remember. But she cares more about plants than people. She gets sleepy in winter. She has green highlights in her hair!"

"In the right light, so do you," I said. "And your magic has nothing to do with plants."

"So what is she?"

The question sounded perfectly innocent, and I was just about to respond to it, when I hesitated. It was just one step from that to telling Oona I was oath-bound to a High Fae, and that wasn't something I wanted to trust to someone I'd just met. I hadn't even thought through all the ramifications myself yet, though I could feel something uncomfortable around my neck. "Not a dryad," I said, and made myself shrug as carelessly as I could. "I wasn't sure exactly what you were, when we met."

"You didn't think I was human?" Oona said, sounding surprised.

"Oh, no, I knew you weren't human."

"Huh," Oona said. "Neat trick."

I shrugged again. "Honestly, it's my one useful skill."

"You talked Tiffany Chang out of a rage," Oona said thoughtfully. "I'd say you've got more than one skill."

"I also write a mean citations list and I make good microwave ramen," I said, and smiled when she laughed. "But I meant in terms of magical skill. I know Felantheril wanted a wizard, but I'm only a Magician First Class. I can barely light a candle."

"You'll fit right in," Oona said. "I'm an oracle who can't see her visions, Hannah's a ghost with a dog and a day job, our IT guy is the least vampiric vampire you've ever met, and Bev's... Bev."

"I'd heard of her before," I admitted. "The time with the vampire age of consent..."

"God, don't bring that up."

"Really?" I asked, my heart sinking.

"Really. Hannah asked about it once, and then Bev didn't talk to either of us for three days. I ran out of Blu Tack and markers, and had to improvise." She read my look. "Bev's in charge of the supply closet."

"You couldn't just go into the closet yourself?"

"Go into *Bev's* closet without her permission? No, Charlie, I could not do that, because I am not suicidal." She waved her hand in a circle, indicating not just our table and the building, but the neighborhood. "Look, Thirteenth Avenue is a weird place. There are a lot of clashing interests, but people kind of get along, despite their differences. Almost everyone wants the neighborhood to work, even if it shouldn't. The rec center's a big part of that. And having Bev gives us..." She thought about it, searching for the right word. "Authority," she decided. "Not officially, of course. But it's real."

"Is that why Tiffany backed down?" I asked. Now that I'd had time to think about it, an enraged werewolf in a territorial dispute wouldn't usually be appeased by some quick rescheduling.

"Kind of? I mean, you did give her a way to back down with pride, and that's important. She's only been pack alpha for a couple of years, since her great-aunt retired, and she's gotta react fast when someone disrespects the pack." She sipped her drink. "Did Felantheril tell you about Lady Seraphine?"

"No?"

"Our major benefactor. You'll need her approval to keep the job."

My eyebrows rose. I was used to the idea of big donators having some sway over operations, but the hiring of low-level employees?

Oona nodded at me. "Completely illegal, of course," she said cheerfully. "But you know the joke. What does a 500-year-old vampire do with her time?"

"Anything she wants," I said, and swallowed my unease with the last of my beer.

***

We went back to the office for the afternoon. Oona talked me through a typical day—"not that we have many of those!"—and I started to feel better about my future co-workers. Oona was sweet, Hannah seemed smart and competent and Bev apparently spent most of her time playing online poker and sailing out for mysterious "procurement operations". Maybe it wasn't what she was supposed to be doing, but if anyone had earned a semi-retirement, it was Bev Thornton. I wasn't sure how I was going to breach the subject of her previous heroics, but it clearly wasn't a task for my first day on the job.

Sam-the-IT-guy set up my accounts. He was, as promised, the least vampiric vampire I'd ever met. I'd encountered a few—universities attracted bored immortals—and the ones that weren't naturally seductive still tended to skulk around smoldering at people. Legally, they weren't allowed to use their eyes or fangs on you without your consent, but like frat boys at a keg party, the law wasn't always a barrier.

Sam was a Black man who'd been turned in his early twenties, and my other-else told me that had been maybe a decade ago. He wore khakis and a polo shirt, avoided eye contact with Oona, and shook my hand limply when I offered it. Many other vampires would have taken the opportunity for a caress, or kissed my palm, promising unearthly delights if I would just give into their allure. Sam promised to talk me through updating the website, issued me a clunky laptop that weighed a ton, sent a test email to my new address, and left the unearthly delights entirely out of the equation.

My final task of the day was helping Oona set up folding tables for bingo night, a twice-weekly event the participants apparently took very seriously.

"Normally we ask people to do this themselves when they hire the rooms, and we do the breakdown, but a lot of the bingo people are ghosts," Oona explained. "Some people have been playing here for fifty years, and they haven't let a little thing like death stop them."

"The rec center's that old?"

"First building on the block. The ribbon was cut just five years after the Cataclysm. Anyway, you know ghosts. Routine keeps them anchored."

From everything I'd read, routine was something that had been in short supply post-Cataclysm. Put bluntly, a lot of things—law and order, civil infrastructure, public safety—went to shit for a while.

It's true that some people and communities had always been more sympathetic to the idea of the supernatural, always more aware of what lay outside and alongside the mundane, observable world. Their Cataclysm had tended to be way less traumatic, although there were more than a few New Agey crystal-bathing types who were truly pissed they'd missed out on getting nifty new abilities.

But for many people, the immediate post-Cataclysm years were *rough*. Fascinating, absolutely, which was why I'd spent so much time researching the period. But while all that rapid social adjustment was interesting to read and write about, I was grateful I hadn't had to live through it. This building probably held some stories worth finding out.

Oona drew a line through the dust on the last table and grimaced. "Grab a damp rag and wipe this down, would you?"

"Sure." I hit the corridor, and realized I didn't know where the nearest faucet was, much less where to find a rag. Presumably there'd be something on the ground floor, but I was getting along well with Oona and didn't want her to have to wait until I found it. I ran upstairs to the employee kitchenette, remembering not to place any weight on the wobbly stair railing, and walked in to discover Felantheril staring intently at the spider plant on top of the fridge.

"I just need a cleaning cloth?" I said, hating the way my voice rose at the end.

Felantheril turned, so smoothly it seemed as if she were rotating in the air. I snuck a quick look at her feet, but they were planted on the old tile. "I hear you did well with Tiffany," she said.

"Oh. Thank you."

"And got her a meeting with me." She waggled a finger at me playfully. "Now I'll need to rub her tummy and call her a good girl."

I sucked in a breath. That was wildly inappropriate on so many levels. But either I let her get away with it, or... "I'd prefer not to discuss our werewolf clients in such terms," I said. My voice was clear and cold, even as my heart sank. I was going to get fired, and I'd still be held by that oath.

Felantheril beamed at me. "*Quite* right," she said, her voice warm with approval.

"Was that a test?" I demanded.

"Yes." She picked up the spider plant. "We're going to find a little more light. You keep working really hard."

The oath tightened around my neck like a heavy collar. I'd been trying not to think about it too much, even wondered if I might have imagined the strangling feeling, but with Felantheril saying the words, my breathing hitched in involuntary response.

She nodded at me. "Until a normal quitting time," she added, and the pressure eased. "I'll see you tomorrow!"

I grabbed some paper towels, dampened them, and headed back downstairs, where Oona was unfolding chairs.

"Everything all right?" she asked.

"Is Felantheril... okay?" I said, substituting for *sane* in the last moment.

Oona straightened. "She's a fae who's been living in the iron world for half a century," she said. "*Okay* might be expecting too much."

Chastened, I wiped down the tables and helped Oona with the chairs. Hannah was hovering behind the reception desk when we went back to the foyer, dutifully uploading pictures to the center's social media sites.

"You two should take off," she said.

"When do we normally finish?" I asked.

Oona and Hannah both laughed, the weary laugh of the cynical and weathered long-timers directed at the clueless newbie.

"Normal," Hannah said, and wiped imaginary tears away. "You work at the Thirteenth Avenue Rec Center now, honey. We don't do normal here."

Chapter Five

My mother was waiting in the lobby when I got back to my dorm.

"Hi!" I said, and got one of the best hugs in the world, plus a hefty whiff of the lavender and peppermint shampoo Mom uses. "I thought you were coming later tonight—did I get it wrong?"

"Oh, no!" she said. "I was just so excited to see my baby girl again! How was the job interview?"

"I was hired on the spot," I said.

Her smile flickered for an instant. "That's great!" she said, too heartily.

Mom's plan, I was pretty sure, had been that we'd load up her Suzuki Swift, and trundle my life back to New Rochelle. Then I'd continue the job hunt, work in the city if I *had* to, but commute back and forth until I fell in love with someone nice, moved in together with them, got engaged a socially acceptable year later, married a year after that, and had a baby or two, timed to avoid impacting my burgeoning career in whatever the heck I did with my History degree.

Marla Kerrigan-Cross is one of the most caring, generous people you'll ever meet, but she was raised by my maternal grandparents, who are part of Sunrise, which is... Well, honestly, it's a cult. Everyone in Sunrise is human, absolutely baseline, but they're sure that they can *become* magicians if they just do the right ceremony on the right day under the guidance of whatever charismatic grifter is scamming them this week. If I'd been brought up by people who did (stupid, useless) arcane "rituals" and were always quitting their jobs to drag their kid to a new "sacred ground" they were trying to appropriate from local indigenous culture, I might also embrace as much normalcy as I could.

When I went through the standard first grade testing and was identified as a magician, Mom's first reaction was to hug me. Her second was to say, "Don't tell your grandmother."

So even though Mom wouldn't say a word, I knew that my desire to stay in the city made her sad, and that made me feel guilty—and irritable, for feeling guilty.

"It'll take at least a week until I can find a room to rent," I added. "Is it still okay if I crash with you for now?"

"Of *course*, sweetheart," she said, brightening again. "What's the job like? Did you actually start today?"

"Yes. I think it's going to be really interesting. It's not like a standard admin job—everyone seems to do a bit of everything."

"Are your co-workers nice?"

"I've only really talked with one of them, Oona. She's training me. I like her."

Mom nodded, and asked more questions as we took the elevator up to my room and started ferrying boxes down. The few people on my hall who remained were all getting ready to go out to celebrate graduation; most of them had already left. I heard a burst of laughter echoing from one open door and poked my head in.

Simone d'Aburnay waved at me. "Charlie! How'd it go?"

"Got the job."

"Of course you did," Simone said, with more confidence than I'd ever had in my life. "Come out with us! You missed the walk, but you shouldn't miss the party."

I smiled at the two other girls sitting cross-legged on her bed, taking sips from a clear bottle, but shook my head. "My mom's here. We're heading back to the 'burbs."

"Not forever, right? Boo the 'burbs!"

I flicked a glance down the hall, hoping Mom hadn't heard. "No, definitely not."

"Stay in touch," Simone said. "You promise?"

I laughed. "I promise," I said, even though I wasn't sure she meant it. I *liked* my dorm-mates, but I hadn't really gotten close to any of them.

Once we got back to New Rochelle, Mom insisted on taking me out to dinner, and we ended up at Fat Tony's, the restaurant that had been the location for many of my birthday parties, Grandpa Cross's wake, my valedictorian dinner, and the night that my parents had sat me down, partway through ninth grade, to tell me they were getting divorced. Tragedy or celebration, Fat Tony's was the place for it.

I didn't know which Mom thought this was. I wasn't sure myself.

But it was still the best pasta alla Norma in the Tri-State area, and I'd stake those cannoli against anything you could find in Little Italy.

"Now, I know you told me not to get you a graduation gift," Mom said, as the waiter cleared our plates.

"Mom, no."

"It's just a small thing, honey," she said, and pulled a smartly wrapped parcel out of her purse. "Don't say anything, I got a really good deal on it, and I want you to be safe."

I pulled the ribbon and folded the paper back to find one of those multi-purpose protection charms. Unlike a lot of the tourist junk you could find in Times Square (New York City! The most magical city in America! If you ignore New Orleans!) this wasn't made of cheap plastic. It was solid rowan wood, inlaid with a black cast iron medallion on one side and a silver one on the other.

If I'd been religious, she could have got me one with a symbol of my faith stamped into it, but presumably the silver would have to do double duty for werewolves *and* vampires. My other-else even registered a faint whisper of spellcraft, which meant the runes around the rim had been properly enchanted as they were carved.

However good the deal had been, I was holding nearly a thousand dollars' worth of protective magic. It had to be at least that for me to feel anything at all. My identification trick didn't work so well on objects.

"It is real, isn't it?" she said, looking at my face. "The salesman swore up and down that it had been spelled by a reputable Fourth Class who specialized in protection charms—"

"It's real," I said, and poked at the little vial hanging off the bottom. "What's this?"

"Rock salt."

"Ah," I said. Salt was occasionally useful as a demon repellant. The problem would be finding a demon willing to wait long enough for me to uncork this tiny bottle and spill a quarter teaspoon of the stuff on them.

Maybe Anton would be willing to wait.

"It's great, Mom," I said. "Thank you, really." I pulled out my keys and added the charm to my keyring, next to the little bottle of pepper spray and personal safety alarm she'd given me when I went to college. I'd never used them, and hopefully I'd never need the charm either, but I was touched by the gift, by my mother's desire for my safety.

When I looked up, she was frowning.

"Is something wrong?"

"Oh, no, I just... I thought you'd wear it. Like a necklace."

I could feel my eyes widen. "Mom, I can't do that."

"It's harder to get to on your keyring, sweetie."

"Only tourists *wear* charms, Mom. Or those Human First weirdos." I put the keys back in my purse. "But thank you so much. It's a lovely gift. Very thoughtful." And in this case, it was definitely the thought that counted.

The rest of the evening passed in "getting me settled in" which meant a silent struggle over how much I should be unpacking versus living out of a suitcase. We compromised with unpacking two bags and a box of books I'd already read and thought Mom would like.

She took the new revised edition of *Broken Windows, Mended Hearts: True Stories from the Hidden City* to read before bed, probably hoping that the anonymous memoirist had added even more scandal. I set my alarm, climbed into my old twin bed, and fell asleep before I could think.

Getting up in the morning wasn't nearly as easy. I had to catch the Metro-North, then transfer at Harlem-125, which meant being not only awake, but showered and dressed and emotionally prepared to handle mass transport at rush hour, two hours before I normally got out of bed. I surged out of the station with a crowd of my fellow commuters, grabbed a coffee and a giant pretzel from a stand, and took a detour through Riverside Park to cheer me up before I started work. Some cherry trees had a few pink blossoms clinging to the stem, but most of them were going that fuzzy, delicate spring green as the new growth came in.

Riverside was still called Riverside, though a lot of it was no longer beside the river, for the same reason New York was called New York even though we'd broken from the British Crown (and York) centuries ago. Even in this city, where people embraced change, or rushed after it with their hands outstretched, they treasured the past too. Thirteenth Avenue only had sixty years of the past to treasure, but from what I'd seen so far, the people were as proud of it as every other neighborhood in Manhattan.

As I arrived at the rec center, Anton was just leaving, looking pleased with himself. I stopped before I bumped into him, this time.

"Hey," I said. "If I was rude to you yesterday, I want to apologize. I wasn't sure what was happening, but I thought—"

"Oona explained," Anton said. He wasn't smiling, exactly, but there was a curl in the corner of his mouth. His lips looked really soft. "You don't need to apologize."

"Okay," I said. "Thanks."

"No worries."

We stood there for a moment. I was on the step below and looking up at him, with the scent of Felantheril's roses rising thick and sweet around us, made me faintly dizzy.

"Um, I should—" I said, and he startled and jumped out of the way. My sleeve brushed against his body as I went past, and the motion set a tingle down my arm.

Oona was at the reception desk, looking equally pleased with herself. "We have a new back stair railing!" she said, then saw my face. "What?"

"Does Anton spend a lot of time here?" I asked. If so, I needed to start bracing myself.

"Yeah. He's one of Bev's kids."

"She has *kids*?"

"Not actual children. People she helped out, when they were kids. People who owe her, or think they do. Anton was one of her last truancy cases. To hear him tell it, she pretty much saved his life, not to mention his soul. So he tries to help out here, when she lets him."

"Oh."

"And when she doesn't let him, he helps out anyway," she said. "Which is why we have a new stair railing, and also why we aren't going to ask where he got it."

The new railing did look nice, a shiny stainless steel that made the worn vinyl and scuffed steps look even shabbier. When I cautiously leaned my weight against it, it was reassuringly sturdy. I headed up, dumped my purse at the desk Oona had said was mine, and went downstairs again.

Today, I was shadowing Oona at the reception desk. She promised that this wouldn't be my only task, but it was the fastest way to make myself visible to clients, and to start getting to know them. There were evidently a lot of regulars; Oona greeted nearly everybody by name, often accompanied by a question about how things were going in their lives. I felt like a charmless lump in comparison, but she praised my efforts. My other-else kept pinging—maybe two-thirds of the clients were supernaturals of some kind, which was high, even for New York's half-and-half population.

In between classes and events, Oona showed me some refinements in the booking system. The park was blocked out for construction for the rest of the week, but there were hopeful question marks over next week's booking slots.

"It's opening soon?" I said.

"Friday evening," Oona said. "We've got the final planning meeting for the opening tomorrow." She grimaced. "That'll give you a chance to meet Lady Seraphine. She'll do the park opening and the dedication speech and bring three dozen reporters."

A 500-year-old vampire, opening parks. If ambition was the biggest problem for wizards, and rage was the biggest problem for werewolves, the biggest problem for vampires was boredom. The less connected to life they were, the less likely they were to care about it—their own, or other people's. Vampires picked up hobbies as they aged. Philanthropy was probably a good one.

I mentioned that to Oona, and she snorted. "Philanthropy? Politics. Lady S wants to run for mayor."

"Seriously?" There'd never been a known non-human mayor of NYC, although everyone had their suspicions about the guy who'd seemed, in retrospect, a bit too goblinesque. A vampire wouldn't be my first pick as a likely candidate to break that barrier. A magician, maybe, which a lot of people thought of as the next thing to human anyway, or perhaps a part-fae with a lot of charisma.

"Seriously. She's been waiting for the right time for years. The philanthropy is to support the mayoral bid."

"Wow. How do you know?"

Oona's smile flickered. "Her PR head, Thomme, lives in the neighborhood, and they volunteer for our litter clean-up program. We've gone out for drinks a few times, and they gossip. But it's not that big a secret, anyway. We've already had reporters trying to get a scoop before the announcement."

An absolutely stunning red-headed woman wearing a diaphanous dress walked in at that point, and I abruptly lost my train of thought. The dress had sparkles and sequins covering the naughty zones, but that left so much smooth brown skin, soft and round, only lightly veiled by gold netting. She swayed towards us in golden heels, unstoppable as the sunrise, glorious as a song, heartbreaking as the bittersweet pangs of your first real love—

"Could you tone it down, Zenith?" Oona asked, her voice an unwelcome intrusion into my reverie. "The new girl's about to pass out."

"My apologies," said the gorgeous vision, in an alto voice that dragged lingeringly over my skin like the caress of a lover's hand. "How about this?"

I blinked hard as I came out of the trance, and found myself staring at a woman in a dress that belonged onstage at a jazz club. Still beautiful, but less overwhelming. My other-else was pinging wildly. *Demon, demon, demon*, and I was sure I knew what kind.

Zenith nodded at me and walked away, and I released my grip on the rim of the desk. My hands ached.

"What's a full-blooded succubus doing in a community rec center?" I hissed at Oona, who cackled at my blatant discomfort.

"Teaching burlesque and dance to people who want to find joy in their bodies," she said. "Her heels class is really popular."

"I bet!"

"Don't worry, it's really just the first time that it hits you that hard. She also volunteers for the clean-up program, and helps out with donation drives and some of our Meet and Mend sessions. She's really nice. And kind of lonely, I think."

"A *lonely* succubus?"

"She's in a monogamous relationship with this guy, Mark. He works a lot, so she has time to fill."

I'd never heard of a monogamous succubus, but I'd never heard of one doing volunteer work, either. Succubi didn't need to work unless it amused them. Most demons operated on a strict exchange basis, this for that, but people tended to just give succubi everything they wanted, often before they even bothered to ask for it. They were very popular in LA.

"Mark's a wizard," Oona added. "Rumor is that he summoned Zenith directly from the demonic realms and they entered a contract."

What would you have to promise a succubus in return for an exclusive relationship contract? This Mark must have some serious assets.

"Also, she told me that she loves him," Oona said, looking mystified. "Like, for real." She shook her head, as if shooing a bug away, and people started filing in, wearing athleisure wear and carrying lace-up stilettos. Oona showed me how to charge per class, or how to charge their multi-pass for those who had bought a slate of classes. A lot of the programs we provided were free, or had a nominal fee, but Zenith was charging real money, and people were paying it. And because we hired out rooms on a sliding scale, the rec center was making money too. Zenith was one of the few clients bringing in a profit.

The phone rang while Oona was talking to a customer, and I glanced at her for permission before picking up.

"Thirteenth Avenue Rec Center, this is Charlie. How may I help you?"

I heard a masculine chuckle, and then a smooth, deep voice said. "Hello, Charlie. This is Ian Kelly, of the Committee to Improve Avenue Thirteen. You may help me by explaining what's happened to our booking next month."

Oh, right. "Certainly, Mr Kelly. It turned out there was a prior booking for the gym that hadn't been recorded properly. In order to restore that reservation, we unfortunately had to move your booking to the dance studio, which should meet the identified needs for your meeting. It's a smaller, but much more comfortable room. We can provide the same tables and seating we'd booked for the gym, and there are also A/V links available."

All of that information had been in the email I'd sent him yesterday, but after two years work-study at the Butler, I knew not everyone read their email.

There was a patient sigh. "Well, I'm afraid that just won't do," he said.

"I apologize for the inconvenience, but unfortunately that's the only solution we can offer. We'll be more than happy to explain the misunderstanding to your guests and direct them to the appropriate—"

"You misunderstand me, Charlie," he interrupted, and his voice was no longer smooth. "I don't accept your 'solution'. You need to restore *our* reservation, now."

Oona shot me a worried glance, but she was dealing with a woman buying a multi-pass ticket.

"As I explained, there was actually a prior booking, and that had to take precedence," I said, keeping my voice pleasant with some effort. "If you're sure that you need the gym, I'll be happy to send you other dates—"

"No. Our booking, in the room we reserved, for the time and date that we reserved it."

"I'm afraid that won't be possible."

There was a chilling silence. I thought I knew what he was doing, but I let the silence stretch before I politely inquired, "Sir? Are you still on the line?"

"I'm here. I was waiting for you to realize the stupidity of what you'd just said to me."

I could feel my eyes narrowing, and my own voice shifted—still polite, but no longer conciliatory. "As I've explained several times, someone else reserved the room first. Again, I apologize—"

"Save your apologies for this supposed prior booking. Kick them out."

"No."

There was an inrush of breath. "*What?*"

"It's a child's birthday party, sir. I will not be 'kicking them out'."

"Child!" he said, his voice alive with scorn. "I heard it was a pup."

I made a fist so tight my fingernails dug into my palm. So he was *that* kind of asshole. "If our solution doesn't work, sir, I will be happy to cancel your booking and return the deposit."

"Who is it?" Oona mouthed, and I mouthed, "Ian Kelly," back.

She grimaced, and reached for the handset, which I gladly gave her. "Hello?" she said, and then rolled her eyes. "He hung up."

"What a—" I said, and then bit down tight on the cuss. Probably swearing about the clients on your second day was frowned upon.

I caught a glimpse of black leather and gleaming chrome outside the door, and then Tiffany Chang strode in, her thick hair ruffling in the rose-scented breeze.

She was right on time, but she hadn't toned down her look any for this meeting with Felantheril. In fact, I thought I spotted a new piercing high on the cartilage of her left ear. It looked silver. I knew it couldn't be, of course, because for a werewolf, that would be the equivalent of begging for a deadly sepsis infection, but it did look impressive.

"Is she here?" Tiffany asked me. Oona was evidently still in her bad books.

"Felantheril? Yes, she is. I'll walk you up."

"I know the way," she said, but the sneer was half-hearted, and she followed me without further protest through the staff-only door. "My niece is really excited that she gets to have a big party. It's dinosaur-themed, and now she's insisting on costumes."

"I thought she had a dress?"

"She plans to wear the dress over the costume. She's got a real thing about velociraptors."

I laughed, feeling better about my phone confrontation with Ian Kelly. It was worth a little conflict to make an eight-year-old happy. "That sounds super cute."

"She's a great kid." Tiffany seemed to be in a good mood. Maybe her meeting with Felantheril would go well.

I took three steps up the stairs, holding onto our pretty new rail.

Behind me, Tiffany howled.

It was a spine-chilling noise that raced up the back of my neck. I froze in an automatic cringe, clutching the rail to stop my legs from giving way. It was horribly difficult to turn around. Every instinct told me that behind me was the wolf, fangs bared, saliva dripping from her open jaws.

But when I turned, I saw a small woman hunched against the far wall, cradling her left hand against her chest. When she lifted her eyes, to mine, they were golden and angry, but with the rage was also pain.

Oona opened the stairwell door, Hannah popped through the wall, and Bev appeared at the top of the stairs, her hand diving into her leather purse. Tiffany's lips curled back, exposing her gums, and teeth that were too sharp and too long.

She held her hand out, and I winced at the weeping red welt across her palm. It looked as if she'd tried to pick up a hot cast-iron pan, bare-handed.

"Why the fuck," she said, her voice gravelly and low, "does your supposed *community* center have a stair railing full of silver?"

Chapter Six

"I'll find out," Bev said. Tiffany looked past me and locked eyes with her, and I felt very much like a small creature between two large predators. I was taller than Tiffany, and probably healthier than Bev, but I wasn't fool enough to pit myself against either of them.

Especially because Bev still had her hand hidden in her purse.

"I want to know who did this, and why," Tiffany growled.

"I'll find out," Bev repeated, and Felantheril wafted out behind her.

"Everything all right here?" she asked, peering down the stairwell over Bev's shoulder. "Oh, dear! That's a nasty wound. Let me fix that for you."

She took a step forward, but Tiffany snarled at her and she flinched back.

"Don't pretend you didn't know," Tiffany said, her voice rasping.

"Know what?" Felantheril asked, sounding hurt.

Tiffany was no longer listening to her. She'd refocused on Bev instead. "Take the new girl," she said.

It wasn't phrased as a suggestion. Bev's face didn't change, but the muscles in her forearm shifted, gripping tighter... then released. She took her empty hand out of her purse. "Charlie, you're with me," she said. "Oona, get back to the desk. Hannah, if you could fetch the first-aid kit—"

"I can handle a little burn," Tiffany said, and brushed past Oona. She was trying to move with ease, but she was stiff, bracing against the pain, and my other-else felt a hot red wire pulsing through the wild citrus glow it recognized as Tiffany. Anything that could hurt an alpha werewolf like that with just brief contact...

I sat on the steps.

"Are you okay?" Hannah asked.

"Mm? Sure." I was looking under the rail, first with my eyes, and then when that didn't show me anything, sliding my fingers along the cool metal. There, just at the edge of my awareness, a slight ridge, and a tiny shiver. "It's enchanted."

Bev was walking down the steps. "What kind of spell?"

I got up. "I can't tell. But pure silver would tarnish, and it's too malleable to serve as a real railing. If you wanted it to work, you'd need magic to hold it together. I think this might have been juiced up beyond that."

Bev made a thoughtful noise. "Most silver bullets are enchanted or a silver alloy, preferably over sixty percent. And they're expensive."

I looked at the railing, and tried to imagine how many bullets you could make out of it. It was a lot of silver.

"And Tiffany's no fool," Bev added. "She knows what silver looks and feels like. She wouldn't have touched it if she'd noticed, and she'd usually have noticed."

"I was distracting her," I said, feeling guilty.

Bev shook her head, and flicked the metal with her fingernail. It rang like a bell. "Not that much, you weren't."

The railing was enchanted, and not just to make the silver strong and shiny, but to hide what it was. Even from the senses of an alpha werewolf in her own pack's territory. Magic that powerful didn't come cheap.

"Money," Bev said, spitting the word like a curse. "Money and politics."

"Do you think An—" I said, and I seriously got less than a syllable into his name before Bev's hand was clutching my chin, cutting me off.

"Not here," she said tightly, and releasing me, walked down to ground level. "Basement. Come on."

I hadn't known the rec center had a basement, but it turned out the entry point wasn't from the stairwell, but through a door I hadn't noticed in the storage room and down a narrow set of steps. Tucked in beside the intimidating boiler was a workbench and two whole parking spaces. They were tiny, and both were half-occupied by one enormous car, a Ford with wood-grain panels that looked like the weird offspring of a coupe and a pickup truck. At first, I thought the "wood" was vinyl, but when I looked closer I realized it was actually thin sheets of real wood, varnished and polished.

"My driving glasses are in the glovebox," Bev said, a clear instruction, and I rummaged around for them while she reversed up the ramp I also hadn't noticed was there. I clearly needed to improve my observational skills. There was a ton of stuff in the glovebox—a half-empty crumpled packet of cigarettes, tissues, drive-thru napkins, two dried-out lipsticks in the same shade of neutral pink-brown. And charms. A whole bunch of protective charms, all easily as high-quality as the ones in my purse, but none of them with the same frisson of active magic. Half of them were charred, or had components missing. One looked like it had *melted*.

I found the glasses and handed them over, and we joined the traffic with a throaty roar.

We crawled through the streets. This wasn't exactly Midtown, but even so, traffic in Manhattan was always dicey. Courier cyclists swerved around us, a few pedestrians stopped to gape at Bev's wheels, and I spotted a pixie flitting above us at second-story level, his diaphanous wings blurring as he ignored all the congestion of the ground-bound.

I was still thinking over the events of the morning—and was maybe a little overwhelmed to be sitting in a cracked vinyl seat next to *Bev Thornton*—so it took me a while to realize that Bev was taking a circuitous route to wherever we were going. She took three right turns in a row, then a left, which sent us in the direction we'd come from. At one set of traffic lights, she suddenly signaled for the left turn just as the lights went green, which prompted a chorus of indignant honking.

"Do you think someone's following us?" I asked.

"Not sure." She parked, in magnificent disregard of the sign that prohibited parking on this side of the street on Tuesdays and Thursdays, popped a blank black card on the dashboard, and got out. "Come on."

I hustled after her as she walked into a deli, past the line, and into the back room. "A gutn tog, Judith," she said to the gnarled and wrinkled woman playing solitaire on a fold-out table.

"Morning, Bev. Back door?"

"Yep."

"Haven't seen you." She flipped a card, and muttered something in Yiddish, shaking her head. As we left, I looked over my shoulder to glimpse Judith hiding the card at the bottom of the draw pile, grinning like a delighted child.

We walked through a space too narrow to be an alley, hopped a low brick wall into a concrete square the size of my childhood bedroom, then dodged between two full and smelly dumpsters. When we emerged onto a street again, it wasn't until I spotted a sign for West 103rd that I realized we'd only gone a few blocks uptown of the rec center. The trees of Riverside Park were at our backs, which meant that Thirteenth Avenue was right ahead of us.

Bev checked over her shoulder to make sure I was with her, and then turned into an unmarked door, the window blacked out with either paint or grime. A bell jingled cheerily as we entered, and I blinked rapidly, trying to make my eyes adjust to the dusty dimness. I had the impression of shapes moving around us, but Bev didn't seem alarmed, so I decided it was nothing to worry about.

We were in a garage, with oil stains on the floor and a red muscle car hoisted up on a hydraulic lift. The shapes resolved into the bodies of three white men of varied age: a teenager with greased-back hair, a balding dad type with a paunch, and an elderly man so wizened I wondered if he might be part gnome. My other-else pulsed, as if it were as uncertain as I was. 'Not-ex-actly-human' was the best it could do.

The three of them regarded us for a moment, and then the old man spat meditatively on the concrete and nodded at the youngest one, who hitched up his skinny jeans and meandered towards a door in the back, giving Bev a respectful nod and me a quick up-and-down that managed to exactly trace the line between appraisal and appreciation. He couldn't have been more than seventeen.

I wished I'd brought my purse with me. The charm might not be effective, but I would have liked to know my pepper spray was close at hand.

"Beverley," the old one said, his voice like the creak of an open door. "You look wonderful. When are you going to make an honest man of me?"

"When Fenrir's son eats the moon, Rafn."

The middle-aged man laughed, and then turned it into a cough as Rafn's sharp black eyes cut towards him. "I'll be out the back, there?" he suggested, in the distinctive sing-song of a Minnesotan native.

Rafn nodded. "Bring tea, Bjorn."

"We can't stay long," Bev warned him.

The old man spread his hands. "Long enough for tea, and for me to warm my eyes on your face!"

"Next time," Bev said, and Anton walked out, wiping his greasy hands on an old rag. He brightened when he saw Bev, and me beside her, but as he walked over, I saw him register her expression and slow down, his mouth turning down at the corners. In that moment I knew Anton hadn't meant to hurt Tiffany, or anyone else. He looked like a kid who'd built a painstakingly detailed diorama for his favorite teacher, and was realizing too late that the assignment had been for a five paragraph essay.

"Ah," Rafn said. "Next time, then." And he left the three of us there, me confused, Anton shifting from foot to foot, and Bev stone-faced.

"What's up?" he asked.

"Where did you get the railing, Anton?"

He tried to give her a winning smile, but there was a worried set to his shoulders. "Ah, you know, from a guy."

"Which guy?"

"Not like, a *guy* guy. Might have fallen off the back of a truck."

"Which truck, where?"

"It's really important, Anton," I said.

His eyes fastened on me. "Am I in trouble?"

"Not yet," Bev said. "But I have to know. Where?"

He grimaced, then caved. "From that new park build. There was a truck parked outside the building site with some stuff that hadn't been unloaded yet."

"Which you lifted," Bev said. It wasn't a question.

"I only took the railing. I figured that everything belonged to the rec center anyway."

"The park build is from a vested fund. The things bought with that money aren't supposed to go to just any project."

Anton's eyes narrowed. "I don't see why you guys should have to deal with a death trap on your stairs while Lady Seraphine makes a big deal out of her shiny new park."

"What were you going to do if Lady Seraphine recognized the railing?" I said curiously. "She comes to the center, right?"

The look Anton gave me suggested that he hadn't gotten that far in his thinking. "It still isn't fair," he said stubbornly.

"That's how it goes," Bev said absently. Her eyes were flicking back and forth, as if she were thinking hard.

Anton sighed. "Do you need me to take it back?"

"Did you notice anything weird when you picked it up?"

"No."

"It wasn't noticeably heavier or lighter than usual?"

"I don't usually lift railings. Bev, what's going on? What's the problem?"

"That railing had a silver content high enough to burn an alpha werewolf on limited contact," Bev said crisply. "You turned our stairwell into a werewolf trap. You're lucky Sam wasn't in this morning."

I hadn't even thought about our resident vampire, but she was right; he'd be susceptible too. Silver wasn't quite as bad for vampires, but there was also whatever enchantment had been laid into that metal.

"Who?" Anton said, his olive skin looking a little pale in the dim light.

"Tiffany, of course."

I wasn't imagining it; the blood really was draining from his face. "Ah, crap. What do I do?"

Bev dismissed him with a wave. "You lie low for a while. I'll handle it."

Anton frowned. "I messed up, Bev. I should fix it."

"I'm on it," she said. "Okay. Let's go."

She walked out, but I lingered long enough to give Anton a sympathetic look.

He sighed. "She still thinks I'm the fifteen-year-old she needed to bail out of a demon gang."

"I thought the railing was really nice," I said. It was a truly generous act, if you ignored the whole 'fell off a truck' angle. "I felt much more secure, going up the stairs this morning."

He brightened. "Yeah? I'll see what I can do about a replacement."

"I didn't mean that you had to—"

"Hey," he said, and spread his hands. Wide, strong hands, I couldn't help noticing. "Your security is my pleasure."

It should have been corny—and it totally was—but his voice went smoky, and his eyes gleamed, and I was suddenly very aware that we were alone together. No curious co-workers, no passers-by, just the two of us in this dim and dusty place.

My skin tingled, and it wasn't entirely unwelcome.

"Charlie!" Bev called from the door, and I jumped, which would have been embarrassing if Anton hadn't startled as well. We exchanged awkward smiles, and I scurried out, blinking in the sudden bright light of a New York spring.

Bev didn't say anything as we retraced our steps, though I noticed that she took the direct route back to the center.

She parked in the basement and sat there for a moment. "Are you any good with tools?" she asked.

"I can do minor repairs," I said, by which I meant I could sew on a missing button or replace the O-ring in a leaky faucet. Power tools made me nervous, but I wasn't going to admit it.

"Right," she said, and started upstairs. The silver railing was still there, but someone had draped yellow warning tape all over it and taped on several handwritten signs that read "Danger: DO NOT TOUCH" in neat printing.

I trailed Bev to the admin area, where she headed to her desk, and the supply closet behind it. Mr. Scruffles was asleep under Hannah's desk, but he shook himself awake when we came in and trotted over to me. I bent to offer tribute in the form of head scritches, and so missed the moment when Bev opened the closet, but I felt the cessation of a hum I hadn't actually noticed until then, like the wind suddenly falling silent.

The supply cupboard was warded. *Heavily* warded.

I straightened, but Bev's broad back was blocking my view, and when I stepped closer, Hannah popped into view in front of me and shook her head, placing one finger against her lips. Right. Bev's private domain, then.

Bev backed out with a toolbox in hand, and reengaged the locks, both supernatural and mundane.

I spent the next miserable hour holding various bits of railing while Bev methodically unscrewed them. The stairwell was an unairconditioned, unventilated chimney shaft, and I was sweating before we'd got the first section down. By the time we reached the foot of the stairs, I was damp all over and panting for air.

Which, of course, was when a gorgeous man in a gorgeous suit walked through the staff-only door and blinked at us.

He looked like Hollywood's idea of a Viking, as if the Vikings had spent a lot of time eating superfoods and getting expensive facials, and considerably less time rowing warships in horrible weather and pillaging monasteries. He was easily six foot two of good looks, all broad shoulders and deep blue eyes. His hair was the color of wheat, gleaming even in the shitty stairwell fluorescents, parted neatly to the side.

"My goodness," he said mildly. His voice was rich and resonant, and he had an accent like a BBC newsreader.

He was absolutely delicious.

Unfortunately, he was a vampire.

Chapter Seven

Okay, yeah, I'm wary around vampires.

Partly, it's because my best friend is a werewolf with werewolf parents, and weres and vamps have bad blood going back before the Cataclysm, which *post*-Cataclysm weres and vamps eagerly adopted as at least one thing to give structure to their suddenly unmoored lives. You're unlikely to find a werewolf pack and a vampire nest occupying the same neighborhood, and when they do there's always trouble. I heard a lot of stories growing up, and I'm sure that influenced my prejudices.

Partly, it's the atavistic fear of being *food*. Vampire attacks for feeding purposes have really dwindled since the mid-70s, when some powerful vampires put their feet down, very hard, on bad vampire necks. There are plenty of willing donors for vamps who prefer their blood from the vein, and there are free blood banks to make up the gaps, which is one of the most successful social programs of the last sixty years. Even the most fervent opponents to the welfare state came around when they realized it was in their own best interests to make sure vampires got fed. But still, you know and they know that what runs in your veins is their three-course dinner.

And finally, it's the sexy sexlord thing, which is hugely annoying. I know a lot of people love it, and I like flirting as much as anyone, but if I go to a club I'm going there to *dance*. I'm not looking for some guy to shout over the music, trying to entice me with the wonders of the night. I'd almost rather they talked about Bitcoin.

I'm aware I sound like an asshole. I can't even claim that I'm worried they'll make *me* a vampire. Magicians can't be turned any more than they can grow fur every full moon, and vamps are very quick to point out that even for humans, turning has to be a choice. It doesn't seem like much of a choice if you're, say, bleeding out and desperately want to live, but you do have to fundamentally accept the transformation.

We know this, incidentally, because of some horrible studies that came out of France in the early 80s. In Lyon and Saint-Étienne, two ancient rival vampires, delighted by the possibilities that opened up post-Cataclysm, tried to amass a lot of followers very quickly. They discovered that even on the brink of death, a lot of people *did not* want to be vampires. One of the generals, who'd been an Enlightenment philosopher before he was turned himself, got methodical about it and kept notes, which were discovered after both of the original vampires and most of their new recruits were brutally slaughtered by the Alliance des Chasseurs.

History is full of these fun little stories.

Logically, I know that these days most vampires are law-abiding folk just trying to get by, the same way that most men are decent people who would never think of harming their wives and girlfriends. But fifty percent of female homicides are committed by male intimate partners, and nearly forty percent of homicides committed by supernatural means are vampire attacks. I don't leave my drinks unattended in bars, I don't date men who try to make me feel shitty, and I don't feel entirely comfortable around vampires.

And now there was this golden god who'd just walked through the staff-only door wearing a suit that cost more than I would make in a month, looking calm and collected and in his mid-thirties, not the several centuries my other-else told me he was carrying. I was all too aware of the strands of hair sticking to my face and the spreading patches of armpit sweat under my sensible button down.

"Can I *help* you?" I said, in my snottiest tone.

He smiled at me, flashing the tips of his fangs, but I was too sticky and frustrated to flinch, and also, I already knew he was a vampire.

"I'm here to meet with Felantheril," he said, and then looked at Bev. "Or am I meeting with you in her stead, Miss Thornton? Again." He said the last word like it was an inside joke.

Bev didn't return his smile, but she was equally dry-voiced. "Not this time, Raphael."

Oh, of *course* he was named after an archangel. And the coolest Ninja Turtle.

Raphael gave Bev a quizzical look—evidently this wasn't the answer he'd expected—but made a move towards the stairs. Which I was blocking.

I could try to edge around him, or let him edge around me or—forget it. I went up the stairs ahead of him, trying to pretend like that had been my next move all along.

"You're the new hire?" he said conversationally.

"Yep."

"Ah. What were you doing with the—"

I opened the door in the middle of his sentence, and said, "Hannah, Raphael is here to meet Felantheril."

Hannah looked up from her screen. "Oh! I think Bev's downstairs somewhere."

"I'm apparently to meet with the lady herself this time," Raphael said. "But I'm not positive I remember the way."

That was dumb. There weren't that many doors.

But Hannah only said, "Charlie can show you."

"Charlie," he said, his accent light on the R. "How lovely. Short for Charlotte, I presume?"

"Presume away," I said, and dutifully led him to Felantheril's door, rapping twice before I opened it. "Felantheril? Raphael is here to see you."

Felantheril was sitting on her desk, her long, bare legs tucked under her skirt. For a second I saw panic flash across her face, and then she went straight into ditz mode. "Oh dear," she said, looking flustered. "Surely Bev—"

"Told me to see you," Raphael said. He didn't show any surprise at her unusual position, but sat down in the chair across from her desk without asking. "Lady Seraphine is looking for an update on the park situation, and you have not responded to my last three emails."

Oh *crap*. I should have realized, and probably would have, if my brain had been less cooked. A vampire in a business suit, known to the staff, who had business with Felantheril? Of *course* he worked for Lady Seraphine, who had the final say over my employment. And of *course* I'd been borderline rude to him. It was absolutely that kind of day.

I reached for the doorknob, meaning to cut my losses and close it behind me as I left, but Felantheril said, "Stay here, Charlie."

It was an order, and just in case I thought about resisting it, my oath tightened around my throat like a choke-chain. I stepped into the room and closed the door on the three of us instead.

Raphael had apparently not noticed the by-play.

"Previously, you had indicated a park opening date of—" he began, and began one of the politest scoldings I'd ever witnessed. If I'd had any doubt about who held the power at the rec center, Felantheril's reaction every time he said the name "Seraphine" would have corrected me. Lady Seraphine wasn't just a major donor; she was essentially Felantheril's boss.

The mountain-sized chip on Tiffany's shoulder was beginning to make more sense. We had vampires and werewolves in the same neighborhood, negotiating the use of the same territory, and at the moment, the werewolves appeared to be losing.

Felantheril tried wide-eyed bemusement, then implied that she'd forgotten all the previous dates without quite saying she had, and then finally admitted that yes, she'd taken a little longer winding up the previous construction company's contract than Lady S had expected, and her apologies if she'd given the impression things were on track for the previous three dates.

Raphael showed neither frustration nor any inclination to call her on her bullshit, and I was reluctantly impressed. He just kept doggedly pointing out gaps between what Felantheril had indicated might happen and what had actually happened.

"Lady Seraphine's calendar is tight," he said finally. "I must ask for assurance that the park *will* be ready for the scheduled dedication ceremony on Friday."

"The new construction company assured me everything would be ready."

"Which representative of the company?"

"Oh, who can recall these things?" Felantheril said vaguely.

"I would like to speak to the project manager."

"I don't think I have her number."

This dodging back and forth was incredibly annoying. Fortunately, I'd been doing some quiet snooping at the reception desk earlier.

"The company's Callahan Construction," I said. "The park wasn't in their gallery of recent projects, but they had contact numbers listed on their website and a general enquiries email, so I could easily find out who's in charge of the project."

They both looked at me like they'd forgotten I was there at all.

Raphael recovered first. "Excellent," he said, and stood up. Felantheril gave me a betrayed look, but I wasn't feeling very sympathetic. She'd tugged on the leash of my oath to make me stay here so she didn't have to talk to the scary man alone. I wasn't an emotional support animal.

"May I borrow Charlie?" he said, and Felantheril blinked.

"Why?"

"I'll need a representative of the center with me while I inspect the site," he said. "No need to trouble you."

Augh, *no*. They were supposed to send me back to my desk, where I could use my degree to write a nice email to Callahan Construction.

"Now?" Felantheril said, and glanced out her window. It was mid-afternoon, and bright daylight.

"I assure you, my wards will be sufficient," Raphael said briskly, and yeah, if he could afford that suit, he could definitely afford top-dollar wards to protect him from sunlight. Smart vampires who were active in the daytime got at least two sets of wards, layered on top of each other, from two different wizards. That way, if one wizard was incompetent or got bribed to take their work apart, or had a massive heart attack, the other ward was still current and the vampire wasn't a smoking skeleton on the sidewalk.

"Shall we?" Raphael asked me.

I effectively had no choice, but I appreciated the courtesy of the question, so I nodded and got up. At least I'd stopped actively sweating. I tried to comb my hair into some kind of order with my fingers as we went down the stairs.

Oona was still on the reception desk, and I guiltily wondered if anyone had relieved her for a lunch break. I'd been supposed to do that, and then the day had gotten completely out of hand. I couldn't do anything about it now, but I gave her an apologetic look.

Raphael held the door open for me, and we fell into step. "I'm afraid I don't know the exact nature of your position," he said.

"Administrative assistant. I started yesterday."

"Ah, one of those cheerfully broad job titles that can mean you do almost anything."

"What's yours?"

"Aide-de-camp. Another general dogsbody title."

He probably hadn't wanted to come to the rec center and try to get information out of Felantheril, but his boss had told him to, and he'd had as little choice as I did. Our eyes met in our first genuine moment of mutual empathy.

"Um, well, the park is here," I said, and stopped outside the gate, with its AUTHORIZED PERSONNEL ONLY sign and a notice underneath to sign in with the site supervisor.

"I see," he said, and stood there for a moment. I waited for him to take the lead, then realized he wasn't going to. I reached for the gate latch.

"Lady Seraphine is really very keen on recreational opportunities," Raphael said suddenly, and I paused. "She feels that in a metropolis like this one, it's important for children in particular to have access to outside play spaces."

"I agree," I said politely.

"Adults, too, can benefit from green spaces. Our fae community members are particularly fond of areas of natural growth, but even manicured landscapes improve their physical and spiritual wellbeing."

"I've heard that as well."

Raphael was looking at me, but his eyes were a little out of focus. "It's important that the dedication ceremony to her illustrious ancestor go well."

"Which ancestor?"

"This is to be the Jeanne d'Arc Park." He smiled, flashing more fang, and looking more like himself. "My apologies for the rhyme."

"Lady Seraphine is descended from Joan of Arc?" I said. "*Saint* Joan?"

Raphael coughed. "Not directly. The Maid of Orleans was, of course, a maid."

"Yes, she was examined by the women of the court to prove her virginity," I said impatiently. "And then again in that sham trial. Not that a physical examination proves anything but that she still had her hymen, but that was considered firm proof in the time period, and there was never reason to doubt her word. Witnesses at the rehabilitation trial did claim that once she started wearing women's clothes—"

"You're well-informed," Raphael said.

"Oh. Sorry, History ma— recent History graduate. I took a special seminar on historical oracles."

"Also a rhyme," Raphael murmured.

I smiled. "Anyway, no kids."

"Lady Seraphine is descended from Jeanne's sister, Catherine." He said it as if he expected the statement to be challenged, but I didn't know anything about the family tree. The seminar had focused on Joan's visions, not her relatives.

"Wait a minute," I said. "There's already a Joan of Arc Park! It's a few blocks that way, on Riverside. It has that statue of

Joan on a horse in her armor. It was one of the first statues in New York to depict a real woman. It was *by* a woman, too, Anna something. Anna Huntington!"

Raphael blinked at me. "You're not wrong," he said.

"Then why—"

He shrugged. "Lady Seraphine wished it so." And that, his tone implied, was that.

"Okay, cool," I said, and reached for the gate latch again.

"You're not beautiful, but you're rather clever, and there's something about you that's very attractive," Raphael said.

I spun on my heel. "*Excuse* me?" He'd done so well avoiding the sexy sexlord thing up until then. And now he was pulling out a clumsy neg?

His eyes were wide and shocked. "I— Do forgive me," he said. "I didn't mean to say that."

"That was *completely* inappropriate," I said firmly.

"I agree. My sincerest apologies." He looked genuinely appalled. On closer inspection, there was moisture on his upper lip, and a tremor in the corner of that perfect mouth. His hands were gripped together at his stomach, like something was hurting him.

I eyed him carefully. "Are you feeling all right?"

"I've recalled that I need to take care of some urgent business," he said, and took three steps backwards. He shook his head, hard, like he was trying to jostle his thoughts together. "Could you please... inspect the premises without me? My business card. Call me." He was thrusting it towards me at arm's length.

"Uh. Sure?" I took the card, an embossed cream thing with a plush texture.

"Thank you. I just need confirmation that the dedication ceremony can proceed as scheduled. Er. Sorry again." He took another step backwards, nearly tripped over a stroller, scattered more apologies in his wake, and took off, walking just a little faster than human standard.

What, as they say, the fuck.

I reached for the latch again, this time without interruption, and pushed the gate open. The park was swarming with a bunch of people in hardhats and hi-vis, many of them wearing tool-belts, all of them looking beyond busy. I took a guess that the pre-fabricated cabin to the side was the site office, and headed over, moving cautiously and looking around as I went. It was going to be a small park, tucked into the corner of a city block, but it seemed pretty nice to me, even in its unfinished state. There was some children's play equipment, benches, steps leading up and down to a couple of vantage points, and even a fountain at the center of a little circular pond. The fountain basin was currently dry, the trees in the back corner were on the spindly side, and a lot of the garden beds were still just loose soil, but I could imagine how pretty it would look when everything was finished.

No silver railings were visible. The truck had been parked outside, Anton said, so maybe he'd been mistaken that it was for the park. I wasn't sure how I felt about that. Re-appropriating materials that came out of rec center accounts had made sense to me, despite all the talk about vested funds. But maybe Anton had accidentally taken materials for something else. A prison, maybe? I couldn't think what else you'd want enchanted high-silver-content metal for.

A man carrying a clipboard came out of the cabin as I approached, settling his hard hat on his head.

"Hi," I said. "I was sent to check if everything will be ready for the opening ceremony on Friday."

He nodded, looking slightly surprised. "You're the wizard?"

Hannah must have called ahead to give them a heads-up. I didn't feel like going into the vocabulary—most people really didn't care if you were a magician or a wizard proper. Neither did I, though wizards sometimes cared a lot. "Yep, that's me."

"Dave, site manager. Sorry, I thought you were a guy."

My gender-ambiguous nickname had struck again. "I get that sometimes."

"And I thought there were two of you. Boss not coming?"

I tamped down the urge to snap that Raphael wasn't my *boss*, and shook my head. "Sorry, just me. I don't want to take up too much of your time. I only need to confirm that—"

"Let me give you the tour," he said, and reached back inside the cabin to grab me a hardhat and hi-vis vest of my very own. I wavered for a moment, thinking about Oona bravely womanning the desk without a break, and then complied. I didn't want to screw this up, and the more complete report I could give Raphael, the better.

Also, I was curious as hell. I'd only been at the rec center for two days, and this pleasant urban park had been the source of a lot of conflict already.

Dave was a man of few words. I gathered that he was the second in command, while the actual project manager was off-site, dealing with some dispute. He pointed out features I'd already noticed, and made some comments about the water table and the difficulty of boring through Hartland schist. I hoped I was nodding in the right places. I'd left my phone behind, or I'd be taking notes in an effort to look like I knew what he was talking about.

"It looks like you've made amazing progress," I said. "Especially compared to what I've heard about the previous crew."

He snorted. "Well, what did they expect?"

I had no idea what this meant. "Right, exactly."

"All that diversity crap. Just slows down the work." He glanced at me. "No offense."

"None taken," I said brightly.

"You people have done good work. I meant, you know, generally speaking." We went up a set of concrete steps, where a bench was being bolted into a platform with something noisy.

"Rowans are going in now," he said, pointing to a group of four people digging holes and moving little trees around. "Ten years to full growth, more or less."

"Mm," I said. Who had he meant by "you people"? Women? Magicians? The people working at the rec center? In any case, I wasn't flattered by being the exception to the diversity-is-bad rule.

"Okay, the fountain," he said. "The statue's arriving tomorrow, and the plumbing's nearly done. Jackie said the plants shouldn't go in until just before opening, but it'd help if we could do it a day earlier, so they've got a chance to bed in overnight. That work for you?"

"Sure."

"So, new statue in tomorrow, couple days to let the concrete set, then we can put in the ornamental stone and test the water again." He frowned at a chisel that had been left on the fountain rim and bent to pick it up.

A charm swung out of the top of his vest. It was similar to the one Mom had given me, except his had a crucifix stamped into the silver side.

And mine was in my purse, whereas he was actually wearing it. And he definitely wasn't a tourist, which meant he was probably a Humans First sympathizer, or maybe even a party member. If that was the case, "you people" probably did mean magicians.

Ugh.

It struck me that I'd been walking around this space surrounded by people for nearly half-an-hour, but my other-else had been quiet the whole time. I crouched, pretending to inspect the rim of the fountain, and deliberately sent my senses out.

Nothing. Not even a hint of demon blood or a whisper of fae charm. Unless I was mistaken, this entire construction crew were completely human.

I straightened, shading my eyes from the sun. Now that I was looking, there were more charms visible, hanging around necks or swinging from workbelts. One man reached up to take something from a pick-up bed, and I saw the tattoo inked on his inner bicep.

It was a little red orb, joined with a black bar to a little white orb.

On the surface, it was totally harmless, just an illustration of something hundreds of thousands of kids played with in science classes all over the country. Molecule model kits, where red meant oxygen, white was hydrogen, black was carbon, and so on.

If you knew anything about militant anti-supernatural groups, it meant something else. Hydroxide. OH. Only Humans.

Humans First weren't my favorite people. They wanted law enforcement to "do more" about incidents of supernatural violence. They wanted legislation that would exclude certain supernaturals from certain jobs, partial or complete bans on further migration from the Fae and Demon Realms, and a host of other things that they'd politely debate with you as if they weren't talking about limiting people's right to exist in our world. They would tell you they weren't *anti-supernatural*, they just wanted to *exercise caution*, and while we were discussing this, did we really think voting rights should extend to ghosts when dead people voting had once upon a time been viewed as a clear example of election fraud? They were bigots who would vociferously protest that label, but they were at least bigots who were trying to enact their bigotry through mostly democratic means.

Only Humans didn't want to *restrict* supernatural rights. Only Humans wanted to exterminate supernaturals.

They wouldn't always say it out loud. They talked about the great American nation, the proud tradition of the Hunters who had protected us in the dark days of the Cataclysm. If only someone could raise the torch and be a beacon for the *people* of this great land... and then some asshole would bomb a wizarding academy or go on a shooting spree in a werewolf daycare center. When the Only Humans ties were found, their smug leaders would go on TV and claim it was *abnormal and disturbed individuals, acting alone, in response to supernatural provocation.*

The man who was now carefully lowering a tree into a hole looked very normal. Very undisturbed.

And he'd inked a hate group symbol onto his skin.

My skin prickled, and I concentrated on breathing normally as I took another, slower survey of the park. Rowan trees were fast growing and ornamental, but a lot of fae had severe allergies to the wood, flowers, and berries. Two of the garden beds were lined in feathery bushes with little yellow and white flowers. Grandmother Cross had made sure I could recognize my herbs.

"Are those yarrow?" I asked casually.

"Yup. Growing well."

Another plant used against the fae. I glanced at the dark concrete path beneath my feet, where light glinted off something glittering embedded in the material. There were sparkling sidewalks in the city, and I'd assumed it was more of the same. "How's that going?" I said, nodding towards my feet.

Dave scratched his head. "The quartz was no problem, but I'm not going to lie, the silver dust was kind of an issue. It's going to wear."

"Right, of course," I said. Silver dust on the pathways that werewolf kids might run along, rowan and yarrow to turn the fae away... I turned slowly, looking not at the paths themselves, but at how they were laid out.

A ring in the middle for the fountain, and then four paths at right angles along the cardinal directions, the south path longer than the others.

"Celtic cross," I murmured. A vampire repellent.

"Yeah, ripping out the winding paths the previous crew put in was a pain in the ass, but we got her there." He nodded at a patch of grass. "You can barely see where we laid the turf down to cover it."

This was not a friendly neighborhood park, not for any neighborhood in this city, but especially not for Thirteenth Avenue. Lady Seraphine wouldn't be happy to present it to the public. She wouldn't even be able to walk its paths.

I couldn't feel any magic, which should have been reassuring. But I remembered the way Raphael had sweated and hesitated and run away from the gates, and thought instead that it was a very bad sign.

"What have you got for ghosts?" I asked, so very nonchalant. I felt as if I were floating numbly above myself, watching some other me ask casual, damning questions.

Dave squinted at me. "Isn't that your department?"

"Sure," my mouth said. "I was wondering if you'd done anything special with the construction, though—helps us know what the materials are before we lay in enchantments."

"No, nothing special. Just the salt circle buried around the border." He squinted again. "Didn't you already enchant it?"

My other-else was quiet, but my ordinary instincts were yelling very loudly that I had to get the hell out of here. Dave had mistaken me for someone else, someone who knew all about this awful plan. In retrospect, I realized, neither he nor I had said I was from the rec center.

Callahan Construction were working within high wire-mesh fences, hidden behind opaque plastic sheeting. They were changing paths at the last minute, planting something hideous around the fountain, and preparing for a dedication ceremony that would humiliate and undermine one of the most well-regarded vampires in the city.

Their crew were all human, and many of them were Only Humans sympathizers.

And I knew, without having to be told, that they were working with some very dangerous wizards.

Chapter Eight

"Well, this all looks great," I said, while icy beads of sweat rolled down my back. "I'm happy to go back and report that to my boss."

Dave nodded, taking due recognition for a job well done. "It'll be nice to have a safe space for the kids."

I wanted to vomit, or maybe punch him in the face, but instead I nodded back. "Anything in particular you want me to pass on to the higher ups?" I said. I wanted a name, if I could get one. He'd said something earlier, and I'd missed it while I was still confused by the general weirdness.

"I don't think so," he said, and then his face brightened. An older woman in a pant suit was coming through the gate, pulling her hair back into a ponytail as she swapped her suit jacket for an orange vest.

"That's Jackie," Dave said. "The project manager. She'll know about anything else you'll need."

Jackie was talking to a man who'd run up to her with a clipboard, evidently talking through a list of items. She asked a question and he pointed in our direction.

Even from this distance, I could make out the sudden tension in her body.

"Actually, I'm afraid I have another appointment," I said. Was there another exit? Yes, there, another gate opening onto the cross road.

"It'll just take a minute," Dave said. Jackie was striding towards us, her sensible pumps eating up the ground.

"Sorry, I'm already late," I said, and took off, walking as fast as I could without actually running.

"Dave!" Jackie shouted behind me. "No visitors on site!"

Dave said something.

"What?" Jackie said. "She's not—"

She cut off abruptly, but I didn't dare look behind me to see why. I was only yards from the gate. I tripped the latch and pushed it open.

Or tried. There was something heavy on the other side, blocking my exit. *Fire hazard*, I thought, giddy with adrenaline, and then shoved as hard as I could. The gate opened a sliver, and I shoved again, thrusting desperately at the narrow gap. No time for pretense now; I was trying to escape, and I didn't care if they saw.

Why couldn't I have *real* magic? A little bit of telekinesis would really do the trick right now.

I shoved harder. Something on the other side crashed to the ground. There was suddenly less pressure on the door, and a gap just wide enough for me to wriggle through, if I was motivated.

I was *really* motivated.

A bony hand came down on my shoulder. I abandoned all decorum and shrieked, turning sideways and forcing myself through the gap. Something scraped my hip and back. The hard hat I was still wearing banged against the gate poles and then fell off as I clawed at it.

The hand on my shoulder clutched harder and then slipped away as I wriggled out of that stupid hi-vis vest and ran for my life.

***

I was panicking and scared, but I wasn't a big enough idiot to run straight back to the rec center. It was on the very next block and they wouldn't have to catch me to find out who I was. They'd just have to step outside the construction site, look up and down the street, and watch the red-haired girl disappear into the building with the roses outside.

Instead, I took a page out of Bev's book. I raced down the first cross-street, then doubled back on myself. I didn't know any deli owners who'd let me use the back door, but I had been introduced to at least one other place in the neighborhood.

I was in luck. The werewolf barman from yesterday was on duty today, and he looked up in startled recognition as I barreled down the steps and through the door. "I'm Oona's friend," I said, just to make sure, and then went for it. I didn't have time to be subtle. "I think I'm being chased by Only Humans. Can I use your back door?"

There were four patrons in the bar. My other-else pinged *human, werewolf, werewolf,* and something fae that my eyes told me was a bridge troll. The werewolf closest to the door was moving towards it before I was even fully inside, and the bridge troll was rising to his massive feet.

"This way," the barman said, and jerked his head towards the door behind the bar. I heard the clunk of a heavy lock behind me. The two werewolves were peering through the glass panel.

I didn't have much pity for any Only Humans creeps who tried to chase me through that door.

"What happened?" the barman asked as he took me through the kitchen. Baz, that was his name. The human guy at the grill looked up.

"I saw something I shouldn't have," I said. "That park, the one they're building down the block? It's a supernatural death trap."

"Oh, okay," Baz said. It was too casual a response, and I stopped to stare at him. His eyes were just a bit glazed. He could have been distracted or bored, but I knew, with a sensation like swallowing rocks, that that wasn't the answer.

Just how effective were the wards on that building site? This was *big* magic. Maybe even beyond Tenth Class.

For wizards, beyond Tenth Class is when things start going very wrong.

"Wait," Baz said, looking at me suspiciously. "What are you—"

"Only Humans is after me," I said, sticking to what had worked before. "Back door?"

His eyes cleared with the reminder. Words are powerful things in their own right.

"Right," he said, and led me past a big walk-in refrigerator to a heavy back door. I suspected the bar didn't have much in the way of warding, because when a bar is the hangout spot for the local pack, it doesn't need wards. A few lights and whistles aren't nearly as big a deterrent as several dozen pissed-off werewolves. But that door tingled against my hands as I shoved it open, and I got the distinct impression I was leaving a place of safety.

"Are you going to be okay?" Baz asked.

"Don't worry," I said, with far more confidence than I felt. "I'm going somewhere safe."

But just in case, I ran for it as I went up the steps and down the alley.

Good thing, too, because even as I left the narrow gap, I saw three people wearing hi-vis rounding the corner of the block. One of them was Dave. There was a shout behind me, but I took off, accelerating from fast jog to dead sprint, through the indignant traffic, and into Riverside Park. I could have tried to lose them there, among the trees and other people, but I had a destination in mind: three blocks up and to the left.

Maybe I lost them anyway, because I didn't see any hi-vis behind me when I risked a quick glance over my shoulder. The building I wanted had gray stone steps, and heavy oak and glass doors. I could feel the building's aura before I even hit the door, but the second I was in, it folded over me, warm and comforting as a weighted blanket.

It was such a relief that I could have cried.

Instead, I straightened up, raked my fingers through my hair to even it out a bit, and exhaled.

I was standing in the foyer of the newest branch of the New York Public Library.

Chapter Nine

L ibraries have always been special places.

I don't mean that just as a historian, although we'd never be able to do our jobs without them. I mean all those gathered words, made available to anyone who can access them, have *power*.

The words don't have to be written, either, or even what most of us might consider words. Societies with a strong oral or visual culture have similar repositories of knowledge. There are meeting grounds where the earth has absorbed the power of generations of oratory, buildings where complex metaphysics and history are relayed through the carvings on the eaves and the patterns woven into the wall panels. I've never been invited to one of those places, but I'm told by people who have that they have a similar feel, that weighted, awe-inspiring sense of power held in trust.

The New York Public Library system is a series of magical refuges. Each branch has a genius locii, a sort of spirit that comes from all that accumulated knowledge and the community it serves. No one's succeeded in establishing reliable communication with a library, and they probably don't think in a way we can access or even comprehend, but as much as libraries can want anything, they seem to want to serve their patrons. Even people who rate baseline for supernatural sensitivity can feel the weight of a library. Even pre-Cataclysm, people got poetic about how good libraries felt.

Plus, ever since I'd done that favor for the ghost of Butler Library, all the university and city libraries I'd visited had felt, well, friendlier towards me. This kind of implied that libraries could communicate with each *other*, which was both thrilling and kind of scary.

Metaphysically, libraries are safe zones. I wasn't protected against *all* harm within the branch walls, but magically speaking, I was fine. The wizards that Only Humans had hired wouldn't be able to drop me with a lightning spell or even scry on my location. Unfortunately, the Only Humans goons themselves could technically still jump me, even though they'd be stupid to try.

Because a defining characteristic of Only Humans was that they were stupid enough to think humans were the only kind of beings who should exist, I wasn't placing any bets on their intelligence. I went up to the fourth floor, where the reading cubicles were. They were about half-full, which I figured was enough people to make a fuss if someone got violent. People will tell you that New Yorkers don't care, but it's not true. And they *really* care if your business intrudes upon theirs.

I was about to take a seat in a cubicle near the end of the row when the light at one end of the shelf flickered. I walked towards it, and another light flickered, a little further on.

I can take a hint. I followed the blinking lights through the shelves and around several corners until I found myself blinking at a bare wooden panel on a wall. It was flanked by shelves on both sides, and I hadn't seen it until I was practically face-to-face with it. The panel didn't have a handle, but there was a small brass plate and a keyhole.

I put my palm against the wood and pressed.

The narrow door opened easily. I walked into a room with a tight floor plan and a high ceiling. It held a desk, one of those leather chairs on wheels, a filing cabinet, and two shelves of books that went all the way up. There was a casement window that let some light filter through the dust. The air smelled empty and dry, as if it hadn't been disturbed in a long time.

I sat in the chair with what I hoped was appropriate reverence. "Thank you," I said quietly.

Look, just because we can't communicate doesn't mean we can't be *polite*.

I let my bones melt into the chair, took a deep breath of the dusty air, and settled in to think. My hands were shaking, and my heart was pounding, and not just from the exercise. Whatever I'd stumbled into, it was big, and it was dangerous. I let the panic come and go in waves, and when it died down again, I started tracing the thought to its logical conclusion.

Realistically speaking, a ward from a halfway-decent magician, say a Third Class, could make it harder for people intending to do damage to enter a specific place, or provide some protection for a particular person. That was the whole theory behind protection charms. A ward that could hide itself, so that nobody *knew* there was a ward, was exponentially more difficult—you were looking at Fifth Class work for that. And that was still over a small area—a home safe behind a hidden panel, for example, or a single VIP who didn't want anyone to know they were important. The construction site had a ward that covered a corner of a city block, made people stay away, wasn't recognizable as a ward, *and* was sufficiently complex and powerful that people couldn't even recognize they were being turned back.

Raphael the hot vampire had really needed to get into that site. He'd been sent by his patron to check on it; disobeying that order could have had nasty consequences. I'd watched him in that meeting with Felantheril. He wasn't easily deterred or swayed by glamor. And yet, the closer we'd got to the gate, the more uncomfortable he'd become. He'd brought up new conversational topics, he'd said I was attractive, and then, when it was clear I still intended to enter the site, he'd claimed urgent business elsewhere and hurried away.

The real kicker was Baz the barman. Half a block away, and the ward had still been strong enough to fuzz his brain and make him momentarily forget what we were doing and why I was there. That was, frankly, just too much magic.

But the ward had let *me* in. That was the one bright note, because it meant the wards hadn't been keyed to particular people, but to particular species. Wizards and humans were okay. Everyone else, I was betting, was being pushed away. So the people who were able to walk in were the same ones Only Humans expected to actually use the park. Presumably, just before the opening, their pet wizards would drop or adjust the wards, and then the supernatural community of Thirteenth Avenue would realize exactly what was happening in the heart of their neighborhood.

And Lady Seraphine would be cutting the ribbon on a park that made a mockery of everything the community rec center stood for. I couldn't predict the exact repercussions of that, but, for just one example, I didn't think Tiffany Chang would react to this kind of provocation with some polite emails.

I finally let myself understand what was going on.

Callahan Construction had hired mauvais wizards. From what the site manager had said, they'd hired *two* of them.

Here's the thing about magicians. Whether you think of us as human or not, we have human biology and mostly-human limitations. The only quantifiable difference is that we have an extra sense, the other-else, which manifests slightly differently in everyone. The Abbot-Grace scale measures roughly how much power you can call with your other-else, and you get whatever power you're born with.

There are a few workarounds. Some magicians have an affinity for a particular element, or a field of magic—fire spells, scrying, nature magic—and can do things in that field that might normally be considered out of their class range. Trained wizards can combine power for complex workings in circles of three, seven or twelve, essentially chaining spells together.

But your personal class—the raw power you can access alone—never changes. And in the same way that even the fastest human sprinter will never run a five-second 100 meters or the most powerful human gymnast will never land a quintuple flip on their beam routine, there's an upper limit to how much power even a Tenth Class wizard can access.

Unless, that is, you decide to go for the magical equivalent of doping.

There's no charm or potion that'll boost your class, although a lot of grifters make money from that kind of scam. There's only one reliable way to permanently gain more power than you start out with, and that's by giving up your empathy.

That's the bargain mauvais wizards make. They metaphysically cut away their ability to care, and in return, they get to impose more of their will upon a stubborn universe. If I was willing to stop caring about humanity in general, I'd get to Third Class immediately. If I gave up the ability to care about most people I know personally, probably Fourth. If I gave up all of my empathy, I'd lose not only my love for my mother and my best friend, but any recognition of why that was a bad thing. I would regard them, and every other person, as an object, a *thing* that could be good or bad for me. And I would act accordingly.

If I thought the outcome would be good for me, I'd lie, I'd cheat, I'd harm people, and I'd never, ever understand why that was wrong.

I'd also be a Magician Fifth Class, capable of complex illusion, powerful telekinesis, teleportation, emotional manipulation, and some fairly nasty destructive spells.

And that would be *me*, starting out as First Class.

You can't just try it out, either. Once you go mauvais, even a little, you can't go back to where you used to be. Opinion is divided as to whether it's metaphysically impossible, or whether someone with lessened empathy can't care enough to change. This is why magical academies have the best and most highly paid youth psychologists in the world. They're keeping an eye out for magicians who are already less empathetic than the norm, and they're especially watching for high-class magicians who might *go* that way, out of greed, or rage, or the kind of misery that makes you want to just *stop caring*. That's a kind of misery that teenagers are especially prone to, and it's not great regardless of species. But when it's a wizard-in-training, it can be explosively terrible.

What I was dealing with at the construction site were two deliberately sociopathic wizards, at least one of whom had started out pretty high on the Abbot-Grace scale to begin with, and was now orders of magnitude more powerful than a single benign wizard could ever be. They wouldn't see anything wrong about working with Only Humans, as long as it was to their benefit. They'd do the work and get paid, and if you couldn't beat the offer, it might take a full Circle of Twelve to stop them.

(If you ever want to give yourself the screaming horrors in the middle of the night, think about what could go down if mauvais wizards eventually figure out how to circle up. Personally, I don't think it'll ever happen, because they wouldn't be psychologically capable of maintaining an empathetic link with eleven other magicians, much less sharing power with them. But thinking about it is a good way to stay awake at 3 a.m.)

The worst thing was that I wasn't even sure an actual crime was taking place. It wasn't against the law to plant rowan trees, or use silver in construction, or form religious symbols out of pathways. It wasn't illegal to throw a salt circle. It *was* illegal to exert mind control on people without their consent, so the wards could be an issue for them—another reason why they'd probably drop them before the park opening. But most of what Callahan Construction was doing with that park was deeply anti-social, incredibly bad for the community, and, as far as I could tell, completely within the law.

Honestly, from a certain point of view, it might have been better if the Only Humans assholes *had* caught me. Abduction and assault were definitely crimes.

I wasn't quite socially conscious enough to wish they had, but I could see the pragmatic appeal.

I rubbed my eyes and stretched painfully out of my slump, only then aware of how long I'd been sitting in this chair, thinking through the implications. The daylight was dimming, and the library had helpfully upped the interior lighting in response.

I had to go back to the rec center. For one thing, my phone, wallet and keys were still in my bag. For another, the oath was a shackle I couldn't escape.

And for a third, I might be able to *research*. There had to be a brief for the project somewhere, and even if Callahan hadn't committed any crimes, they definitely weren't delivering something fit for purpose. If they'd broken the terms of their contract, Lady Seraphine could probably sue them into oblivion. Come to think of it, Raphael definitely had lawyer vibes. Maybe that was part of his aide-de-camp duties.

But I really, really didn't want to walk back to the rec center by myself.

The door to my little room opened.

I shot backwards, the wheels on my antique chair screeching in protest, before I could register the presence in the doorway. It wasn't a hi-vis wearing thug. It was Anton, who was carrying a stack of thick pink and peach books and wearing a bemused expression.

"Whoa," he said. "Are you okay?"

"How'd you get in here?" I demanded. "What are you *doing* here?"

He hefted the pink and peach books. "I'm picking up Rafn's holds. I saw the panel and was curious, so I pushed. Is this like a secret room?"

"I think it's just well-concealed," I said, recovering some of my equilibrium. "Uh. Hi."

"Hi."

We stood there for a moment, just looking at each other.

He was hot, okay? I'd dated a bit in college, but mostly other nerds like me, who liked discussing source authenticity or debating the historical impact of obscure legislation. The furthest I'd gone out of my comfort zone had been my three weeks of dating Patricia Klein, an MBA student who played soccer on the weekends. I'd been totally smitten, overwhelmed by her charisma and athleticism.

Then she'd dumped me. She was nice about it, but I think she thought I was boring.

A well-muscled mechanic with a wide smile, who liked doing other people favors and helping them out... Well, that was also out of my comfort zone, but maybe in a good way. And from the pink in his cheeks and the glint in his eyes, I thought he liked what he was seeing too.

Demon, my other-else reminded me.

"I'm heading back to the rec center," I said. He hadn't asked me what *I* was doing there. Either he was less curious, or much more polite than I was. "Um, any chance you'd like to come with me? For the walk?"

"Sure!" he said, beaming, and I felt bad for taking advantage of his interest to draft him into bodyguard duties. Not too bad to do it, though. He checked out Rafn's books—all large-print romances—and we hit the street. I felt exposed the second we walked out the door. I scanned for hi-vis vests, and tensed at a flash of bright orange across the street, but it was just an electrician getting into her van.

"So why the romances?" I asked.

Anton laughed. "Rafn will tell you it's because women are a mystery, and you must study their deepest desires if you wish to unlock the puzzle box of their hearts." He'd dropped into a pretty good Nordic accent, so it was likely a direct quote. "But I think he just likes them. People finding love, guaranteed happy endings. Who wouldn't feel good about that?"

"Do you work for him full-time?"

"Not really? Technically, I'm an apprentice. I'm supposed to be going to community college to learn automotive repair." He shrugged. "I'm a little too old for both, to be honest. It's been tricky, finding something I wanted to commit to."

"How old are you now?"

"Twenty-six."

"I'm twenty-three."

He grinned. "So old enough that I can take you out for a drink?"

"Technically, that is possible," I said primly, then coughed against the sudden heat in my throat, and looked away. "Uh, about that handrail."

"I know. I fucked up."

"No. I mean, yes, but... where was this truck?"

"Parked on the curb near the new park site."

"Just outside the site?"

"Yep," he said. His eyes were clear and honest. But that was well within the boundaries of those crazy-powerful wards. He shouldn't have been able to get anywhere near that truck without finding an urgent reason to go somewhere else.

"Can I ask you something kind of personal?" I said.

"Sure."

"Um, you've got some kind of demonic heritage, right?"

He stopped dead in the street. This was a bizarre thing for any New Yorker to do, and he realized that at once, stepping smartly into the lee of a trash can so we weren't impeding the foot traffic. "Uh. Yeah. How'd you know?"

"I have a knack," I said. His olive complexion was flushing dark red. "I'm sorry, I didn't mean to embarrass you."

"You're not supposed to be able to... I have a suppressor." He fumbled in his jeans pocket. "Unless the damn thing's dead again. I thought I'd got that fixed. Faiza told me it was good for six months at least."

It was my turn to blink. Suppressors were powerful, very rare, *very* expensive charms. Most of the time, they were government-issued for adolescent supernaturals who hadn't learned how to fully control their powers, powerful fae who were new to our realm and needed a reminder not to glamor everyone they met, or people whose parole conditions included not doing certain things their powers enabled. Suppressors had limitations—nothing was going to stop a werewolf from turning at the full moon, for instance—but they generally damped things down and made it much harder for anyone to do anything especially impressive or dangerous.

Anton pulled his keys out of his pocket. There was a small circle of dark metal dangling from the fob, with a symbol I didn't recognize inlaid in gold. "You're a wizard, right?" he said. "Can you tell me if it's working?"

And before I could make my usual disclaimers about not being a *real* wizard, he pressed the damn thing into my hand.

My other-else blinked out.

It was such a weird sensation that I couldn't quite process it. It was like an electrical grid blackout, maybe, or the way it feels when a machine making dim noise in the background suddenly powers down. I instinctively pushed *back*, and felt my other-else flicker like a faulty light bulb, and then disappear again. I was standing on a busy street on the Upper West side, with dozens of people flowing past us, and I couldn't tell you a damn thing about any of them. Well, okay, the seven-foot-tall woman with the impressive horns was probably on the demonic side of the supernatural spectrum, and the hobgoblin teenagers holding hands couldn't be anything *but* hobgoblins, but almost everybody else felt... like nothing.

Was this what being human was like? If I'd been born baseline, instead of barely a magician, was this what my world would have been?

I shuddered, and thrust the awful thing back at him. "It's working," I said, my voice clipped and harsh.

And then there was a moment when the suppressor let go of me and hadn't yet settled over Anton. It was just a split-second where my power had come back online, and his hadn't been muffled, and my talent got a clear view of his.

Part-demon, yes, my other-else had been right about that, and now I knew what kind. Heat flared up the back of my neck, shot down my spine, wrapped around my breasts and between my thighs. For that fraction of a second, I wanted Anton with a desperate, aching hunger that pressed every other thought aside.

I stepped towards him, needing to touch, to kiss, to *devour*, and his eyes widened, pupils blowing wide and black. And then the suppressor in his hand kicked in, dampening his aura, and he was an attractive man with great forearms, and I was a stupid magician who'd been momentarily more turned on than I'd ever been in my entire life.

Incubus, my other-else informed me.

Yeah, I thought back. *No shit*.

"You okay?" Anton asked. He was clutching the suppressor in his fist, as if that would make it work better.

"Yes," I said, and then checked to see if it was true. Yes, I was okay. Sure, I still thought he was hot, but I was a normal amount of horny, instead of blazing from the inside out. I was trying very hard not to be embarrassed about it. It wasn't anyone's fault.

Although... "You could have given me a heads up," I said.

He looked abashed. "Sorry. It's worse when I, uh, when I have reciprocal, uh—"

"Okay, don't worry about it," I said, deciding that *reciprocal* was something to think about later.

There was no longer any mystery why Anton carried a suppressor. If he didn't have tight control, every time he saw someone he thought was cute, he risked overwhelming their will and dragging them towards him, like a magnet pulling iron filings. And he was *strong*. When I'd held that suppressor, it had blanked me out completely. He was wearing the thing every day, and he was still leaking enough power for my other-else to ping on him.

But maybe not enough for the *wards* to ping on him. He'd walked right up to the truck sitting beside the park and stolen their vile silver railing.

"The new park construction is an Only Humans project to install a metaphysical toxic waste site in the middle of the neighborhood. It's designed to stoke community tension, seriously discredit the rec center, and embarrass Lady Seraphine in front of the press," I said, and watched Anton carefully.

"Whoa. Really?"

"Really."

He looked taken aback, but not fuzzy or dazed. "That sounds bad," he ventured.

"Oh my god," I said, so relieved I could have hugged him. So I hugged him. After a hesitant moment that made me wonder if I'd read this wrong, his arms came around me, warm and strong, pressing me against his broad, powerful chest. I got a whiff of clean cotton and grease, the salty tang of fresh sweat and the complex smell of benzene. I let myself enjoy the hold for a moment, then pulled back. He let me go at once.

"Yes, it's terrible. And you're the first person I've been able to talk to about it. There's at least one wizard off the Abbot-Grace scale working with them, and they've put some kind of really complex warding system in place that stops people from recognizing what's going on. It doesn't work on you, because of the suppressor. That's how you stole that railing in the first place."

"Reacquired," Anton corrected. He was still looking kind of stunned, but I couldn't tell if it was the result of the information or the hug.

I abruptly realized we were still standing out in the open, way too exposed. "Uh, yeah. Can we talk about it back at the center? I think a bunch of Only Humans goons might be gunning for me."

Anton's face went from concerned bafflement to protective fury in no time flat. He threw his arm around me and stepped us back into the flow of traffic, hustling me along at a pace that was only just under the speed at which New Yorkers start to get alarmed. Which is to say, pretty damn fast.

I was breathless by the time we got there, partly because of the speed, and mostly because I'd been explaining as we went, gabbling out what I'd seen and the deductions I'd drawn from it as fast as my tongue would let me. It had occurred to me that being the *only* person who knew this stuff was an incredibly dangerous position, and not just for my own physical safety. Callahan Construction was counting on the surprise effect. The more people who couldn't be surprised, the better.

I explained that too, not very coherently, as we went past the roses and through the center doors, into the empty reception area. There was a sign on the desk that told people to ring the bell for service. I wasn't sure that I'd conveyed the information clearly, but Anton was nodding, eyes narrowed, as the doors closed behind us and the wards—*our* wards—kicked in.

"Got it," he said. "One thing, though. You can't tell Bev."

"Can't tell me what?" Bev said, standing up from behind the desk.

Chapter Ten

I stared at Bev, my mouth opening and shutting with all the grace of a fish on dry land. My brain had completely emptied out of everything except the construction project and the danger it posed to Thirteenth Avenue, but of course Anton was right. The park *had* to be the source of Oona's vision, the thing I'd been brought on board to deal with. And everyone had been very clear that Bev couldn't know about it. Or she'd act on the information alone, like the hero she was, and according to Oona, she'd die.

"Well?" she asked. "What can't you tell me, Charlie?"

Fortunately, Anton was quicker off the mark. His arm was still slung around my shoulders, and he tightened his grip, tugging me closer.

"That we're dating," he said, and even managed a decent blush. "Uh. Hi."

Bev's eyes narrowed further. "Why would I care about that?" she demanded, but from the look on her face, it was clear she did. Oh, hell. Tread lightly, Charlie.

"Because it was pretty fast?" I offered. "I only started work yesterday..."

Bev transferred her attention to Anton. "Are you sure?" she said, her voice oddly gentle. "Does she know?"

Anton fidgeted. "Yes," he mumbled. "I showed her the suppressor. We're clear."

"Right," Bev said, and then glared at me. Somehow, I didn't collapse at the knees. "Congratulations, I guess, and where the hell have you been all afternoon? Oona covered for you as long as she could, but she had to go meet her idiot boyfriend. Hiring you was supposed to make *less* work for her."

"I was inspecting the park construction site with Raphael," I reminded her. "I'm sorry, the whole thing took longer than I was expecting."

"A *lot* longer," she said, and her eyes were clear—no ward-daze. Anton's arm tightened around my shoulder again, this time in warning.

"I'm really sorry," I said. "I didn't have my phone with me, or I would have given Oona a heads up." It wasn't hard to look humble. I truly *was* sorry to have dumped the afternoon reception desk in Oona's hands.

"It's right next door," Bev pointed out. "You could have excused yourself for five minutes to let her know."

Oh, damn. She was right.

And Anton was with me. It didn't look as if I'd been toiling away to please a vampire and his high-powered patroness, but as if I'd skipped out of work to make out with my new boyfriend.

On my second day in the job.

"I'll take over for you now, Bev," I said.

She waved a dismissive hand. "I'm here now, aren't I? Hannah put a pile of paperwork on your desk. You'd better read it."

"Um, right," I mumbled, and shot Anton an agonized look.

"No worries, babe," he said cheerfully. "I'll wait for you."

"Don't you have night classes?" I heard Bev say, sharp as a blade. I slipped through the staff door and went up the now rail-free stairs, hugging the wall and feeling sorry for myself.

Being scolded was never pleasant. Being scolded by your heroes, it turned out, was even less so.

Hannah had either gone or was doing something somewhere else in the building—or was invisible at the moment, something I would need to keep remembering. There was light glowing under the door of Felantheril's office, and I hesitated. Weird as she was, a High Fae would be a formidable ally.

But first things first. I ignored the paperwork, which really was a pile, and uncovered my phone in my bag, dialing the number on Raphael's business card.

He picked up before I had time to consider what I was actually going to say.

"Raphael Bergsen."

"Hi, it's, I'm Charlie. It's Charlie. Cross. From the Thirteenth Avenue Rec Center?"

His voice shifted, from generic polite to amused. "Yes, Ms. Cross?"

"You wanted me to report on the state of the park? Whether it was ready for opening?"

He hesitated, as if he was trying to access a memory from weeks ago, instead of this afternoon. "Ah, yes. Well?"

I crossed my fingers. "It's a front for some kind of Only Humans operation," I said. "The construction crew has redesigned the park layout so that it's actively hostile to most supernatural beings. Including vampires."

There was a pause, long enough for me to hope that the message had got through. "And is it ready?" he said at last.

"What?"

His voice gained an edge of impatience. "The park, Ms. Cross. Will it be ready to open on time?"

I clenched my fists. The wards had constructed some kind of story in his mind, and I couldn't shake it. "No," I said.

"You're lying, Ms. Cross," he said, his voice silky-smooth, and the hairs on the back of my neck stood up. Some vampires *could* tell truth from lies, though they usually had to be making eye contact or at least be in the same general area as the speaker. Being able to do it over the phone would be an incredibly useful skill for an aide-de-camp.

"Seraphine shouldn't come to the opening," I said. "It won't work out well."

"Interesting. *That* was true." His voice hardened. "Ms. Cross, I am not sure if you're aware of Lady Seraphine's status as a key benefactor to the rec center. It literally would not exist without her support. Your *job* would not exist without her support, am I clear?"

The invisible collar around my neck chose that moment to tighten. "Yes," I choked out. Oh god. Could the oath hold me to a job that didn't exist anymore? Would I become Felantheril's personal servant instead?

"So. The park will be ready to open on time, but you think something about that opening will negatively impact Lady Seraphine. It is therefore your task to make sure it does not." He paused. "I understand you are still in the trial period of your employment?"

I got the hint, you bastard.

"Yes," I said.

"I see." He actually sounded sympathetic. "Well, if you wish to acquire a permanent employment contract, I suggest that you ensure the opening ceremony goes as smoothly as possible and takes place at the appointed time."

"I'm not talking about stale canapés or dull blades on the giant scissors!" I blurted. "Please, you've got to take this seriously."

"I am," he said. "That's why I'm making it your responsibility. Good night." The line went dead.

I stared at my blank screen for a second, furious and terrified, and jumped to my feet to do... I wasn't sure what. Something! Something that would make it clear this disaster in the making was well beyond my grasp, whatever Oona's visions had told her. I wasn't a spell-slinging combat wizard, or a Hunter, or even a scrappy street fighter with a lot of heart. My resources were a nice part-demon, great research skills, and the ability to write a paper overnight if I had enough energy drinks. It wasn't as if the last two were going to do me any good.

I paused. Actually...

Felantheril's door opened and she came out, looking more flustered than usual. "What did you do?" she demanded. "I sent you away with Raphael, and he just called to say you're to be put in charge of the park project!"

"I don't want it," I said, too upset to be diplomatic about it.

"Well, too bad!" My skin prickled at the power she was gathering. "You are to ensure the park opening ceremony goes as smoothly as possible, and takes place at the appointed time."

It was a direct quote, the same wording Raphael had used to me, but it came with the extra whammy of my oath. I literally stopped breathing as the compulsion took hold, every muscle in my body locking down from the metaphysical force.

This, if you're wondering, is why you don't make oaths to High Fae.

"Okay," I said, when I could get enough air to speak. "Is Sam here?"

"I don't know!" She flounced back to her office, and the door slamming behind her made it very clear that this whole mess was my circus and my monkeys. I didn't know why she was so mad about it. I was the one she'd just doomed to fail an impossible task.

I felt very much like bursting into tears, but that wouldn't get me anywhere helpful. Instead, I marched down the corridor to Sam's IT closet and knocked on the door.

He peeked into the corridor, and seemed relieved that it was just me. "Hi." After a moment, an internal search query must have thrown up my name, because he added. "Hi, Charlie."

"Hi, Sam. You're in charge of filing and data management, right?" Those weren't typically IT tasks, so I thought I'd better check.

"Yes," he said ruefully. "On my first day I made the mistake of telling Felantheril I was kind of like an archivist, and she took it literally."

"That sounds about right," I muttered. "Felantheril's asked me to take care of something. Where can I find the files on the park construction project?"

"In here somewhere," he said, and fell back from the door. I followed him into the airless, windowless room with its humming server cabinets. It was about ten degrees hotter in there, and I started sweating again immediately. Sam, of course, was unaffected by the heat. A dark, private space like this was probably a pretty good deal, if you were a vampire who really liked computers.

"I can email the folder to you," he said, sitting down at his set-up. He had five screens and three keyboards, which seemed excessive for a community rec center, but who was I to judge? "The physical files are over there," he added, and waved at an enormous filing cabinet, which was a dingy avocado green and looked as if it might have been donated by an ad agency in the late 70s as they updated their look.

I opened the cabinet and started pawing through the files. About a third were unlabeled, and many documents appeared to be in the wrong category altogether, but I kept going, beads of sweat rolling down my back, until I found the familiar Prussian blue paper of older architectural drawings. I pulled that file folder out and went through it methodically.

First in the pile were the formal blueprints for the original center construction, dated 1969. Wow, it really had been the first building on the block. Other blueprints from the 70s and 80s tracked the addition of the indoor basketball court, and a roof renovation after a minor pixie clan war. Then the architects had adopted computers, and we went from painstakingly drawn white lines on blue background to computer generated grey lines on white. The second most recent blueprints were for a bathroom overhaul to comply with accessibility legislation, and the most recent blueprint was... a park.

I pulled that free. Even a cursory glance was enough to tell me that this was not what I'd seen inside those fences.

"I'm taking this," I told Sam.

"Mm? Yeah."

I straightened up to look at him. He was playing a game on one of his screens, little red dots swimming over little blue dots, and drinking from an insulated mug with a straw poked through it.

"Did you send me the folder?"

"What folder?"

I counted to five, because it wasn't Sam's fault he was being magically turned away from complying with a co-worker's reasonable request. "Oh, don't worry about it," I said lightly, and reached for a keyboard. "I'll just sit here and find it myself."

That woke him up. I've never known anyone in IT to be happy about letting you use their keyboard to type in a password, much less handing over access to their system architecture. He spun away from the game, eyes alarmed, and a touch of fang at the lip. "Uh, no, that's okay, I can help you find what you're after. What was that, again?"

If I said the park construction project, he'd find another way to get distracted. "All the contracts and scope-of-work briefings from the last two fiscal years," I said.

For me, that would be a hideous amount of folder-clicking and back-tracking, but Sam had apparently written some really nice search parameters. He pulled up the files swiftly, and I hovered over his shoulder. I knew the close supervision was making him uncomfortable, but I needed to make sure I had what I needed. I saw the file name Callahan Schedule Update included in the sweep, and let myself relax a little. Then Sam went vague on the crucial emailing-the-zipped-file-to-Charlie part.

"I can type in my email," I said, as casually as possible, and reached over his shoulder.

I didn't see him move. One moment, he was nervously click-ing through a file directory, and the second he was holding my wrist. I instinctively pulled back, which achieved absolutely nothing. Sweet and self-effacing as he was, Sam was a vam-pire, with vampire strength. He was looking up at me, his deep brown eyes absolutely blank, holding my hand four inches from the keys.

"Sam," I said quietly. "You're hurting me."

He wasn't. The grip was immovable, but not painful.

But at my words, panic bloomed in his eyes. "Oh, God," he said. "I'm not— Charlie, I'm—" and then he was gone, racing out the door.

I felt like a complete heel as I typed in my email address and clicked send. I stuffed the paperwork pile and the park design plan into my bag, grabbed my new (second-hand) heavy laptop, and headed downstairs. The Potions Anonymous meeting was just letting out. Bev was playing online poker on her phone. Anton was nowhere to be seen.

I glanced at Bev, and decided that walking to my stop alone was way less scary than interrupting her to ask where he'd gone.

But halfway up the block, Anton was leaning back against a streetlight with one foot propped up, smoking a cigarette. I watched the smoke drift from his pursed lips into the still night air. He could have been James Dean's Stark, Judd Nelson's Bender, Heath Ledger's Patrick. Bad boy with a heart of gold, at your service.

Then he saw me and smiled, hastily putting out the cigarette, and he was Anton again.

"I took a look at the site," he said, by way of hello. "Well, I tried to, but they've got a watchman on duty now." He grimaced. "Probably because of the railing."

I patted his shoulder. I thought it was far more likely to be because an unknown magician had turned up and asked a lot of nosy questions. "Did they see you?"

"Don't think so. I went around the side and tried to hop the fence, but I couldn't get over it. That salt circle must be right inside the property line." His mouth scrunched up as if he were tasting something bad. "Salt isn't always that effective, you know. They've juiced it."

"Dave said their wizards had enchanted the salt before they buried it," I said. "Okay. My first thought is that we need more suppressors. I know we can't talk to Bev, but we need more people to know about this, and I need help to shut it down. I think we've got to tell Oona, and if I can get Raphael to believe me, I'm sure he can do something about it." With luck, he'd take the whole problem off our hands. At that point, I could concentrate on making Lady Seraphine's opening the success I'd been ordered to provide.

Anton made a face at Raphael's name, but nodded at the idea. "Sounds smart," he said, and I'd be lying if I didn't say that gave me a warm little tingle. I'd spent most of the day feeling ignorant, slow, and completely out of my depth.

I knew it was normal. I felt that way every time I started something I didn't already know how to do. But it was nice that Anton, at least, seemed to think I could be trusted to provide some solutions.

We fell into step together, walking down the block—away from the park. I didn't want the night watchman to catch a glimpse of me and figure out the nosy magician from earlier today was from the rec center next door.

As it was, I should probably think about some sort of disguise. Did I still have the blonde Marilyn Monroe wig I'd worn for Halloween last year?

"Charlie," Anton said, and then hesitated.

I kind of liked the way my name sounded in his mouth. "Yes?"

"I just want to say... You don't really need to be doing all this. I mean, I know Oona had that vision, but maybe finding out about the park was all you needed to do. I can take it from here."

The oath tightened in warning. I wasn't allowed to walk away on his say-so.

"That's really sweet. But I think I have to see this through." I wasn't going to tell him about the oath, so I added, "Oona's vision said I was *there*, remember? That was the difference be-tween Bev dying and not. And she must have been there too, so we need at least one suppressor, for Oona." And those didn't come cheap. I thought about my empty bank account and sighed. I could probably ask my mom for a loan, but she'd want to know what for. "Where did you get yours?"

"I know somebody," Anton said. His lips were pursed in thought. It was a good look on him. "Let me talk to her and see if we can make a deal. I might get more than one."

That would be some deal. "Sounds great," I said. "If we can get another one for Raphael..."

"And if we can't, you and Oona can dig up the salt circle and I'll start taking the place apart," he said confidently. "Probably can't dynamite anything, but a couple of sledgehammers could do a lot of damage."

I flinched. "No. We have to do something, but we can't totally ruin the park. Besides, what about the night watchman?"

Anton shrugged. Personally, I wouldn't be that casual about facing someone who was probably armed and definitely hated supernatural beings, but maybe he had reason to be confident.

"Anyway, the opening ceremony has to take place as scheduled."

"How come?"

"It just does," I said lamely. "I mean, Lady Seraphine is the rec center's main source of funds, right? We can't piss her off. Raphael and Felantheril both ordered me to take care of it. If we can't get a suppressor for Raphael, I'll work it out." Somehow. I had to. I really didn't want to suffer the consequences of breaking an oath to a High Fae.

We were nearing the next subway entrance, and I felt some of the tension drop from my shoulders. I'd read that pre-Cataclysm, violent crime in the subway hadn't been uncommon. Now it was one of the safest places in the city. Three rotating teams of fae and wizards worked round the clock to keep the wards in place through the barrage of constant motion in a vast and expanding network. Every werewolf pack in the five boroughs had declared the subway safe from territorial disputes, no matter whose turf you were traveling under, and the human gangs had agreed to the deal, all of it set down in unbreakable demonic contracts with hefty metaphysical consequences. It might be a different story once you got off the tracks, but as long as you were on the iron road, you were protected.

I was about to say thank you and good night, when Anton took a swerve towards the corner.

"My stop's down there."

"Nah, come back to the shop. I'll drive you home." He hefted a tote bag with the rec center logo stamped on it. "Besides, I have to drop off Rafn's books."

"I'm kind of a long way out," I admitted.

"No problem. Unless it's Staten Island."

I made a face. "No, I'm in the suburbs. New Rochelle."

"Oh." He thought about that for a second. "Hey, still better than Staten Island."

Only Humans couldn't touch me in the subway but a ride did sound nice.

"Okay," I said, and smiled at him. "I'm game. Show me your wheels."

Anton's wheels did not disappoint.

They were, he proudly told me, a 1970 Plymouth Road Runner, with wide blue bench seats, Monroe shocks, and the original V8 engine modified by a Gonzalez Spectral Chamber to make the emissions street-legal. There were a lot of other details that I couldn't repeat if my life depended on it, but he seemed happy to talk, and I was happy to relax into the passenger seat and feel the engine purr under the sound of his voice.

"—had a hard time with the frame rails, though, the old wheel jacks really—" He stopped. "Just tell me if you're bored."

"I'm not bored," I told him. "I don't really understand what you're saying, but I like listening to people talk about things they're enthusiastic about."

"Oh, okay! Do you drive?"

"I have my license. I don't really use it, except to get into clubs."

"You like clubbing?"

"I like to dance. Clubs are mostly where that happens."

"Right, yeah." Anton tapped his fingers against the skinny wheel, and then did something hair-raising with the gearstick welded into the floor to shift us up a gear. We were driving over the Henry Hudson Bridge. It's not the most dramatic bridge leading from Manhattan, but I've always loved that steely, elegant curve.

"I'll give you cash for the toll," I said.

"Nah, I've got it."

"No, you're the one doing me a favor, I should—"

"My yiayia would beat me to death with her sandal if I let you," he said solemnly. "You've gotta save me from that."

I laughed. "Okay."

"Okay." He tapped his fingers again. "She's where the demon side comes from," he added. "My grandfather was one of the first guys from his realm to make contact after the Cataclysm, and she seduced him."

"She seduced *him*?" I tried to imagine a Greek babe with Anton's flashing eyes and dark, tumbling hair, laughing up at a handsome incubus.

"That's the way they tell it. My mom's baseline, because apparently the incubus powers don't mesh with the double-X chromosomes, but I got the whammy." He coughed. "I didn't, uh... I don't handle it very well."

We were flashing through the streets, Anton's hands moving confidently on the wheel and the stick. I could feel a humming tension building between us. We paused at a red light.

"You don't need to tell me this if you don't want to," I said, just in case he needed an out.

"I want to," he said immediately. "Everyone thought I was baseline, and then, pow! Everything kicked off the summer I turned fifteen. It was rough. Grandfather tried teaching me control, but I was so freaked out that I couldn't get a grip on it. Then Yiayia got me signed up for a government suppressor, and that helped some, but not enough. Half the kids in school thought I was dangerous and the other half wanted to make out with me, and I was just this dumb kid, y'know?"

"Being fifteen is intense. I can't imagine how much worse it would have been if I hadn't known I was a magician well before then." Not to mention having sex-demon powers suddenly appear on top of normal teenage hormones. Anton must have been half out of his mind.

He let out a shaky laugh. "Yeah. Long story short, I started fighting, then skipping school. I got involved with some older demons who seemed pretty cool, and they were immune to my pull, which was a massive relief. When I'm not wearing a suppressor, I can sneak around pretty good, melt into the shadows. And I'm stronger, faster. So they had me do some small-scale stuff. Shop-lifting and courier duties, mostly, but they were ramping up to something pretty big. Something that would have needed my name on a contract."

I made a face. Demon contracts, like oaths to High Fae, are not something you can just get out of with a good lawyer and a kill fee. "I'm glad you didn't go there."

"Me too."

"What stopped you?"

"Bev. I was one of her last cases before she got 'restructured' out of government work. She pulled me out of the hole I'd dived into and got me a heavy-duty suppressor that actually worked. I went back to school. I even graduated."

"That's awesome," I said. I kind of wanted the ride to last longer, and not just because I might find out more about Bev. But without me even really noticing, we'd covered the distance, and were heading down Carmen Street. "I'm right here."

He pulled up outside the two story Colonial Cape Cod Revival that my parents had bought for a steal in the 90s. It was white and square and the red door framed with its faux-Grecian pillars felt like both a welcome and a warning of the trap that could gently close on me.

"Wow, nice place," Anton said.

"It's not mine, it's my mom's," I said and then winced. "I live with her. I don't know if I mentioned that? I'm hoping to get a place in the city soon, but for now, I'm here, I guess. I know that sounds lame."

He laughed. "I live with my grandmother. Have for most of my life."

"Oh. I mean, I love my mom. She's the best person in the world. I just— We have different ideas about my future."

"I get it," Anton said, and put his hand on mine, where it was resting against the smooth vinyl seat. I went still, startled by the warm pressure. "Charlie, I just wanted to say... it means a lot to me, that you're doing this for Bev. She's helped a lot of people."

"She's a legend," I said, trying not to squirm too much. I didn't deserve this praise, not when I was acting out of self-preservation as much as anything else. "I know a little bit of her history."

"She's more than a legend," he said seriously. "She's a really great person. And so are you."

He was looking at me in a way that made my heart trip. I was very aware that there was no console or gearstick between us. Just that wide, flat bench seat. I'd released my seatbelt, but I didn't make any move to leave. His hand was still pressed against mine.

The street lamp shone through the leaves of the magnolia and made dappled patterns on our skin, light and shadow shifting with the night breeze.

"You're a great person too," I said. "You got me back to the rec center, you've made sure I got home safely... I truly appreciate it."

Anton's eyes were locked on mine. "No problem. I'm sorry I told Bev we were dating."

"I don't mind," I said, and slid an inch or two closer.

Anton's Adam's apple bounced up and down in his throat as he swallowed. "We shouldn't," he said softly.

I nodded. "So... good night?" I couldn't help making it a question.

"Charlie," Anton said, like my name was a curse. Or a prayer. He took his hand off mine, braced his arms on the steering wheel and looked straight ahead. "Yes. Good night."

"Okay," I said, and fumbled for the door handle.

I heard the click of the seatbelt release behind me, and then the welcome warmth of two hands on my shoulders, turning me back. I was reaching for him, even as his arms came around me and his mouth descended on mine.

Chapter Eleven

M ost of my brain was thinking nothing more complicated than *wheeee!* A tiny portion of it, the part of me that was always watching and always cautious, briefly wondered if he'd put the incubus whammy on me after all. My other-else said nope, no supernatural force at play here. This was good old-fashioned lust.

At that point, I stopped questioning it and just sort of dove into the experience. Anton's lips were soft and full, moving gently on mine. I opened my mouth under his and teased the pointed tip of my tongue along the seam. He made a noise, low in his throat, and deepened the kiss. I was aware of the strength in his body, the power in his arms, and I was aware that he was holding back, his arms actually trembling with the effort.

I loved that he was so restrained, and I desperately wanted to make him lose control.

I slid my hands up under the back of his shirt to find bare, hot skin. The muscles of his back bunched and shivered under my greedy touch, and I was suddenly lying half on my back while he braced over me with one arm. His eyes were wild and black in the shifting light.

"You okay?" I said breathlessly.

He nodded, and kissed me again, and this time he wasn't restrained at all. I was gone, spiraling down into a bottomless pool of desire, all my senses going haywire. It did occur to me that if this was just natural talent, Anton without his suppressor would be completely overwhelming. Then he licked the hollow of my throat and the thought fell right out of my head.

I wriggled down beneath him, tugging at the hem of his shirt until he stopped kissing me long enough for me to yank it up and off him. God, he was beautiful. I stroked the broad planes of his chest and let my fingers trail down the dusting of hair which darkened to a line pointing towards his belt.

Anton watched me, his eyes drowning-deep, his skin shuddering under my touch.

And that's when my best friend's mother rapped sharply on the car window.

Both Anton and I screamed, me with perhaps just a touch more volume, and scrambled upright. Ms. Borouka, peering through the glass, recognized me and recoiled, her face aghast.

"Oh, shit," I said. "I've got to go."

This was shaping up to be one of the all-time embarrassing encounters of the neighborhood, almost worse than the time my mother and Mr. Salamanca had brought the same salad to the Livingston's Fourth of July party.

Anton was holding his head with his hands, taking deep breaths. "I'm sorry," he said.

I grabbed his shoulder, as much to steady myself as to comfort him. "Don't be," I said. "Um, can you follow that lead on suppressors? And I'll see you tomorrow?"

He raised his head. "Yes."

"Okay. Good!" I said and kissed his cheek before I grabbed my bag and jumped out. Oops, a couple of my top buttons had gotten undone at some point. I hastily refastened them, while Anton roared away—still shirtless in the driver's seat—and a beet-red Ms. Borouka waved awkwardly at me from the curb.

Her particular flavor of *werewolf* was so familiar that it barely registered with my other-else.

"Charlie, I'm so sorry," she said. "I was taking out the trash, and thought it was some kids from the high school."

I winced. "We, ah, probably could have chosen somewhere better."

"New boyfriend?"

"Something like that. How's Laurence's job hunt going?"

"You probably hear from him more often than I do," she said dryly. This was a joke. Laurence was a terrible communicator. You had to harass him for days to get a text response. "Well, good night." She headed back inside, but not without a final glance at the space where Anton had parked. I was definitely going to come up at book club.

Which meant my mom probably deserved a heads-up, provided I could figure out how to phrase it. But when I unlocked the door, she was waiting for me in the hall, grinning.

"Charlie Anna Hope Cross, what time do you call this?"

I did a dramatic eye roll. "Jeez, Mom, did I break curfew?"

She laughed. "No, but who gave you a ride? Dare I hope that my sweet, nerdy daughter has been making out with a leather jacket-wearing bad boy in the back seat of his muscle car?"

"He wasn't wearing leather, he's a nice boy, and we were in the front seat," I said. "The making out part I will neither confirm nor deny."

"Well, come in and have dinner, and tell me all about your first full day."

For a moment, I contemplated doing just that. I could lay it all out for her, explain the terrible constraint I'd laid upon myself and what it had led to, let her know about Only Humans and the poison they were bringing to the city. I could cry on her shoulder, and she'd support me as best she could. She'd done it before.

But it felt like I'd be giving in. It would be like admitting that my own plan for my future was too hard, that the city was too big and dangerous and that I couldn't handle it.

And like it or not, I wasn't a kid anymore. I had to take responsibility for the consequences of my own choices. Besides, what could she do? Call Callahan Construction and yell at them? Call Felantheril and yell at *her*? Actually, she probably *would* call Felantheril, and that could lead to all sorts of bad places. There are a lot of stories about humans trying to save their loved ones from fae bargains, and they don't always end well.

"I'd love to give you all the gossip," I said. "But unfortunately, your nerdy girl has homework." I hoisted my bag, weighed down with both the paperwork Hannah wanted me to address, and the research I had to go through for the park.

"On the first day of school?" Mom asked, widening her eyes, but she relented when I sighed. "I'll fix you a plate."

I went up to my bedroom, still full of boxes I hadn't unpacked, and set up my laptop on the desk that had been the site of so much frantic study for the SATs. That had only been a few years ago, but it felt like a lifetime. How much help were my extended vocabulary and hard-won research skills going to be for a real-world problem?

It was going to be a long night.

***

I woke with a headache, gritty eyes, and a nasty taste in my mouth. It felt sort of like a hangover, without the fun part beforehand. Honestly, during four years of college, I'd probably suffered more all-night study aftereffects than I had actual hangovers. This was either a testament to my work ethic or a scathing indictment of my inability to have fun.

Either way, I was tired and irritable, and even after a hasty shower, I felt grubby. I put together a kind-of professional outfit from my dwindling choices, grabbed a protein bar from the pantry, and walked out into the far-too-early morning.

Anton was leaning on the hood of his car.

I stopped dead in my tracks. I'd meant "See you tomorrow" at the rec center, not outside my mom's house. He wasn't... Did he think we were together? I mean, I was open to the possibility, but a couple of kisses didn't make a relationship, at least not among the people I hung out with. That would take longer, and probably more than three conversations.

Some of this must have shown on my face, because he hurriedly said, "My source on suppressors said to bring you in, and I thought before work...? I would have texted, but I don't have your number."

I theatrically slapped my forehead, partly because I'd meant to give him my number, and partly out of relief that he didn't think we were going steady. "Right, of course. Thanks for the ride." I climbed into the big seat and belted up, trying not to think about what we'd been doing in there, not too long ago. "Sorry, I'm out of it. I was up late researching."

"Did you find out much?"

"Some," I said, and settled in to explain while Anton navigated us through not-quite rush hour.

Callahan Construction was a real company. They'd done a lot of small-scale stuff like this park project, and they had a reputation for being nimble, able to pick up half-finished jobs and see them through. It didn't advertise having an all-human crew, but all the photos of smiling workers on their website were people who looked human. That didn't necessarily mean much—a lot of supernaturals looked baseline—but in New York, especially in construction, it was unusual.

Callahan's connection to the rec center had been a lot harder to figure out. Sam's zipped folder had included a lot of emails back and forth between Hannah and the previous construction company, Zeeland International. Zeeland had been the lowest bidder by far, and as I read through the archived emails it had become clear why that was. The park design had been completed late, with Hannah having to point out missing features and agreed-upon changes that hadn't been included. They'd fudged the budget in places, which Hannah had caught and politely called them out on, and then, once construction actually started, they kept adjusting the schedule, back and back and back. Delays for supplies, delays for weather, delays for council approvals that should have been completed weeks earlier. The park fell weeks, then months behind schedule.

Reading between the lines, the final straw had been a meeting between Hannah, Bev and Raphael, where he, as Lady Seraphine's representative, had told them to pull the plug on Zeeland and seek more bids, which explained why he was so keen to see it finished. His boss was probably hissing down his neck about the delays. In the minutes of the corresponding staff meeting—and I was proud of myself for that bit of cross-referencing—Felantheril had personally taken over as project liaison.

And that was pretty much it. Callahan had proposed an updated budget, and a new timeline. I didn't know much about construction, but it seemed optimistically fast—Callahan had obviously committed a lot of resources to the project.

There was no updated design for Callahan, although they presumably should have been working off the same plans as

Zeeland. Even worse, there was no updated contract outlining their scope of work. No documented parameters on the kind of plants they should be using in landscaping, or the materials for railings and pathways. Not even a paragraph saying something like "for general community use".

"So the rec center can't sue?" Anton asked, narrowing in on what I'd realized at about 3 a.m.

"I don't know."

"How did Callahan get away with not signing a contract?"

"Felantheril took Hannah off the project. If Callahan planned this from the start, one of their mauvais wizards might have enchanted Felantheril not to make any records."

"You don't think so, though?"

"Maybe." It wasn't very likely, to be honest. High Fae had some natural resistance to mind-magic, since they came from an environment absolutely saturated in competing glamors. "Mostly, what I think is that Hannah was careful and responsible and got everything from Zeeland in writing, and Felantheril probably didn't even think about asking Callahan to sign anything." Was that too catty a thing to say about your boss? Ugh, I needed coffee. "There might be a verbal agreement. Or who knows, maybe she wrote something on the back of a napkin and got them to sign, and then accidentally mulched it for her plants."

Anton grimaced. "That sounds right."

"So I'm back to not knowing what to do. I could dig into Callahan a little bit more, or get Sam to do it, if we can undo the ward effects. I know a journalist who owes me a favor, but she's kind of the nuclear option." Tilly would enthusiastically splash this story all over the front pages, but I was sure that wouldn't suit Lady Seraphine at all.

More to the point, it might not fulfill my need to "ensure the park opening ceremony goes as smoothly as possible, and takes place at the appointed time". The oath tightened around my throat even as I thought it.

"Maybe Oona or Hannah will have an idea," I said, and crossed my fingers.

***

Anton's suppressor contact was in Alphabet City, which I discovered when we parked in front of a store on Avenue B. Among the hip cafes and pop-up art galleries was a narrow storefront that was doing, as far as I could tell, absolutely nothing to appeal to foot traffic. Newspapers were plastered over the inside of the window glass, which was already almost opaque with grime. Some thin gold letters, mostly scratched off, might have once spelled out the store's name.

To replace them, someone had taped a piece of printed paper to the peeling paint of the door. "EPHEMERA," it read. "ODDITIES AND CURIOSITIES."

Underneath, someone had added, in spidery handwriting, "No tourists!"

Anton pulled the door open and gestured me inside. I entered, blinking against the dim light. The narrow store was absolutely full of *stuff*. Multiple vintage bureaus and closets were shoved against the walls, while various end tables and bookshelves were crammed between, allowing the tiniest aisles of clear floor space for any customers to squeeze through. Every surface was covered. I saw tableware, clocks, books, old vases, battered pots and pans, a butler's tray of antique watches, a rack of silk ties, a pile of tartan cloth, a box of vintage post-

132

cards with weathered corners, a corkboard covered in enamel pins—everywhere I looked I saw something that had seen better days. Lampshades and chandeliers were suspended from the ceiling. Framed art and mirrors were hanging crookedly on the walls.

In the midst of all that mess, leaning on a glass counter, was a pretty, dark-skinned young woman in a long-sleeved silver shirt and loose black linen pants, her hair concealed by a black hijab. She was engrossed in a paperback, and didn't even look up as the doorbell jangled. I noticed that she was wearing black gloves. They were thin leather, and matched the rest of her outfit, but gloves, in this weather?

"Welcome to Ephemera," the girl said in a monotone, and then she *did* look up, as I stepped closer and crossed some invisible line. "No tourists," she said sharply.

"Charlie's not a tourist, Faiza," Anton said, entering behind me. "I told you about her last night, remember?"

Faiza's eyes narrowed, focusing on my bag. "If you're not a tourist, why are you carrying an all-purpose protection charm?"

"My mom gave it to me," I said.

"Oh, your *mom*," Faiza said, and relaxed. "Yeah, I know about moms. Okay, Charlie-who's-not-a-tourist. You need three non-government suppressors, medium to heavy charge, ideally portable?"

"That would be amazing," I said, and snuck a look at Anton. I'd been hoping for *one* suppressor. Three would be incredible: one for Raphael, one for Oona, and one for Hannah. If Raphael couldn't come up with a solution, I was sure Hannah could.

"And you don't have ten thousand dollars lying around?"

"Ten *thou*— No. I don't."

"Come on, Faiza," Anton said. "We just need to borrow them for a few days. Jeremy doesn't even have to know."

"Uh-huh," she said, sounding unimpressed. "Anton, does the sign on the door say Rent The Runway?"

"No."

"Does it say Public Library?"

"No."

"No. We do not allow people to *borrow* things. We are not a *rental* operation. These suppressors will bond to the first person who holds them."

"Irreversibly?" I asked.

"No," she conceded. "They can be reset. But that's a lengthy process that involves them sitting under the full moon in my secret recipe of herbs and spices. It's not like you can take them out for a quick joyride. It takes work to get them shop-ready again. And if my boss finds out before then, I'm in deep shit."

Anton scuffed his foot along the floor. "Like I said, I'll owe you one."

"More than one," Faiza said dangerously. I got the feeling this was a game they were playing, and that despite her tone, Faiza was enjoying herself. "Why do you need these suppressors, Charlie-who's-not-a-tourist? Why should I risk my job and my livelihood and my own mom's displeasure to do you a favor?"

I'd made my way closer to her by then, and my other-else was registering something. Not a ping the way I normally experienced it, with a bright burst of extrasensory information I then had to translate, but a low shiver-hum. Similar to the way Oona felt, or at least closer to that than anything else. "Are you an oracle?" I asked.

She jerked. "Not exactly."

I looked again at the gloves. "Clairvoyant?"

Her mouth flattened. "Yeah."

Well, that explained it. She'd be able to read the history of any object she touched with bare skin, magical or mundane. And if she could feel my protection charm halfway across the room, she had to be good.

"How'd you do that?" she said suspiciously. "I know you didn't cast anything."

That was interesting. She must have something on her—or somewhere in this cluttered room—that was able to detect spells. "I have a knack, that's all."

"She knew I was part-demon," Anton said.

"Through your suppressor?" Faiza asked, and whistled when he nodded. "That's some knack, girl."

"It's just a party trick." I had, in fact, pulled it out at parties in high school. At least, until I'd confidently identified Eileen Sorrento as part-fire demon, and she'd gone home to have a fight with her dad, who'd turned out to be her adopted dad.

Oh, I should explain something about demons. Despite what the more conservative churches like to proclaim, 'demons' aren't demonic in theological terms. They don't live in hell, they aren't fallen angels, they haven't been condemned by a deity, and they're not trying to stop you from achieving nirvana or heaven or whatever afterlife you're aiming at. The Demon Realms are no more damned than the Fae Realms (though according to some churches, fae are also demons, and so are ghosts, and don't get them started on vampires and were-wolves). The one thing most of the Demon Realms do have in common is that their culture is extremely transactional. If you know a demon's name, you can try to summon them, make a request, and pay—or not—the price they name in exchange for their services, all written down in this carefully itemized contract, please sign on the dotted line.

The price is sometimes steep. Sometimes, it's your soul. I have no opinion one way or another on the everlasting soul or the existence of an afterlife, but if you sign your soul over to a demon, your choices after that in *this* lifetime are not entirely your own.

Nowadays, most demons who want to bother with mortals have offices downtown and get pissed if you try to summon them outside working hours. They also swear up and down that of *course* they don't undertake contracts to do anything illegal. Why, that would be against the Faerie Accords! I'm just trying to operate a business here!

Anyway, Christianity and Islam and various other faiths have a name for a troublesome entity you can ask for help, with a cost. Demons have other names for themselves, but here they use our words for reasons of their own. Honestly, it might just be because they think it's funny.

Part-demons, who are exclusively the descendants of demons and humans, can be trickier to define. The powers refract in strange and unpredictable ways, resulting in excellent contract negotiators or brilliant lawyers far more often than they do people like Anton, with wild power he can't reliably control.

"Okay," Faiza said. "Three suppressors. Three favors. Number one, Anton, I need a date to my sister's wedding."

He blinked. "You don't want to take Maryam?"

She rolled her eyes. "Of course I want to take Maryam! But my mom insists that I take a boy, don't shame us in front of the in-laws, how do you know if you won't try, blah blah. So I figure if *you* show up, they'll compare this white Christian guy throwing his demon allure around the place to my beautiful, Muslim, human girlfriend, and be like, you know what, now that we think about it, Maryam's pretty great."

I glanced at Anton, who didn't seem enthusiastic. "How much demon allure?" he asked.

Faiza waved a gloved hand. "Just wear your government suppressor instead of your normal one. Base level allure is fine. I'm not asking you to seduce my grandmother."

"If you don't want to—" I began.

"No, it's okay," Anton said, and gave me a lopsided smile. "And the food will be good."

"That's the spirit," Faiza told him. "Bring your car and dress inappropriately. Now, favor number two. Give me your hand, Charlie-who's-not-a-tourist. I'm curious about your knack."

My eyebrows rose, but I obediently stepped closer, while Faiza peeled her glove off her right hand. "Only if you call me Charlie without addendums from now on," I told her.

"Your codicil is accepted," she said, and reached over the counter.

Faiza's hand was soft and dainty, but there was nothing delicate about her grip. The hum that was her presence in my other-else got stronger until it was a buzzing in my ears, then a vibration that shook my body. She was pushing at me somehow, trying to learn more about me and my power, and my other-else pushed back, and we *connected*. I could feel what she felt—her rough affection for Anton, her deep love for her girlfriend, her curiosity about me.

And for just a second, I could also feel the magical objects in the store. There were so *many* of them, far more than you'd expect to find outside of a museum or a private collection, all of them sparkling and vivid to my other-else, each of them with a provenance, a story to tell, if I'd only reach out my hand...

Faiza let go. I stumbled back, about to get mad that she hadn't warned me, but then I saw her face and realized she was as shocked as I was.

"That was unexpected," she said, and hastily pulled her glove back on. Her fingers were trembling.

Anton hovered, looking alarmed. "Everything okay?"

Faiza ignored him. "Do you know what that was?" she asked me.

"I have no idea."

"Hm. I'll have to think about it. You're an interesting puzzle, Charlie-without-addendums."

I frowned, and she smirked at me, regaining some of her spark. "Okay," she said. "Your suppressors." She pulled out a small black box and placed it on the counter before opening it ceremoniously, the way you might display precious jewelry. Inside were a medallion with a squashed impression of an ugly baby, a delicate bracelet of twigs wrought from silver, and a safety pin. "Go ahead. Test them. As long as you don't actually hold them they won't go off, but you should be able to feel the effect."

I didn't want to, but she was right; I couldn't just hand these over unless I was sure they'd work. I hovered my pointer finger over each in turn, and my other-else faded and buzzed like a broken strobe light. It made me feel nauseated, and I wiped my fingers on my blouse when I was done, as if they'd been contaminated.

Faiza closed the box with a snap and handed it to me. It was heavier than I expected; there was probably a thin layer of lead or gold acting as insulation. "Full moon is in three days," she said. "You get those back to me before then, so I can reset them to neutral and my boss never knows."

"Got it," I said. Three days was a tight deadline, but it wasn't as if delay would make things any better for me.

"What's the third favor?" Anton asked.

"Hm? Oh. You'll owe me one." Her eyes rested on me for a moment. "Or maybe *you* will. I'll see you later, Charlie Cross."

We were halfway uptown before I realized I hadn't given her my last name.

Chapter Twelve

I was late, of course. Anton dropped me off, and headed to the garage, promising to return at lunch for a council of war. I had until then to get Oona and Hannah to take their suppressors and listen to my story. With some luck, they'd be able to get Raphael to come uptown, and we could talk him into taking his.

Unfortunately, Hannah was the only one who'd arrived. I apologized for being late and slunk to my desk, unsuccessfully trying to hide my yawns while she went through the paperwork I'd filled out the night before. Her fingers occasionally drifted through a page instead of picking it up.

"Okay, good," she said at last, squaring the pile neatly. "The final sign-off has to wait until the end of your trial period, but we can at least put you into payroll now." Mr. Scruffles emerged from his nest under her chair, and she scritched between his ears. "How are you finding everything? Felantheril told me she put you in charge of the park project, which is pretty impressive for your first week." The tone was calm, but there was a question in her eyes.

I took a deep breath. "About that," I said, and opened the box. "There's some funky magical interference happening with the park."

"What are those?" Hannah asked, focusing on the suppressors.

There was no natural-looking way to get the damn thing out. I pulled my sleeve over my fingers and gingerly picked up the ugly medallion. I could feel it buzzing at me through the cloth, but it needed skin contact to work.

"Could you hold this, please?" I asked.

Hannah didn't move. "Why?"

"It's important," I said, and played my trump card. "It might help us save Bev."

Hannah glanced at Mr. Scruffles. He cocked his head at her and yawned. "All right," she said, on a sigh, and held her hand out.

I dropped the suppressor into her open palm.

Hannah vanished.

Mr. Scruffles yipped. His back legs stiffened and he stared at me, his little black eyes alarmed.

"She's okay," I said, hoping it was true. I knew that a suppressor couldn't exorcise or disintegrate a ghost, and I'd deliberately handed her the one with the lowest charge, but I was still nervous. I should have waited until Oona had come in. And maybe I'm slow, but it only came to me then that a ghost without access to her powers might have some trouble communicating. There had been plenty of ghosts hanging around pre-Cataclysm, but most of them hadn't been able to manifest anything stronger than a strange noise or unusual smell.

There was a faint movement of air, just enough to ruffle the ends of my hair and stir Mr. Scruffles' fur. The tension went out of his small body, and he went back to his nest under the desk, turning around three times before he settled down.

"Okay," I said, keeping a wary eye on the door, just in case Bev was coming early today. "I'm just going to assume you can hear me, and the reason you haven't dropped the suppressor is because you now realize you haven't been able to think about the park project. There's a reason for that." I sketched out the problem of the wards, and then the malignant work inside them. "I think that has to have been what Oona's vision was about," I concluded.

There was a pause, and then a clink, as the medallion hit Hannah's desk. She faded slowly back into view, looking concerned.

"Will I remember without holding the suppressor?" Her voice was a shadow of her usual crisp tones. "I can't work like this."

"I think so? Maybe if you trip the wards again it'll reset, but... do you still remember?"

She waited a moment, then nodded.

"Isn't it a beautiful day?" Oona asked, almost dancing through the door. "I think we're going to have great weather for the clothes swap this weekend! Charlie, have I told you about the clothes swap yet?" She stopped, and looked at us: Hannah obviously shaken, and me probably jittery. "What's going on?"

Sam came up the stairs behind her in the broad-brimmed hat and cloak that were *de rigueur* for the cautious vampire in daylight, spotted me, and went stiff and wide-eyed all over, a baby deer waiting for the eighteen-wheeler to mow it down. I caught Hannah's eye, jerked my chin at Oona, and said, "Sam, can I talk to you in your office for a second?"

"Sure," he said, with a heroic effort at being casual. His hands were opening and closing. "Um, I mean, if you want to bring a support person, or a manager..."

Oona was looking even more suspicious.

"I'm so sorry," he blurted. "Everyone, I assaulted Charlie last night. I was coming in to give Felantheril my resignation, but—"

"You what?" Hannah said, in blatant disbelief, at the same time that Oona said "That can't be right."

"That's not what happened," I protested.

His pupils were blown wide and black. "I held you down. I hurt you."

"You held my wrist for maybe two seconds," I said. "It didn't— You weren't hurting me, and it wasn't your fault."

"I don't know why I did it." His face was contorted with guilt. "I'm so sorry, Charlie. I promise, you'll never see me again."

"I know why you did it, and it *wasn't* your fault," I said, but I could see he wasn't really listening. "Sam! Please don't resign."

"I have to," he said miserably. "I could do it again."

Oh, *hell*. I looked at the two remaining suppressors, one destined for Oona and one for Raphael, and made what was probably a very bad decision. But I just couldn't let Sam think he'd assaulted me out of nowhere. Getting Raphael on board wasn't worth Sam's distress.

"If you want to make it up to me, you'll pick up that safety pin," I said, with all the authority I could muster.

"Stop! Daylight!" Hannah said sharply, and I jerked the box away just in time, my heart pounding. I wasn't sure if the suppressor would stop Sam's personal wards against daylight, but Hannah was right; it absolutely wasn't worth the risk.

"What's going on?" Oona asked.

Hannah jerked her head at the box. "Oona, you take that bracelet. Charlie, take Sam into his office and give him the safety pin there."

Sam was looking lost and bewildered, and I wanted to hug him. I never wanted to hug vampires. A quick daydream about grabbing Raphael by the tie didn't count.

"Just come with me," I said and hustled Sam down the hallway to his windowless office, brushing off more apologies on the way. "It'll all make sense in a moment," I promised, and checked the door was securely closed, without a hint of daylight making its way inside. "Okay, I think we're good. Take the safety pin."

Sam did. After a minute, he stiffened and touched his forehead, like someone waking from a strange dream. "What?"

I gave him the now-practiced spiel, and he collapsed into his chair, spinning from the impact. "Those assholes!" he said.

"Yep."

"And I really didn't hurt you?" His eyes searched my face anxiously. "I did hold your wrist. You said—"

"It didn't hurt. I just said that hoping it'd break through. I'm sorry I lied."

He waved that off, still frowning. "They messed with our heads!"

"They'll do more than that, if they get away with this," I said. "We need information, Sam. I need to know who Callahan Construction are and who they're working for. This could just be some Humans First publicity stunt, but mauvais wizards don't come cheap. They're paying a lot for those wards, and I have to think it's not just to embarrass Seraphine."

"Shouldn't we tell her?"

I sighed. "Even if we had another one, do *you* think a 500-year-old vampire will let me hand her a suppressor without explanation?"

"Uh," he said. "She might do more than hold your wrist if you tried."

"Right. We have to take care of this ourselves." I resolved not to tell him that I'd planned the third suppressor for Raphael—Sam was dealing with enough misplaced guilt at the moment. "And then there's Oona's vision."

Sam's frown got deeper. "What vision?"

"Ah," I said. "Um, okay. We definitely have to talk to the others."

***

Sam's office was even stuffier with all four of us crammed in there, but it was obviously Sam's safe space, and no one wanted to take that away from him right now. He'd reacted with increasing alarm as Oona explained her vision.

"We need an order of operations," Hannah said. She'd claimed the other chair, so Oona and I were standing up, trying not to lean against anything too expensive. She gestured at the map of the park I'd hastily scribbled out, with my best guesses of where the various supernatural hazards were. "The biggest problem is the wards, which prevent us from explaining the problem to many people who might be able to assist." She hesitated, then looked at Oona. "Humans and magicians are both unaffected. We can't tell Bev, of course, but would Blake be willing to help?" She glanced at me. "Oona's boyfriend is a wizard."

"Um," Oona said, and twisted her fingers together. "We're kind of taking a break at the moment. I've been pretty clingy, lately, and he needs some space. Honestly, it might be for the best. Sometimes I'm not sure that we're good for each other."

I recognized the look on Hannah's face, because I'd made it—and seen it—a few times myself. It was the look of a woman who had plenty to say about her friend's boyfriend, but knew she wasn't ready to hear it.

"What's Blake's class?" I asked. It was rude to ask, but this was kind of a crisis situation, and I didn't think a Third or Fourth Class was going to be much help here.

"Tenth," Oona said.

I sat up straight and looked at Hannah, who nodded in acknowledgment, her lips pressed tightly together. "That could be great," I said cautiously. "The spell is probably bound to some kind of artifact on site. A Tenth Class could unbind that."

"Um," Oona said, and looked at her hands again.

"We'll keep that as a backup option," Hannah said, and Oona nodded in relief.

"Or we could just smash the artifact," Sam suggested. "That'd break the wards."

Sam seemed to be taking this especially hard. I didn't want to be the one to point out that even if the wards were down, he wouldn't be able to enter the park until that cross-shaped pathway was broken up. If you want to use religious symbols to repel vampires, you have to be an adherent of that religion, and a lot of Humans First people claim to be Christian. There's a huge theological debate on whether the Christ himself would have condemned supernaturals. As a devoted agnostic, I stay out of that kind of discussion, but I draw the line at invoking your god to justify harming other people.

Anyway, the point was that the cross had almost certainly been built by true believers in order to keep vampires away, which meant that it would work. Until it was gone, Sam couldn't smash anything.

And the rest of us weren't really smashers.

It was a clever, nasty feedback loop. Build the wards to protect the park, and the park to protect the ward artifact. I was just about to suggest that maybe one of us could approach this Blake, if Oona didn't want to do it, when Bev opened the door.

Sam jerked backwards. Oona squeaked, "Hi, Bev! You're in early!" looking as guilty as if she'd been caught with her hand in the register. I probably didn't look any less suspicious. I'd gone stiff, a guilty chill racing over my skin, and I had to consciously close my mouth.

Practiced conspirators, we were not.

"What are you four plotting?" Bev asked, her eyes tracking slowly over the tableau.

"Definitely not your birthday party," Hannah said. She was the only one of us who looked calm, and judging from the way Bev's eyes narrowed, it was exactly the right thing to say.

"Waste of time," she growled. "At my age, birthdays don't need celebrating. Anyway, you don't know when it is."

Hannah buffed her nails, which were exactly as polished as they'd been the day she died. "All employees are required to enter date of birth—and death, where applicable—in their personnel files, stored securely in the company servers."

Bev looked at Sam, who looked ready to burst into flame on the spot. "Don't," she said. It seemed to be a general instruction.

Hannah was a *genius*.

"Seraphine's here," Bev said, and then, when we all looked horrified, "For the *meeting*? Everyone except Sam is supposed to be there."

"Oh no!" Oona said, and Hannah blinked out of existence as she passed through the wall.

"I'll uh, I'll just work on that thing," Sam stuttered, and turned back to his screens.

In the corridor, Bev let Oona hasten past her, but pinned me with a look as I tried to do the same.

"You and Anton," she said.

"I don't really want to talk about that at work."

"You think I do?" she said, sounding more tired than mad. "Just... go slow, okay? For both of your sakes."

I thought about Anton hovering over me in his car, his weight on my lower body, the desire in his eyes, and couldn't repress a shiver.

"He's been through a lot," Bev said. "And I don't know you, but you seem like a smart kid. So *be smart*." And with that, she ushered me into the conference room, and the next disaster I had to deal with.

***

I was trapped in an enclosed space with three powerful vampires, and I didn't like it one bit.

Raphael was there, in all his golden Nordic handsomeness, and the round, purple-haired person beside him had introduced themselves as Thomme, Lady Seraphine's PR rep. I caught the conspiratorial smile they sent at Oona, and remembered that they were friends. Thomme felt older than Raphael, coming close to four centuries, though they were dressed up to the minute in the boho-punk look.

But Lady Seraphine outclassed both of them.

She wore designer black, presumably to signal that she was fashion-conscious, but not a slavish trend-follower. The soles of her high pumps were blood-red, and so were her nails. She wore no makeup, because that flawless, ageless face needed no decoration, but I hated to think how much maintenance was required for her sleek, long black hair.

No doubt she could afford it.

"How very nice to meet you, Charlotte," she said, and took my hand in hers.

I decided now was not the time to insist she call me Charlie. "You too," I said, and shook.

Raphael's eyes sharpened on me, and I remembered he could tell if I was lying.

So could Felantheril, but she'd shrunk right into herself, a dull presence at the head of the table when she should have been leading the meeting. Lady Seraphine took charge instead, smiling brilliantly around the room. Not a glimpse of fang showed, but it didn't need to. Her presence beat against my metaphysical awareness like someone hammering on a door.

"Raphael assures me that the opening can go ahead on Friday as scheduled," she said. "The purpose of this meeting is to go over the last-minute details, and make sure everybody's in the loop."

Oona was holding her pen in a white-knuckled grip. Hannah was looking much wispier than usual.

"Charlie's in charge of that now," Felantheril said, her voice colorless.

"Uh, yes," I said. "There are a few final issues with the construction, but we're working to address them." There, that was the truth, even if it was grossly understating the problem.

"Excellent!" Seraphine said. "Thomme, how are we placed for press?"

"Representatives from all the major papers will be there, my lady. All the local networks, of course, plus some of the nationals." They looked at me. "Shall I coordinate with you regarding refreshments?"

Oh, shit, we had to feed the press? I had the feeling they'd be fattening themselves up on a juicy story, vulture-like. Would

Tilly be coming? There was no way to ask her without looking suspicious.

"Yes, thank you."

"Now, the schedule," Seraphine said, and looked at me expectantly.

I stared back. I'd been handed this task at the end of business *yesterday,* on my second day in the job. Did she really expect me to have organized a schedule for the ceremony I wasn't even sure could *happen*?

Evidently, yes.

"Right, the schedule," I said, and looked around the table in dismay. Bev was frowning at Felantheril. Oona was wincing. "I'm afraid that—"

"If I may, my lady," Raphael said, and withdrew a sheet of paper from a folder. "Ms. Cross took the precaution of sending the schedule to me for vetting. I believe that with these changes, this will suffice?"

It was a good thing Seraphine had turned towards him, because my face must have broadcast my shock. I managed to smooth out my expression by the time she looked back at me.

"Splendid work, Charlotte." Her voice was clear and sweet. "You're clearly a wonderful addition to the team."

I wanted to crawl under the table, where those sharp green eyes couldn't see me. She couldn't have the same talent Raphael did, to tell truth from lies, but I didn't think she was easily fooled. "Thank you, um, my lady."

"And I believe that draws this meeting to a conclusion," she said, standing up. She'd been in the building for all of twenty minutes. "Thomme, coordinate with Charlotte. Raphael, you'll accompany me back to the office."

"I'll just have a quick word with Ms. Cross regarding the schedule," Raphael said, and Lady Seraphine's eyebrows arched. She said something in quick French, her tone light and teasing, and Raphael responded in the same language.

I'd taken four terms of French as my language requirement, but the listening tests had never been my favorite. Nevertheless, I caught *amourette* and *badinage*, which was enough to be sure Seraphine was implying Raphael was staying to flirt with me. My cheeks burned as she swept out.

Almost everyone filed out after her, Thomme gaily chatting with Oona, but Raphael lingered.

"Thanks for the schedule save," I said.

"It seemed the least I could do," he said, his voice rueful. "Charlie, will you look at me?"

I made eye contact. It was an effort.

"What's wrong?" he asked. "I know something is. Will you tell me?"

This would have been the *perfect* opportunity to give him a suppressor. I tried to stifle my regret. Sam had needed it more. ""There's no point in telling you anything. You won't believe me."

"I can sense that you believe that," he said slowly. "But try me anyway."

I rolled my eyes. "Only Humans is trying to embarrass your boss by making her open a park hostile to supernaturals, and between you and Felantheril, I'm on the hook for it."

Something flickered over his face, some kind of strain, and I watched with a sudden hope.

Then he shook his head, looking cool and calm and infinitely frustrating. "I warn you, Lady Seraphine won't be impressed by excuses."

I held back a sigh. "Right. Good to know."

"I'm sure you'll do your best," he said.

I would. I was.

I was just not sure if my best was going to be enough.

***

Thomme and Oona were deep into a discussion on the implications of this year's hemlines, but they both perked up when I entered the office.

"Charlotte!" Thomme said. "Come and join us."

"It's Charlie," I said, and dropped into my chair. "Hi."

"Hi!" They grinned at me, flashing bright white fangs. From them, it just seemed like a smile, not a threat display. "I don't suppose you know if there's a line item in the park budget for catering the opening?"

"There isn't really a budget anymore," I said, sending a baleful glare in the direction of Felantheril's office.

"Ahhh," Thomme said, looking sympathetic. "Well, let me send you the details for the caterers I get in for last-minute office events, and I'm sure we can cover it in the PR budget for the month."

"Wow, thank you." I sounded more sarcastic than sincere, and I tried again. "I mean it, that's super nice of you."

"No problem! Raph said you'd kind of been dragged in last minute."

"Did he tell you he did the dragging?"

"No, but he didn't make eye contact, so I knew something was off. That guy is *the worst* for taking seminars seriously. Eye contact! Firm handshake! Appropriate business attire!" They fluffed out their purple curls and adjusted the denim jacket slung over their embroidered peasant shirt. "I drive him right out of his mind. It's good for him. Okay, that should be in your email now."

I hadn't even logged into my laptop yet today. We might be getting closer to fixing the park situation, but doing my actual job had been pushed right down the priorities list.

I had twenty-seven emails. Thomme's was at the top, right above another from... ugh.

"Ian Kelly," I said, and scowled at the screen.

Thomme jerked. "You know Ian?"

"Not really."

"He's being a dick about a booking we had to shift," Oona said. She was watching Thomme with interest, and there was a silvery sheen over her eyes. "How do you know him?"

"He runs the Committee to Improve Avenue Thirteen," Thomme said. "You know me, I'm community-minded, so I went to a few meetings." They smiled, as bright and wide as ever, but it seemed off, somehow, and the shimmer in Oona's eyes was getting stronger. "He used to be a Hunter, you know? A good one, side of justice and all that. Took out a lot of bad actors, supernatural and otherwise. Anyway, I thought he had some good ideas, but the group wasn't super welcoming, so... You've got the caterers, Charlie?"

"Yup."

"Great! Oona, cocktails next Thursday? You want to come, Charlie? I know this great place in Hell's Kitchen."

"Sure, sounds fun."

Thomme jumped up. "Okay! Gonna love you and leave you. Hannah, Mr. Scruffles is looking fab. Bev, my queen, my goddess, I hate to leave your glorious presence but—"

"Out," Bev said, but her lips twitched at Thomme's elaborate bow as they exited.

Oona and I exchanged glances. "Well, we'd better get the doors open!" she said, and we headed downstairs. Oona held her finger to her lips, but I knew better than to talk in the stairwell.

We were all taking things carefully; we didn't have a replacement railing yet, and the stairs seemed more treacherous than ever.

Oona unlocked the main doors and headed purposefully for the reception desk.

"What did you see?" I whispered.

She looked frustrated. "Not much. I got a whiff of that weird smell, the same one I had in the park vision. Then I saw Thomme, looking scared, and Ian Kelly, looking ready to kill."

I gasped. "He's going to kill Thomme?"

"No!" Oona said, and then frowned. "Okay, rejecting that was automatic, but it feels right. God, I have the stupidest power. I don't know why Callahan would even bother to ward their park against me."

"I think it's a general ward against any supernaturals, wizards excepted. That would be the hardest part, actually. The artifact probably contains both baseline human and magician biological material."

Oona made a face. "Like blood? Gross."

"Dark wizards are pretty gross," I agreed. "So, is it just me, or does an ex-Hunter running a community organization that wasn't welcoming to a community-minded vampire feel pretty suspicious right now?"

"Mm-hmm." Oona's fingers were flying over the keyboard. "Okay, I've got Ian's details here from the bookings. Let's see what the internet thinks."

She turned up a picture of a silver fox at his sixtieth birthday party, surrounded by his family. A brother, equally foxy; a sister who looked vaguely familiar; a loving blonde wife; two adult daughters, one holding a baby... "He runs a consultancy and public speaking business."

"Consulting on what?" I demanded. "How to hunt? That's not legal anymore!"

It had been, less than ten years ago. Hunters had been phased out gradually under the Faerie Accords Act, and the timeline for that phase-out had been one of the bigger problems with getting the Accords signed. Werewolves wanted hunting outlawed immediately, which made a lot of sense, given how often—and how unjustifiably—they were targeted. Vampires advocated for a slow fade, possibly because it helped them keep their own more violent factions in line, or possibly because it pissed off the werewolves. A lot of human-focused lobby groups had wanted Hunter divisions incorporated into the military and police forces, arguing for oversight instead of abolition.

Like a lot of the Faerie Accords Act, the end result was a compromise. A thirty year phasing-out of Hunters, with increased restrictions on licensing and much more equipment oversight until they were finally outlawed. No more cowboys with a silver-chased shotgun, a bandolier of stakes, and a grudge.

I wasn't someone who'd argue there'd never been a need for Hunters. In the initial post-Cataclysm chaos, these vigilantes wielding silver and salt had saved a lot of lives. And they weren't all human, either; wizards like Tamatha Grace and the vampire known as Still Water had been effective, and downright heroic Hunters.

But as the world got back on its feet with a new understanding of how everyone could co-exist, Hunters had become a dangerous, almost entirely human hammer for an increasingly complex nail. The lack of oversight and accountability had meant a lot of nasty xenophobes had signed on, and then basically murdered hundreds of innocent supernaturals. Abolition was the only response that made sense.

Except to Humans First, who kept agitating for "sensible" reinstatement, and to Only Humans, who idolized them. Every time one of their horrible terrorist shitheads committed an atrocity, they were lauded like the Hunters of old. If you wanted to see how badly Hunter-worship could fuck up a nation-state, you only needed to look at France and the Alliance des Chasseurs, who ran nearly every branch of government there.

"He promotes like, self-actualization, 'be the best you that you can be' stuff," Oona reported. "Oh, here's some stuff about exploring the best humanity has to offer."

I snorted. "Humanity."

"Yup. But... I don't know. There are a few old pictures of him in his Hunter gear, but no details on targets or cases. There's nothing on social media. His history's pretty clean."

Hm.

"The committee meets here monthly, right? What's he like in person?"

Oona shrugged. "He's just, like, a guy? Not quite as handsome as the photo, but pretty close. Not friendly, but always polite, up until now. His wife is nice. Um... She's called Marjorie, I think."

"Okay," I said, and cracked my knuckles. "Move over."

She relinquished the keyboard, and then had to greet the first booking of the day, a moms and babies yoga class. I held my breath, crossed my fingers, and logged into my Columbia Library account.

Yes! My password was still being accepted, and that meant I had digital archive access. I set up several search strings, and started cross-referencing. I used the photo to throw in a photo archive search as well. Columbia had some of the most up-to-date archival scrying spells in the business.

There wasn't much. Either Ian Kelly was an ordinary guy who'd turned his old job into a lucrative speaking career, or he was an extraordinary guy who'd gone to some effort to disguise it. I genuinely had no reason to think it was the latter, except for Oona's vision, and my own heightened sense of anxiety.

"Maybe I'm just paranoid," I muttered, and then the photo archive search returned a hit.

Oona came back to find me staring at the screen.

"Turns out Ian's big on travel," I said.

Oona squinted at the picture. It was Ian, maybe twenty or fifteen years younger, standing with two other men. They were in combat fatigues, each with a tri-color flag on their left pocket flaps. Ian had a US flag pin on his right.

"He went to France?"

"He signed up for a Chasseur mercenary company. See the lettering under the French flag?" I zoomed in for her.

"PCL?"

"*Les Pauvres Chevaliers de la Lumiere*," I said. "They claim to be the spiritual successors of the Knights Templar. It's one of the most selective—and most brutal—of the Chasseur organizations. Foreigners usually aren't even considered. Ian must have been something special."

Oona whistled.

"Yeah. I did some cross-referencing, and I have names for those two guys. Pierre Martin is listed as one of the honored dead, and Bastien Guillot is retired from service. But Ian isn't on the PCL register at all. He went under another name, or he was removed from the records." I grimaced. "Either way, it's sus."

"I don't suppose he could have just been dressing up in a spare uniform? For a fun photo?" She made air quotes around "fun".

I shook my head. "No PCL chevalier would allow that kind of stolen valor. They'd have beaten the shit out of him, not stood there with their arms over his shoulders."

Oona blew out a breath. "Okay. So, there's this thing Thomme does sometimes," she said, her voice so low I had to lean in and concentrate. "Lady S occasionally sends them to scope out people and organizations. People she's thinking of doing business with, potential rivals... that kind of thing. They call it reconnaissance. Showing up to a few meetings and starting a conversation with the committee leader sounds like reconnaissance to me."

"Thomme liked him," I said.

Oona pointed at the photo. "I bet you a million bucks Thomme didn't know about this, though."

"A potential rival to Lady Seraphine," I said. I had a sinking feeling in my gut. "A political rival? Someone who might want to embarrass her?" Someone who might kick up a stink about being kicked out for a werewolf's eighth birthday party. Somebody who probably had some opinions he'd been keeping really quiet about the place of supernaturals in Thirteenth Avenue, waiting for the right time to make his move.

"Maybe," Oona said, and I could tell we were thinking the same thing. "Can you handle the desk? I'll run up and talk to Sam."

"I've got it," I said, with more confidence than I actually felt. She was up there a long time, probably pulled into some other task, and I answered the phone, went through emails, confirmed the caterers, and booked a room for a Stitch'n'Bitch'n'Witch group who were looking for a new location.

The use of "witch" startled me at first—it was usually an insult leveled at magicians, especially female magicians. But the nice lady at the other end of the phone must have heard my hesitation. "We're reclaiming the words, dear!" she said. "We're mostly werewolves and magicians, you see. Well, and a few humans. And Yossel." Whatever Yossel was had to remain a mystery as she blithely continued:

"The bar we used to meet at said we were scaring the other customers, what with all the sex talk. So a private room would probably suit us better."

"Privacy," I said, making a note by the conference room booking. "You've got it. We'll be looking forward to hosting you."

"Aren't you sweet?" she said, and hung up before I could respond.

Privacy. There was a thought. I wasn't sure I was ready to have any kind of relationship talk with Anton, but we had to at least pretend to be a couple so that Bev didn't get suspicious, right? Maybe he'd be interested in some light making out, somewhere that wasn't parked outside my mom's house?

I was daydreaming about that when I heard the raised voices outside. I lifted my head, and then heard the meaty thud of bodies colliding and the crash of breaking glass.

By the time I heard the first howl, I was already running for the door.

Chapter Thirteen

I'm not the most athletic person in the world. I can dance for hours, but competitive sports bore the hell out of me, and I don't think I've run a race since sixth grade.

And yet I was outside and onto the sidewalk so fast that I could have given a werewolf a run for her money.

It didn't help much, because, in fact, there were three werewolves. Two of them were keeping Anton back, while the third was taking a baseball bat to his car windows

"Hey!" I yelled, which did nothing to stop the werewolves, but pulled Anton's attention towards me. His face went from frustrated fury to fear.

"Get back inside!" he said.

"Nope," I said, and focused on the werewolf holding his arms. "Let him go right now!"

That guy ignored me, but the dark-skinned woman who was shoving at his shoulders looked at me. "Or what?" she asked.

Uh. It was a decent question. Theoretically, I could call the police, but the werewolves could do a lot before they got here, and adding cops to a bad situation often made it worse. Anton had red marks on his face and his shirt was torn, which I hated, but they hadn't drawn blood. They weren't beating him. Just holding him while he struggled and stopping him from intervening in the blatant destruction of his beloved Road Runner.

The werewolf with the bat brought it down on Anton's side mirror. It exploded in bits of mirrored glass and steel, and Anton made an anguished noise.

"Hey!" I said, and jumped between the bat and the car, my arms outstretched. "Stop it!"

The werewolf was a ruddy-faced guy in his forties who looked like he'd be more comfortable behind a desk in a Midtown insurance office than swinging a Louisville slugger. He lowered the bat. "Get out of the way," he said, not unkindly. "This'll only take a minute."

"Did Tiffany order you to do this?" I demanded.

The woman snorted. "She didn't have to. You don't hurt our alpha."

My jaw clenched. "It was an *accident.*"

"That's why we're not breaking *him.*"

The guy with the bat took advantage of my distraction to swing his bat again, beating a dent into the driver side door. I made a startled yip in protest, and lunged in to grab his arm.

It was beyond stupid. I'd be lucky to take down an unarmed baseline guy his size, and this was a werewolf with a weapon. If I'd thought about it for a fraction of a second, I'd never have done it, but I'd been doing a lot of impulsive things lately.

With more luck than skill, I caught his arm, and threw my other-else at him through the contact. It wasn't a spell. It was barely a thought. Mostly, I wanted him to *stop*, and that incoherent desire pulsed out of me, a feeble attempt to put my power to some goddamned use. A real wizard might have frozen him in place with that, but I got a surge *back*. My heart hammered as a feeling of enormous strength flowed into me, along with a prickling expansion of my senses. I could smell the roses lining the path to the rec center, the artificial jasmine of my deodorant, the salty tang of Anton's fear-sweat, sharp and rising.

Then the werewolf brushed me away, with no more effort than I'd take to flick a fly off my arm. Disoriented, I staggered back and bounced off the car. I flung my hand out to break my fall, and felt my palm scrape raw against the asphalt.

"Charlie!" Anton's voice was resonant and almost painfully loud. He jerked one arm free, actually tugging the werewolf behind him a step or two toward me. The female werewolf went for his free arm, and he kicked her in the gut. It was a solid blow. She staggered back.

I was still trying to push myself upright when the guy kicked Anton in the back of the knee.

Anton hit the ground hard, and the guy was on him, pinning him while the woman straightened, one hand to her stomach. She was growling, her eyes going pale yellow. It was three days until full moon. If she lost control, we were all fucked.

Something blasted through the air.

It felt like a lightning strike made of sound, a piercing, pain-inducing shriek. I clapped my hands to my ears and cringed back, just as the man pinning Anton did the same. The woman was made of sterner stuff, but even she flinched, some of the aggression bleeding out of her face.

I staggered upright, leaning on the battered car, and saw a woman in her late sixties with a fussy blouse and tightly permed hair limping out of the rec center. She had her handbag over one shoulder and a silver whistle in her hand.

My other-else was quiet. The whistle was probably enchanted, but Bev Thornton was baseline to the bone.

Her presence could make you doubt it.

"You know better than this, Mina," she told the woman.

"You know he can't get away with hurting our alpha," Mina countered. Bev's eyes hardened. After a second, Mina muttered, "Ms. Thornton."

"And he hasn't," Bev said, eyeing the car. Her gaze passed over me like the collateral damage I was. "But this wasn't the place."

For the first time, I became aware of how many people were around. The florists at the shop across the road had come out to stare. Baz's customers were on the street, one of them still clutching a pint glass. And there was a little huddle of parents and kids, halfway down the block, clustered protectively together.

Mina saw them too, and flinched again. Bev let that rest a beat. "Leave," she said.

Mina grimaced, then nodded. I shot a look over my shoulder, and the guy with the bat was already walking away. But the guy who was kneeling on Anton's back frowned.

"He kicked—"

"You're done," Bev said. It wasn't a threat. It was a flat statement, delivered in a level voice, and all the more effective because of it. "Go home, Nicky."

"You're not my fucking mom," Nicky snarled. He was young, blue-eyed, freckled, and my other-else felt the ripples of power spreading out of him, like someone had tossed a rock in a pool. Alpha potential, definitely.

"We're leaving," Mina told him, and held out a hand to help Nicky up. After a second, he took it, and she slung her arm around his shoulders, talking quietly to him as they walked off. Anton pushed himself up to hands and knees, and then halfway to his feet, bracing his forearms against his thighs. His ribcage expanded and collapsed as he sucked in air.

I headed straight for him.

"Hey," I said, putting my hand flat on his back. "Are you okay?"

He turned to look at me, and his eyes were on fire.

It wasn't a metaphor. Anton's dark brown eyes had been supplanted by flickering orange, red and yellow flames, a burning gaze that seared right through me.

Heat raced over my limbs, clenched between my thighs, settled heavy and liquid in my belly.

He must have dropped the suppressor to fight back, I thought fuzzily, and then I was pressing close to him, unable to live another second without his mouth on mine.

He'd described his power as a *pull*, and that was exactly what it felt like, as if I was being yanked towards Anton by some invisible force. On some level, I was aware that I was acting out of character, that I didn't usually make out with guys on the street. At least, not sober, and not in the middle of the day.

But that didn't matter. Everything dimmed in importance compared to the taste of his mouth and the strength of his hands. Energy spiraled up inside me and spilled into him.

Then Anton jerked forward, his mouth mashing uncomfortably into mine. The pain cleared my thoughts for a second, and I pulled back in time to see Bev's handbag smack into the back of his head again.

"Ow!" he said.

"Suppressor," Bev said, by way of a warning, and clapped her other hand against the side of his neck.

She must have had the suppressor in her palm. The flames in his eyes died immediately, and the pull disappeared.

This didn't mean I wanted to stop kissing him. It just meant I was suddenly really embarrassed about it.

"Oh, shit," Anton said, backing away from me. He'd pressed me against the side of the car. "I'm sorry, Charlie."

My lips were tingling, and not just because he'd jarred them when Bev hit him. I was light-headed, more tired than I should have been on an adrenaline rush, and I remembered that feeling of energy being drawn out of me. Incubi could get energy from desire the same way vampires got energy from blood.

"Why didn't you pull Nicky or Mina?" I asked. My voice was shaking more than I liked. It was a slightly weird time for the question, but given the choice between research and an awkward conversation, I'd choose curiosity every time. Huh, my bra clasp was undone. I folded my arms behind my back to redo it.

Anton was staring at the ground, red-faced, while he fumbled the suppressor back into his pocket. "Because I'm not into them," he mumbled. "I wanted to stop them— I'm stronger without the suppressor. Harder to hurt, quicker to heal. I wasn't planning to use my uh, my other powers."

And then, while he was hurt and struggling, a girl he liked had walked up and touched him. That was my own damn fault—he'd told me himself that his shaky control got even shakier when he reciprocated attraction.

"*I'm* sorry," I said. "I should have known better, or at least checked."

"Yeah, okay, everyone's sorry," Bev said. "Could you two get off the street?"

Anton got even redder. I was pretty sure my own cheeks were flaming. "Is Tiffany gonna—" I began, and then caught a glimpse of orange out of the corner of my eye.

It seemed the construction workers at the park site had also been drawn by the sound of the scuffle, though it had maybe taken them a little longer to hear it over their own noise. There were four guys standing in the open gate, their arms folded, watching us with derision and contempt.

And in front of them, staring directly at me, was Site Manager Dave.

My hand went to my hair, that literal red flag announcing my identity. For a moment, I wondered if I could pretend to have been passing by. But Bev was talking to me and pointing to the rec center, and I had to accept that my anonymity was well and truly gone.

And because Bev *was* talking to me, she didn't miss his interest either. "Who's that?"

"Dave. Site manager of the construction site. I met him when I visited. I don't think he likes me much."

Bev snorted. "No, really?" The bystanders were moving again, pedestrians who had missed the main event striding by with no more than a curious glance at Anton's poor car, Baz's customers wandering back into the bar. One of the girls from the flower shop ran across the road with a sample of herbal salve and handed it to me.

"For your hands," she explained.

"Thanks," I said, and felt tears sting my eyes. The kindness of New Yorkers is weird and unexpected and not always reliable, but it can also stun you with the grace of people just looking out for each other.

Dave wasn't looking out for me. He was looking straight at me. I followed Bev inside like a duckling, because I couldn't tell her why I didn't want Dave knowing I worked right next door. The number of secrets I was keeping felt like a lump in my throat, like I kept trying to swallow something huge and unpleasant.

Oona was behind the reception desk, her eyes enormous as she took in our disheveled state. Bev limped over to the staff-only stairwell. "I'm going to call Tiffany," she said, without turning around. "Make sure this is done with."

Anton nodded, even though she couldn't see him. "I'll call Jafr and get him to bring the tow-truck."

"I'm so sorry about your car," I told him.

His smile was weak. "I can fix her. That's what I'm for." He hesitated a moment, then said, "Not that I don't appreciate you trying to help, but—"

"No, I know. I shouldn't have jumped in there. I just... I saw you in trouble, and I didn't think about it."

"Oh," Anton said. And then he smiled for real. Honestly, that smile was unfair. He had a wide mouth and full lips, and his left incisor was a bit crooked, saving him from being too perfect and giving him a ludicrous amount of lopsided charm.

"Charlie, can I speak to you for a minute?" Oona said, so quickly that the words blurred together. Wait, had I not clued the others in on the pretending-to-date-Anton thing? I joined her behind the desk.

"Don't worry, Bev already warned me," I began, but she shook her head.

"No, not that," she said, her voice fast and breathy. "Sam just called down. He thinks he found the link between Callahan Construction and Ian Kelly."

***

Sam had found Callahan Construction in the city business registry. It was owned by a shell company called Sierra Vista Locations, which was a division of Eventide Enterprises, which apparently did a number of real estate and property investment things. Two of the VPs there were Jackie and Patrick Callahan.

Sam had promptly done a deep dive into those names, and discovered that this was Jackie's second marriage. Her first had been to a man named Peter Bancroft and reported in the society pages.

167

There, she was described as Jackie Bancroft (*née* Kelly.)

"You'd make a good historian," I said. Bev had gone out for her lunch break, and our little cabal had gathered in Sam's office again. Oona was on reception, which should have relieved the crowding issue, except that Anton was in there instead, and his shoulders weren't helping at all.

"I don't have proof that they're related," Sam said. "Kelly isn't that uncommon a name in this city."

"No," I said, and pulled up the Kelly family barbecue picture I'd found on my phone. "But look. Accounting for time and some pretty good plastic surgery, the woman in the wedding dress is the same one standing next to Ian Kelly here."

Sam sucked his teeth. "His sister?"

"Bet your life on it." I grinned triumphantly. "I knew she looked familiar. She was at the construction site yesterday. She was the one who realized I wasn't supposed to be there, which means she's probably had contact with the mauvais wizards, or at least knows enough about them to recognize that I couldn't have been one."

"It's not enough," Hannah said.

"How do you mean?"

"It's a connection Ian Kelly can disavow. His sister works at a company that owns a company that owns a company building the park? She was visiting one of the construction sites and recognized you were an intruder? That's not proof of him trying to embarrass Seraphine."

"It's a pretty amazing coincidence, don't you think?"

"Oh, I *believe* he's in it up to his eyebrows. But I can't *prove* that. And without proof, we're just the employees of Seraphine d'Arc, trying to discredit a potential rival with flimsy rumors."

"We're not her employees," Sam protested. "It's true that she's the major benefactor to the Thirteenth Avenue Community Recreation Center Trust, but technically, she doesn't—"

"'Technically' won't get us very far," I said, my stomach sinking. "Hannah's right."

"Not to mention the optics are terrible. Sneaky rich vampire tries to make a noble ex-Hunter look bad?" Hannah leaned forward and ticked items off her mostly-opaque fingers. "We can't go to the cops, because they haven't broken the law."

"Except for that ward," I said.

Hannah looked patient. "Do you think the cops are going to send a mauvais special investigator for something that hasn't actually hurt anyone? At some point during the next three days?"

"Probably not," I admitted. There was a new story every week about how overworked police wizards were. A manipulative ward would be way down the priority list.

"So take that option off the table. We can't lay suit because there's no contract. We can't fire them because we can't tell Felantheril or Lady S what's going on." *Or Raphael*, I thought, but I no longer felt guilty about my impulse to give the last suppressor to Sam. He'd turned up this missing link.

"And we can't go to the press because it'll make us look bad," I said.

Anton stirred restlessly. "I still think that if you dig through the salt circle, I could do some damage."

It was a terrible idea, dangerous and potentially violent, and not at all likely to result in a park ready for an opening ceremony in two days. "I think that has to be Plan B," I said.

"What's Plan A?"

"We go talk to Ian Kelly," I said, with much more confidence than I felt. "At his home. We threaten him with exposing the connection to Callahan. They've been trying to keep it secret, and that has to be for a reason. Maybe we can pretend we've got more proof than we have."

Sam looked worried. Anton looked disappointed. Hannah looked... calm.

"Or," she said. "We could do nothing." She looked at three startled expressions and shook her head. "Listen. I've been around for nearly a century. Sometimes people catch you unawares and you can't do anything about it. Sometimes the risks of fighting back outweigh the benefits. Sometimes you have to save your energy for something else."

"We can't let them get away with this!" Sam said, his voice louder than I'd ever heard.

"What I'm saying is that actually, we can," Hannah said patiently. "I'm not saying this park is a good thing, but we might be too late to stop it. Even the attempt could have terrible consequences." Anton opened his mouth and she held up her hand. "Anton, half an hour ago you pretty much let werewolves mutilate your car because fighting them would have been worse. And when you did fight, it *was* worse."

"This is different!" Anton said.

"Why?"

Because I was oathsworn to Felantheril. Because Raphael had made my continued employment conditional on getting the job done. Because I didn't want to leave this city or the country or the continent to get away from the consequences of my own stupidity.

But those were just my own reasons, selfish reasons. Would I even be fighting this if I didn't have to?

Yes.

"We have to fight because this is wrong!" I said. It came out a bit squeaky, but I meant it. "This is a *community* rec center! And I know I'm not really a part of this community yet, but I want to be. I want to get to know our patrons, and I want to help middle-aged ladies find rooms for their sexy sewing chat, and do whatever this clothing swap market thing is, and these people *don't* want that. They don't even want us to exist, but they definitely don't want us to be *here*, part of their world, doing burlesque classes with a succubus and helping fae immigrants with their documentation. They don't want there to be a Baby Yoga class where it doesn't matter if the baby has fur or a tail!"

I stopped to inhale. Sam was staring at me. Anton was looking more than a little starry-eyed. Hannah opened her mouth, and I held up my finger to stop her, the same move she'd pulled on Anton.

"And I get it, I understand what you're saying about saving our energy, but this is worth spending it! If these assholes get away with shutting us out of a park, they'll try to shut us out of businesses, or schools, or jobs, or homes, or— or, *voting*. And then supernaturals will have to fight back and we'll be right back to the bad old days, the ones no one sensible wants to return to. But they do. And they *won't* stop, so we need to stop them!" There were angry, hot tears in my eyes, and I wiped them away.

"Then we're agreed," Hannah said crisply. "Plan A, threaten Ian Kelly with exposure. Plan B, physical destruction of the park." She looked thoughtful. "We should check with Oona, of course, but I doubt she'll say no."

We all stared at her.

"You didn't want to do nothing either!" I accused.

Hannah grinned impishly. "No. But I did want you to consider all of your options." Her eyes rested on me, and I felt the prickling sensation of her gaze. "And you *are* new, Charlie. Forgive me for wanting to check the depth of your commitment. As you've pointed out, this group is working with at least two wizards, and many Humans First advocates are more tolerant of magicians than other supernaturals. *You're* not shut out of the park."

"You don't trust me," I said, and tried not to feel terrible about it. As she said, she had no real reason to.

But she smiled again and leaned in. "I do trust you," she said. "You said *us*."

Chapter Fourteen

The problem was timing.

It was Wednesday, a popular day for evening events at the rec center. Sam pretty much set his own hours (and from what Hannah said, actually worked more hours than he was paid for, most weeks), and Hannah was mostly on daytimes. But Oona and I were scheduled on until closing at 8 p.m.

Bev hadn't come back from her lunch break. Anton was looking pinch-faced about it. "If I hadn't—" he said, and Oona made an exaggerated lip-zipping gesture.

"No more blaming yourself for the railing," she said firmly. "I'm sick of hearing about the stupid railing. Bev is probably having the time of her life telling Tiffany how much she's on the hook for your car repairs."

Anton looked doubtful about that, but he did stop blaming himself, at least out loud.

"Rock, paper, scissors?" I asked Oona.

She shook her head. "You're not ready to fly the desk solo."

Well, she had a point there.

"You shouldn't be alone, though," Hannah told her.

"Felantheril will be here."

We all thought about that for a second.

"No," Hannah said. "Sam can stay. It's not like Ian Kelly will invite him in anyway." She pointed at Anton. "And when we get there, you're staying out of sight. Back up only."

Anton looked like he was going to protest, and I wasn't too happy about it either, but it was true that an experienced Hunter would take one look at Anton and peg him as a possible threat. Provided she could stay opaque, Hannah looked like a nice lady in her mid-thirties, and I looked like a clueless girl in her early twenties.

I was hoping that the clueless part wasn't accurate.

We had the Kellys' residential address from the rec center's booking forms. Using it for our own purposes was a breach of privacy law no one else seemed to care much about, but I felt a little tingly about committing my first real crime. The Kelly family were on 110th Street, at the very northern boundary of Thirteenth Avenue. Some residents preferred to claim it was really the Upper West Side, just extended a little bit further west. Sam went hunting for real estate listings online, and found floor plans and pictures for fancy condos.

"Hunting must be more lucrative than I thought," I said.

"The money's mostly hers," he said absently. "His consulting business does pretty well, but Marjorie was the only child of a property developer. Judging from the taxes she pays each year, she's loaded."

I sure hoped Sam would never poke around *my* online record. He could clearly find just about anything, and there were some impassioned articles from my high school paper that I didn't want anyone in my adult life to see.

Or the poetry. Oh, God, the poetry.

We took the subway at rush hour, for our sins. Hannah dutifully paid her fare even though she could have just phased through the turnstile, but opted to dematerialize in the actual car, which I didn't blame her for. I found myself crushed between Anton and a blonde vampire with big poofy hair and a bright pink power suit. She gave Anton an appreciative look and nodded at me, in a kind of "good catch, girl" acknowledgment. Then she went back to playing some match game on her phone, her finger stabbing at the screen so fast it blurred.

Even in the packed car, Anton was maintaining a few inches of distance from me. I hung onto the pole and swayed, feeling sweat prickle my skin under my long-sleeved polyester blouse. It seemed sort of trivial to be worrying about my lack of work clothing options while we were on a mission to disrupt the plans of a human supremacist, but if we succeeded, I definitely needed to expand my wardrobe.

If we didn't succeed, of course, I was out of a job.

Hannah rematerialized once we were back on the street, looking cool and calm as we walked the final two blocks to the Kellys' apartment building.

"I think I should come up with you to—" Anton began.

"No," Hannah and I said at the same time, and then Hannah nodded at the coffee stall across the street. "Get an iced mocha," she suggested. "Get three."

It was the kind of building that had a doorman, a security system with mundane and magical elements, and probably some wards against people acting on malign intent, which were honestly pretty useless. Real estate brokers like to list them in the amenities, but the average person has mild malign intent so often that the wards in a building this many people lived in would decay far faster than anyone was willing to pay for re-enchantment.

Fortunately for us, the doorman was busy with a delivery, and Hannah and I—probably mostly Hannah, who was solid—looked like the kind of people who could belong in this building. We walked straight to the elevators, and the second the door closed Hannah went fuzzy around the edges. Maintaining her opacity had to take a lot out of her.

She noticed my look of concern. "I'm not sure I can pass for an entire conversation," she admitted, and then looked thoughtfully. "Actually. There's an idea."

"What?" The elevator rose smoothly through the floors.

"Get a general invitation," Hannah said. "And keep him distracted." She vanished.

"Hey!" I said. It was incredibly rude, but when she didn't respond, I fumbled at the air where she'd been. My hand met no resistance. What the actual hell? Well, I couldn't stop now. I stepped out into a little lobby space. The Kellys didn't rate the penthouse, but they had the next best thing; one of the four double-story condos with big balconies on the penultimate level. The elegant marble flooring in this foyer had probably cost as much as my entire college education.

I straightened my sweaty clothing, smoothed down my hair, and marched right up to the Kelly residence door. There was a discreet camera set into the heavy wood, and a silvery buzzer and intercom on the wall beside the door. I pressed the button and waited.

The wait was agonizing. Ian technically worked from home, but that didn't mean he had to be there right now. Maybe he was out at a meeting, or had blown off that afternoon to go to a movie. I fidgeted outside the door, feeling small and grubby, and debating whether to press the button again.

I wished Hannah would come back.

"Yes?" a female voice inquired, and even though I'd been listening for the intercom, I startled anyway.

"Hello," I said, and threw caution to the wind. "My name is Charlie Cross. I'm looking for Ian Kelly?"

There was another pause, long enough that I wondered if that silence was my answer.

The door was opened by a human woman, and I instantly felt ten times more disgusting. Marjorie Kelly had aged a bit since the photo I'd seen, but she still had perfect bone structure, immaculate makeup, and a sharp blonde bob. She was wearing a red and white shift dress with a thin black belt.

Those were the colors of Only Humans.

It could have been a coincidence, but the possibility that it *wasn't* stiffened my spine. "I would like to speak to Mr. Kelly on a matter of some urgency," I said.

Marjorie's gaze raked up and down me. "Ian's not here."

"Oh."

"But come in. You can talk to me."

Invitations had power. I hoped that "come in" was enough to let Hannah inside.

I stepped over the threshold and followed her to a living area, feeling as if I were walking into the lion's den. The space was devoid of gnawed skulls and bits of rotting flesh, though it was overburdened with colorful art prints and some nice pieces of mid-century furniture. Somebody in this house had an eye and looking at Marjorie's tailored dress, I thought I knew who it was.

Keep him distracted, Hannah had said, and I had to assume the same applied to Marjorie.

"Um, so, I work at the Thirteenth Avenue Recreation Center," I said, gingerly sitting on the edge of the chair she offered me.

Marjorie sat too. "Yes?"

"And I got put in charge of the park development project next door. The opening ceremony is on Friday."

"How nice."

God, it was like trying to get blood out of a stone. Except that if you knew the right alchemical formula and were at least Third Class, you *could* get blood out of a stone. Marjorie was giving me even less than that.

"I inspected the park yesterday, and discovered some disturbing elements."

"Oh dear." Marjorie's blue eyes were still and calm. "But goodness, where are my manners. Would you like something to drink? Ice tea? A glass of water?"

"No, thank you." I would rather chug rat poison.

Something vibrated across my other-else, a ripple in the fabric of the universe. Hannah was doing something in this home, something powerful enough that I could feel it.

Marjorie couldn't feel it, but something in my face must have triggered an instinct, because her eyes sharpened. "Just what are you doing here, Miss Cross? Why do you want to talk to Ian about a park?"

"You're both members of the Committee to Improve Avenue Thirteen, right?"

"Indeed. But that has nothing to do with the park project. That's entirely under recreation center control. A gift from your generous patroness, as I understand it." She smirked a little, and yeah, she did not like Seraphine. That wasn't necessarily a tell—I wasn't sure I liked Seraphine much myself. But Marjorie was looking forward to her humiliation.

There was a sound above us, where the bedrooms presumably were. A soft thump, as if something had been fumbled or dropped, barely audible, if I hadn't been listening for it. Marjorie was just beginning to frown.

"I know about Only Humans!" I blurted, and I suddenly had all of her attention.

"Excuse me?"

"I know that park's a deathtrap for supernaturals! I know what you're trying to do, and I know you and Ian are connected to Callahan Construction through your sister-in-law. I know all about it!"

Marjorie's eye contact didn't waver, which I felt was more confirmation than a reasonable denial. "I think you must be confused," she said, every word hard and cold.

I rolled my eyes, too angry to be intimidated anymore. "I came to tell you that if Ian doesn't stop what's happening with the park, if Callahan don't stop, then I'll go to the media. I'll make sure everyone knows what you're doing." It was a bluff, but for a moment, Marjorie looked absolutely furious.

"I have no idea what you're talking about," she said, nice and loud. After a moment I realized she meant that for the benefit any recording devices I might have had on me. Damn, I really should have thought of that myself.

"Yes, you do," I said. I was shaking with fury, and my voice was shaking too. "I know, and I'm not the only one."

"Miss Cross, whatever you think you know, I cannot believe that it empowers you to act like this," Marjorie said, and stood. "One might almost imagine that you are attempting to blackmail me, which is, of course, a crime. I have the utmost sympathy for the hard workers of the Thirteenth Avenue Community Recreation Center, but perhaps the exertion of your duties has distorted your thinking. Does Felantheril know that you're here?"

"Yes," I lied.

Marjorie tilted her head at me, almost pitying. "How extraordinary," she said. "I'll have to bring it up the next time we talk. Now, I'm afraid I must ask you to leave. I was just on my way out to an important function."

I stood too. "I know about *Les Pauvres Chevaliers*," I said. "I know Ian went overseas to hunt when he couldn't do it here anymore. What was the problem, too many rules to tie his hands? He couldn't get away with murdering innocent supernaturals, but he couldn't give up the thrill? How you can sleep beside a man like that—"

The condescending smile had vanished, but she still wouldn't break. "Get out of my home."

"With pleasure." I took my time moving towards the door, hoping that I'd provided enough distraction for Hannah to successfully do her thing. Marjorie was right on my heels, her face hard.

Before I stepped out, I whirled around and faced her. "I know what you are," I said, through gritted teeth.

"Me, Miss Cross? I'm nothing at all. Isn't that what the inhabitants of Thirteenth Avenue believe?"

For just a moment I saw the rage in her, hot as a furnace behind her cool eyes, and I recoiled. She used the movement to press forward, forcing me out of her space and back into the hallway. "Have a good weekend, Miss Cross. *I* certainly intend to." And she shut the door in my face.

I stumbled back, pressing my hands against my hot cheeks, fighting back the angry tears. I did know what she was, that was the problem. She was the kind of evil who truly, honestly believed that entire categories of people *weren't* really people, and that they didn't deserve to exist. That kind of person was all through my history textbooks, and they'd done untold damage to the world, pre- and post-Cataclysm. The worst part was that she was utterly convinced of her own righteousness. She thought *she* was the hero.

Hannah didn't reappear in the elevator. Perhaps she'd burned up her energy engaging in her mysterious mission, or perhaps she was trying to be tactful as I sniffled my way back to composure.

The doorman was replacing his phone in his cradle as the elevator doors opened, and he looked up at me sharply. "Miss—"

"Don't worry, I'm leaving." I couldn't really storm out the door, because it revolved, but I gave it a hard shove to relieve my feelings, and had to skip through it like an idiot.

Anton wasn't waiting in the cafe across the road. He was hanging out by a fancy trashcan just down the block, conspicuously loitering. I didn't care that he'd ignored the plan. I hurried right over to him.

"Are you okay?" he said.

"Marjorie Kelly is a fucking nightmare," I said. My hands were still shaking, and I held them out to him. He took them without hesitation. No seduction, no pull, just the steadiness of his strength and the warmth of his grip.

"It's okay," he said earnestly. "You're safe."

I choked back a laugh. "She really hates us."

"We knew that, right?"

I *had* known that. But seeing it was different. "I don't think that was a successful mission," I admitted. "Marjorie wouldn't even acknowledge what I was saying, much less agree to alter the park project. Maybe I should have waited and tried talking to Ian."

A black town car pulled up, and a moment later Marjorie Kelly came out of the building in her perfect tailored dress, a light jacket thrown over her shoulders and a red leather purse in her hand. She didn't look in my direction, but said something to the doorman as he held the car door open for her, and he scowled at me. I'd thought it was just an excuse, but I guess she really was on her way somewhere.

"Let's go," Anton said, tugging gently at my hands. I'd stopped shaking, but he hadn't let go. I wasn't going to point it out if he wasn't. "And where's Hannah?"

"Here," Hannah's voice said. "Get moving. I might have found something we can use."

I pulled one of my hands free and started walking downtown. Anton tightened his grip a little, which I didn't hate at all. We really were going to have to talk about this at some point.

"Are we talking blackmail?" I asked. No one passing by gave me a second look. New Yorkers muttering to the air wasn't even on the top 100 list of weird shit in this city.

"Maybe." Hannah's voice was grim.

It should have been good news. But from the note in her voice, I was bracing myself for the next disaster.

***

While I'd been talking to Marjorie, Hannah had been ransacking Ian Kelly's office. She'd been looking for any revealing paperwork or future leads, weak points where we could apply pressure.

What she'd found were pictures, tucked into an envelope that had been put in a hardcover book.

They were old-fashioned Polaroids, possibly from a pre-Cataclysm camera. Hannah thought they were peel-apart film. I could see why Ian hadn't wanted to use his phone. Far better to keep something like this in one hard-copy format, with no inconvenient shadows online.

There were half a dozen pictures of someone who wasn't Marjorie. They sprawled naked among the mussed-up white sheets of an anonymous hotel bedroom, curving their spine to put their body on display, looking coquettishly over their bare shoulder, and in one blurry close-up of their face, smiling up at the person taking the pictures, just a touch of fang peeking out at the corner of the lip. In one picture, we could make out a shape that could be Ian, reflected in a mirror. Sam had scanned that one and taken it away to do complex facial recognition things in his office. The rest of our little cabal was clustered around Hannah's desk, looking at the wrinkled envelope and the well-thumbed edges on the photographs.

"He must look at them a lot," I said.

"The shelves were pretty dusty, but there was a clear space right in front of that book," Hannah said. "That's the only reason I even thought to check inside it."

And had been so shocked that she'd dematerialized, dropping the book and the photos onto the thick rug. That was the sound I'd heard. She'd managed to pull herself together enough to pick up the envelope and tuck the photos into her blouse, so that they'd vanish when she did, and had phased out of the apartment before I'd finished being shown the door.

"We can't use these," Anton said. "Right?"

"No," Oona said firmly. She pushed back from the desk. "We can't."

The person in the pictures was Thomme, Lady Seraphine's PA and occasional spy.

And apparently, Ian Kelly's secret lover.

I took a deep breath. "Look, I don't want to shame anyone for—"

Oona whirled on me. "Thomme is my *friend.*"

"And sleeping with an ex-Hunter," Hannah said. "Who's apparently in bed with— Oona, I didn't mean it like that, don't give me the stink-eye. *Heavily involved with* Only Humans."

Oona shook her head. "We don't know when these photos are from. Thomme could have stopped sleeping with Ian before that. If they even know." She bit her lip. "If it was even really their choice."

I felt a little sick. Magic for Beginners was just down the hall, working on basic mending spells. Below us, the Thursday night bingo host was calling out various incomprehensible phrases. The occasional bellow or cheer reverberated up through the floor, a wild contrast to the mood in this office. "Do you think Lady Seraphine might have made Thomme sleep with Ian?" I asked Oona.

"I don't know," Oona said. "I think... Thomme liked Ian, when they met him at the meetings. Maybe it just went too far." She pointed at the close-up photo, at Thomme's sleepy eyes and wide smile. "They *look* happy."

"Ian kept the photos," Hannah said. "He's looked at them often, and recently. That says that whatever this was, it meant more to him than a vampire quickie. It was a secret. And that means we can use it, Oona."

Oona's face twisted in distress again, but I was on Hannah's side. Whatever Thomme's motives had been, Ian had kept the pictures. And kept them hidden, in a room that had dust where the rest of the house had been spotless. The housekeeper wasn't allowed in there, and I was betting his wife didn't know about the photos either. Open marriages were one thing—even a discreet affair could be tactfully ignored. But though my encounter with Marjorie had been brief, I just couldn't picture her as someone who'd be okay with her husband sleeping with a vampire.

"So we avoid Marjorie, and go straight to Ian," I said, as firmly as I dared. "Oona, we don't even have to tell Thomme we know about this. We just have to stop that park."

"I don't want to *lie* to Thomme. I don't— Those pictures weren't for us!"

"Then you can tell them we know, if you want to. *After* we stop the park."

"Do you think Thomme would be happy about the park?" Hannah said. "I can't imagine they know anything about it."

"Of course not, but—"

Anton cleared his throat. He'd been silent for a while. "We shouldn't do this," he said. "It would be wrong." He wilted a bit when Hannah glared at him, but the stubborn set of his mouth didn't change. "I mean it. What are you going to do if Ian tells you to fuck off? Tell his wife? Tell the press?"

"Publish and be damned," I said softly.

Anton pointed at me. "Yes!"

I'd been quoting the Duke of Wellington responding to the threat of publishing details of his own affairs—but Anton seemed to take me literally. "Anton, I'm not sure it's as simple as that."

"It's exactly as simple as that. Blackmail is wrong."

"More wrong than theft?" Hannah said pointedly. "More wrong than vandalism, which is our only other option?"

Anton didn't blink. "Yes. That's just things. Blackmail is about *people*."

Hannah narrowed her eyes at him. "You didn't mind when we were ready to threaten them with exposing the link to Only Humans."

Anton looked genuinely confused. "That's something they *should* be ashamed of." He pointed at the pictures. "Do you think Ian should be ashamed of Thomme?"

"No," Oona said. "I mean, maybe he should be ashamed of cheating, but..."

"You're saying that if we threaten Ian with exposure, we're pandering to people who think sleeping with vampires *isn't* okay," I said slowly.

Anton's smile was almost enough to make up for the curdling sensation in my gut. "Yes! Exactly."

"It's the hypocrisy that isn't okay," Hannah said. "Building a park designed to keep vampires out while you sleep with one, *that's* what's wrong."

"Plus, we don't have to go public with any of this," I argued. "Threatening to tell Marjorie, or his Only Humans fans—that should be enough. It's not like the press is even going to care about some guy having an affair."

"Can you *guarantee* that Thomme won't get caught in the crossfire?" Oona demanded.

Hannah and I looked at each other. She grimaced.

"Let's keep thinking," Oona said. "I'm not saying it's completely off the table, but maybe we can come up with something else."

Hannah frowned. "Charlie should be the one to decide."

"Why?"

"Because she's in charge of the park project," Hannah said. "You know we dragged her into this, Oona, and I'm not saying we were wrong to do it, because I'd do a lot for Bev. But if this goes wrong, Charlie's the one who's going to face the consequences. So she gets to make the choice."

I looked at Hannah, with her eyes too wise and old for her face. Did she know something about my stupid oath?

"It's a recession," she said, her tone giving nothing else away. "Jobs are hard to find. I won't feel great if our pure morals get Charlie fired."

Oh, just hell. Part of me wanted to say that Thomme had made their own bed and would have to lie in it. But I couldn't meet Oona's pleading eyes while I said it. And Anton wasn't even pleading; he was already sure I'd make the right choice.

That kind of faith can do a lot to a girl.

"I need to think about—" I began, and then Sam appeared in the room in a rush of vampire speed.

"Come and see this," he demanded. "Come and see it right now!"

I exchanged glances with Hannah as we headed to Sam's little cave, where one of his screens was showing a live press conference.

Ian Kelly was standing on a platform, the New York city flag hanging behind him. Marjorie stood beside him in her blue dress, smiling benignly as he spoke.

"—why I'm delighted to announce my candidacy. I look forward to serving you all as the next mayor of New York City."

His gathered supporters clapped their approval, Marjorie beamed at him, and a dozen reporters asked a dozen questions all at once. I spotted my journalist friend Tilly in the scrum, her scarlet cloche hat set at a rakish angle.

"Turn that off," Hannah said, and Sam fumbled to obey.

"He's running for mayor," I said. "And Lady Seraphine—has she announced her bid yet?"

"No," Oona said, sounding subdued. She must have reached the same conclusion I had.

"Would a park opening with a lot of media be a good time to do that?" I asked.

Anton's eyes were wide and round. "Oh no."

"Oh yes," I said. "That's why Ian Kelly targeted the park. That's why he's got an Only Humans crew in there. He's going to destroy her mayoral campaign before it even begins."

"But how would he know she planned to announce it then?" Anton asked. "She hasn't even told you guys that, right?"

"We could guess," Hannah said slowly. "But I don't think Ian had to."

Oona was staring back down the hallway to where those incriminating photos were sitting on Hannah's desk.

Thomme had told Ian about the planned campaign announcement. And whatever Ian felt for Thomme, he'd used that information to craft a devastating blow against his unknowing rival, Thomme's boss.

Forget the queasy aftertaste of pandering to the pearl-clutching conservatives who thought sleeping with vampires was the fast track to damnation. If this story hit the media, Lady Seraphine would know that she'd been betrayed. And her first target would be her underling.

"Charlie," Oona said. She was vibrating with tension. "You can't—"

"No, I know." I couldn't have that on my conscience. And there was only one viable alternative. "Okay," I said. "Looks like it's Plan B."

Chapter Fifteen

Bev showed up at the end of the shift, while Anton, Oona and I were breaking down the bingo tables and putting them back into the storeroom. She didn't have a permed hair out of place, but she was limping more heavily than usual. I glanced at Oona and she shook her head. Whatever had happened to Bev that afternoon, Oona hadn't seen it coming.

Bev pointed at Anton. "You're with me."

"Now?"

"Now."

"I was going to walk the girls out."

Bev shook her head. "It's time to make your apologies," she said. "We're getting in before the full moon makes everything worse." She glanced at Oona and me. "You two okay to walk together?"

Augh. Bev, of course, had no reason to think we needed to take any extra precautions.

"Sure," Oona said brightly. "Bev's right, Anton. Get it taken care of." They left, and Oona tried to smile, but I could tell it took a lot of effort. Her natural, bouncy energy had nearly drained away.

And that, I was pretty sure, was my fault. "I'm sorry you've had to cover for me so much," I said. "Bev's right. I haven't been making your job any easier."

"You're learning really fast," Oona said encouragingly. "You'll be ready to take reception shifts solo in no time. Oh my gosh, I keep forgetting to tell you about the clothes swap!"

"Right," I said. I'd forgotten too, but assuming we all survived the next three days, we'd still have to do this clothes swap event Oona had mentioned once or twice. "Yeah, fill me in?"

"Okay, so one of the things that can be tricky for supernaturals is clothing, because you know, werewolves need things they can take off quickly around that time of the month, vampires need those UV fabrics, fae often have allergies to artificial materials..."

I nodded. "And ghosts need clothing from their time period, or specially enchanted cloth."

Oona pointed at me. "Yes, exactly! And I thought, hey, everyone gets bored with wearing the same thing every time, but new clothes are expensive, and thrifting is really hard when there aren't a lot of options in the first place. And second hand retailers don't always know how to even label them—I found three ghost-cloth waistcoats in a thrifting run last week, just shoved in with everything else on the rack."

"Mm," I said.

"So, clothes swap! Organized by type *and* size, bring as much as you like—or nothing at all—and take what you need. We'll donate the rest to Weirdo Wardrobe."

"We're not charging anything?"

"Nope! The rec center is donating the space. And our labor, of course. Ooh, let me tell you about the food trucks, though."

We went upstairs to gather our things, and Oona talked the whole way about the specialist vampire butcher who was coming from Queens, and Brownie's Brownies, who she'd somehow talked into setting up a pop-up on the day. That was genuinely impressive. People queued for hours outside the Brownie's flag-ship store whenever they launched a new limited edition flavor.

"You're amazing," I said. I was shoving my stuff into my bag at the time—Hannah had left notes on my paperwork, so I had even *more* homework—but I meant it sincerely, and Oona blushed.

"Oh, you know," she said. "I just kind of try my best. Often you don't know what people will do until you ask."

She'd perked up a lot, like the conversation was pouring energy back into her. There were obviously some benefits to being an extrovert.

Oona locked up, and I felt the overnight wards waver into place. Felantheril was right to be concerned about those wards. Any building with that many people coming in and out has to get them renewed frequently, and it was obviously another thing that hadn't made it onto the budget for a while.

"Oh, I know," Oona said, when I mentioned it. She tugged on the door to make sure it was secure, then slipped the key into her enormous shoulder bag, which had a label I'd seen and envied on some of my much richer classmates. I had an old purse of my mom's and a tote. "Felantheril even tried to bring it up with Lady S, which for her is really saying something."

"Why is she so scared of her?" My pronouns were all over the place. I tried to pull my brains back into some kind of order as we walked down the short, rose-bordered path to the sidewalk. "Ferantheril, scared of Lady Seraphine, I mean."

"I don't know. Hannah thinks it's—"

She stopped talking so suddenly it was as if she'd walked into a wall. I was just stepping out onto the sidewalk, and I turned around to see why she'd halted.

"Wait," Oona said, in a very different voice. In the bright glare of the security light, I saw her eyes, gleaming silver, seeing beyond me.

"What is it?" I asked. "Is it—"

She hurtled forward and grabbed my arm. "Duck!"

I didn't hesitate, and it saved me. Even as I dropped into a low crouch, tugging Oona with me, the spell went whistling over my head, close enough that my other-else could taste it. It wasn't a death spell—those are a whole lot harder than they look on TV—but it was buzzing with mauvais magic. It would have knocked me senseless, maybe, or snared my mind, and left me—and Oona—open to any more mundane attack.

I yelled something incoherent—a curse maybe, or a war-cry—and pushed off from the sidewalk, casting my other-else into the night. The wizard was close by, and he was doing something complicated to stay concealed. I just caught the edges of the illusion spell, enough to know that it was well-cast, with a lot of power behind it.

Half the daytime population of Manhattan leaves every evening. It was late enough that the street was much quieter, but it wasn't completely empty either, and the other pedestrians were starting to look around for the reason for all the yelling. Attacking us like this spoke of either desperation or arrogance, and I wasn't sure which would be worse.

"Left!" Oona shouted in that same ethereal voice, her eyes mirror-bright.

I twisted away from the next bolt of mauvais magic, knowing I wasn't going to be fast enough. I wasn't. The spell would have hit me square on the left side of my chest, right over my heart.

But my bag, dangling heavily from my elbow, flared pure white with a surge of protective magic. It was the charm on my keyring, given to me with my mother's love, and it turned the death spell aside.

My other-else had been frantically sweeping the area, and this time it followed the scent of that spell back to the source, an empty spot across the road that, even now, puzzled bystanders were failing to look at.

"There!" I said, and pointed.

It felt as if I'd flung my other-else towards him like a ball on a string. He caught it, more by instinct than intention, and I felt the contact reverberate down the sudden connection between us. For that moment, I could see him, unblurred by illusion, his eyes wide with shock and more than a little fury that I'd been able to do even that much.

I recognized him.

Three days ago, I'd sat in the office upstairs with this man, where he'd immediately dismissed me as a potential rival. Hannah had poured cold coffee over him to make him go away. I'd thought, even then, that he'd had way too much power for the job, that a Magician Eighth Class shouldn't be chasing after a lowly admin position. But with all the revelations that had followed, I hadn't spared him another thought since.

I was sure thinking about him now.

We were still physically separated by the street, but metaphysically, we were way too close, my other-else entangled with his. I could feel his disdain for Oona, who he thought of as another wizard's toy. Worse was his contempt for me. I was even more pathetic than a baseline human, because I had a tiny touch of useless power, and I'd still stumbled into his excellent work on the construction site. He didn't need a chaos agent around right when he was finally impressing his patron with his capacity for true dark magic. So he'd do what he was being paid to do and snap me out of existence, and my unearned knowledge about the job with me.

I felt like I'd been dumped in an oil spill. There was no empathy in him, not a sliver of interest in anyone except for how they might further or threaten his desires.

I yanked back on the tether. He held on.

My instinct, in feeling something like that close around me, was to get away as fast as I could. His instinct, feeling a victim about to flee, was to stop me from escaping.

So I pulled, and he tightened his grip, and I think we were both surprised when my other-else came arrowing back to me. But it was mine, more mine than anything else I possessed except maybe my name and my sworn word, and it jumped out of his grasp without hesitation.

And because he'd tried to stop it, it tore a bit of *his* other-else off as it went.

That hurt. I felt the first flicker of his pain just as I got free of him, and even that was enough to make me dizzy and nauseated, swallowing hard to keep my last snack in my stomach. He screamed, high and agonized, and the illusion spell dropped.

I didn't think about it until later, but up until then, all the passers-by had been able to see was two girls yelling and fumbling around just outside the rec center. Maybe the more supernaturally sensitive had been able to feel some of the magic whizzing around, but the illusion spell had been several layers deep, and his location had been well-concealed. Now a screaming man had appeared out of nowhere, his face contorted with pain and rage, and they reacted with the usual response of New Yorkers to unpleasant surprises: a lot of swearing and demands to know what the fuck was going on.

He ignored them, in favor of glaring at me. Even wounded and diminished, he could have ground me into the dirt. I could see him deciding to try.

Then a punk angel in a leather jacket landed on the sidewalk, cracking the concrete with her impact. Tiffany Chang must have jumped from a few stories up, but it didn't seem to cause her any trouble. She lashed out at the wizard, her fist moving so fast it blurred. It bounced off some kind of personal shield, a shower of bright pink sparks skittering away from the blow. He wasn't actively casting that—a charm, prepared earlier?

Tiffany grinned—even from across the road I caught the flash of her teeth—and punched again. More sparks, dark red this time. "Not on my turf, motherfucker!" she yelled, and punched a third time. Black sparks. Could she actually break a shield charm through sheer physical force?

The wizard evidently didn't want to find out. He scrambled backwards, touched a spot on a street lamp, and disappeared.

A prepared teleport, after a complex illusion and *two* powerful attack spells, when he didn't even have a whole other-else. I was angry and terrified and on the verge of throwing up, but I still had time to feel some pure, astonished envy for someone being that damn good.

A hand landed on my shoulder and I jerked away, but it was Oona. "Come on, get up," she said. My legs didn't want to work, but I tried, until Tiffany arrived and just picked me up off the ground without any discernible effort.

It must have looked ridiculous, this petite woman hoisting my gangly awkwardness, but at the time all I could be was grateful as she strode towards the building. Oona scrambled ahead of us and got the door open, and then we were back in the building, behind the dubious safety of its wards and walls. I very much needed to be within walls right then.

Tiffany set me down on my feet. I wobbled, but stayed upright. "So," she said. "What the fuck is going on?"

"We literally can't tell you," I said, and she looked thoughtful.

"Some kind of geas shit?"

"Something like that." I remembered I was mad at her. "Why are you here? Neither of us drive."

"Ooh, good burn," she said, rolling her eyes.

"You sent your goons to beat up my— Anton."

Tiffany's eyes sharpened. "You sure about that?"

"Who did, then?"

"I'm not discussing pack business with outsiders," she said flatly. "You're welcome, by the way."

I folded my arms. "You helped us because you can't let someone get away with unsanctioned violence in your territory."

"Yeah, mostly," she said, and grinned at me. "But help's help. Is this the time to be picky about it?"

Oona cleared her throat. "Thank you, Tiffany," she said, and then looked at me. "Speaking of help, I'm calling my boyfriend. We're going to need a wizard tomorrow." She looked pained. "Another wizard, I mean."

"I'm really not one," I said. "A Tenth Class would definitely be handy. His name's, um, Blair?"

"Blake." She was digging through her bag, and pulled out her phone with a triumphant grunt.

"I thought you needed some space?" I was trying to ignore Tiffany, who was leaning against the door with a casual attitude that didn't fool me for a second. She was taking everything in and trying to put the pieces together.

Oona made a face I couldn't quite interpret. "I think this is more important than my feelings, Charlie. That guy tried to kill you."

I should have stayed sitting, because my legs abruptly gave way and dumped me on my ass with an impact that rattled my teeth in my skull. He really had tried to kill me. The first spell had been a snare, but the second would have been lethal.

I upended my bag on the floor and hunted through the pile until I found my key ring, and the remnants of the charm my mother had given me. It was a burnt and blackened ruin, a thousand dollars of well-crafted protection magic gone in an instant. If I hadn't had it with me, I'd be gone instead.

Just minutes ago, I'd nearly died.

I pressed my hands to my temples and sucked in air.

Tiffany knelt beside me. "There we go. That's the shock kicking in."

"I can't be in shock," I protested. "I have stuff to do."

She put her hand on the back of my head and pushed it down between my knees, surprisingly gentle. "Just breathe, tough guy. You can do stuff in a minute."

She was right. My muscles had gone weird and I was shuddering spasmodically, as if my skin might shake right off. I concentrated on breathing. My other-else had curled up tight inside me, wrapped around the piece of the other wizard that had torn away. His scrap of other-else was pulsing balefully, a hot red glow I couldn't see, hatred stuck through it like iron spikes. "I knew that guy," I said. "He was that Eighth Class at the job interview."

Oona frowned. "Eighth? No, I remember him. Robert Luhrens, accredited Wizard Fourth Class. I saw the paperwork."

Robert Luhrens. The man who'd tried to kill me had a name. "Maybe he was Fourth before he met his patron and went mauvais. He was Eighth by the time he came to the interview." I forced myself to consider the implications. "Do you think he was trying to infiltrate us? Make sure everything they had planned for the park was going smoothly?"

There was a pause. Tiffany's hand lifted off the back of my head, and I cautiously straightened up. The world swooped for a moment, but I stayed up. I did feel a bit better.

"Charlie, how did you know he was Eighth Class?" Oona asked.

"My other-else told me."

"It tells you what *class*?"

I frowned at her. "Not in words. But I can feel how powerful someone is, and sort of compare that to how powerful other people are, and he was around Eighth Class. Definitely more than Seventh. I don't think Ninth." If he'd been Ninth, the charm might not have been enough. I put my head down and took a couple more deep breaths.

When I looked again, Oona's eyes were very wide. "Charlie, have you spent much time with other magicians?" she asked.

"Not really. I didn't go to the academies or anything, and the only other magician at my public school was a Second Class boy who mostly used his power for setting fires in the bathrooms. He was kicked out in ninth grade." Karl hadn't seemed like a bad kid, just a lonely, frustrated one. Once he'd seen Laurence and me slipping away from a pep rally, and given me a nod of solidarity instead of telling. But we weren't friends, and we hadn't really talked.

"Okay," Oona said, and sat back. "I thought... You seem to know a lot about the supernatural world for someone without much formal training, that's all."

"I research," I said stiffly. "I don't— I can't do much, but I've read a lot of theory." For all the good it would do me. One thing my research had made very clear was that most wizard training was hands-on. No matter how much I read, there were things

I'd never learn, because no one would tell me. I didn't even want to learn how to *do* them. I just wanted to know what they *were*.

I tried not to be bitter about my magical standing. Most of the time I even succeeded. But the part where being First Class had shut me out of so much knowledge did grate sometimes.

Oona appeared to come to some sort of decision. "Well, I've lived with wizards my entire life," she said crisply. "And I've never met anyone who could tell what class another magician was just by sitting beside them." She looked at Tiffany. "Have you?"

Tiffany shrugged. "Sounds like wizard shit to me."

"It's just a knack," I said. "Your family are wizards, Oona?" Maybe that accounted for the weird almost-but-not-quite-magician feel I got from her sometimes.

She pushed her bangs back. "Sort of. It's a long story. I'll call Blake now." She was being evasive, but I couldn't care that much right then.

"Thank you," I said humbly. I started scooping the contents of my bag back inside. The keys went in my pocket. The charm was totaled, but I still wanted it close.

"And I think you should call in "sick" tomorrow." She made air-quotes around the word. "It's probably better than you don't come in until tomorrow night."

"What's happening tomorrow night?" Tiffany asked.

"More of that thing we can't tell you about," Oona said, and gave me a tight smile. "You have to be there then to... do that thing I saw you doing." Making sure Bev didn't die, she meant. "You can only do that if you're alive."

She was absolutely right. But when I tried to agree, my jaw froze and my oath tightened around my throat. I'd promised to *work really hard*.

Oh, this was *so* unfair. I couldn't even take a sick day?

"I'll come in," I said wearily.

"Charlie, it's too dangerous."

"I'm still on trial, remember? I can't afford to lose this job."

"That's the spirit," Tiffany said, and clapped me on the shoulder harder than I think she meant to. "Show the fuckers you're not scared. Whoever the fuckers happen to be—I'm still confused on that point. And what does this have to with the park? Is it anything to do with that silver railing?"

I took a chance. "Yes," I said, and watched her face carefully.

Apparently, this was indirect enough that it skirted the wards. Tiffany's pierced eyebrow popped, and she looked as if she was thinking up a few more questions. Then, to Oona's obvious relief, she let it go. "You good to get home?" she asked Oona.

"Blake can teleport me."

"Then you're with me, Charlie." Tiffany strode towards the door as if the idea I might not accept her escort had never occurred to her. I gritted my teeth and scrambled after.

She did slow down a little as we went outside. The passers-by had mostly left, though a couple of kids vaping outside the corner bodega perked up when we reappeared. The concrete sidewalk was still cracked where Tiffany had flown into it.

Apart from that, there was no sign of what had almost happened here.

But my body remembered. My legs were wobbling again, and I could feel my heartbeat in my throat. I was trying to force my other-else *out*, extending my awareness, but it stubbornly refused to go. It was still wrapped around that malignant scrap of Robert's other-else.

I thought of the time that Mom, unable to get the battery out of a malfunctioning smoke alarm, had stuffed it into a rolled-up duvet to muffle the sound, and a nearly hysterical snort ripped out of me.

"Easy there," Tiffany said. She wasn't looking at me, but she had other senses at her disposal that were probably telling her much more than I wanted her to know. This close to me, this close to the full moon, she could definitely sense how scared I was. Laurence had been able to tell if I was mad or worried all the way from next door.

"This will be the hardest time," she said, her voice conversational. "You need to do it as quickly as possible, because otherwise the fear builds up. Walking to your stop with me doesn't carry much risk, but letting fear build *is* risky, because it can cripple you, and then you'll freeze at a time when you need to act."

"Easy for you to say. You can punch through walls."

"And one silver bullet could take me out."

"To be fair," I said, trying to sound nonchalant. "One silver bullet could also take me out."

"You scared of that right now?"

"No." I was scared that Robert Luhrens would come back to finish the job. He wouldn't blink at it, because to him, I wasn't a real person. No one except himself was real. He recognized his master was stronger than he was, but he regarded her with wary caution, not respect. And if she ever slipped up or showed him a weakness, he'd strike.

Huh. His master was a she. How had I known that?

Because I'd been inside him. I'd felt what he felt, the same way I'd seen magical objects through Faiza's eyes, and had my senses expand when I'd tossed my other-else at the werewolf attacking Anton's car. What the hell was wrong with me?

"It's okay," Tiffany said gruffly. "Think about something else."

She didn't know that my heartbeat had sped up for a different reason, but it was still good advice. "You really didn't send people to attack Anton?"

"None of your business." She frowned. "Though I can't work out what the fuck he was thinking. If he'd kept his head down for a few days, there wouldn't have been any trouble in the first place."

He'd been thinking that he wanted to help me solve my many problems. "More stuff I can't tell you."

"That's getting really annoying," Tiffany observed.

"Try living it," I snapped back. Ugh, my nerves were so frayed. Tiffany had saved my butt tonight, regardless of her motivations, and I still couldn't keep my temper under control. Even the stamp of my black ankle boots on the sidewalk sounded angry.

She didn't seem to resent it, though. I guessed a pack leader had to deal with a lot of fraught feelings, especially around this time of the month.

And I was safe with her, as safe as if I'd been strolling down the block in broad daylight with a full security detail. People coming towards us nodded and moved out of the way. One teenager with a paper bag full of groceries went bug-eyed, then crossed the street to avoid us. Tiffany huffed a laugh.

"That's Rodrigo," she said. "His mom is pack, and he thinks I'm going to tell her he's been skipping school."

"Are you?"

"Hell, yes. After full moon, though. We try to keep the emotional disturbances to a minimum beforehand."

Crap. That was something I hadn't thought of. If Plan B didn't work, if we couldn't stop the park from progressing, then it would be revealed for what it was at the height of the full moon. Even if Tiffany could keep her cool, could her pack members? I'd been thinking of the community response to the park being pain and anger. What if they turned to violence? Hell, what if Only Humans was counting on that kind of backlash? They were dying for an excuse to spark conflict. If it really popped off, we could all be dragged back to the bad old days of rebel packs and unrestrained Hunters.

"We're nearly there."

"Mm." I was almost grateful to Robert Luhrens, in a way. He'd provided an excellent excuse for me to be constantly veering towards a fresh panic attack.

We stopped beside the stairs leading down to my stop.

Tiffany's eyes were on me, but I had the impression she was scanning the block, alert for any danger.

"I didn't catch a whiff of him," she said, and actually patted my arm. "I think you're okay for now. And if you do need to stay home tomorrow, you should."

It was the unexpected sympathy that broke me. I had no business laying this out for Tiffany when I hadn't told anyone else—not Anton, not even my mom. But I literally couldn't stop myself.

"I *can't* stay home," I said, in what was nearly a wail. "I swore an oath to Felantheril—I swore to work *really hard*. And now I can't take a sick day, not even to avoid an assassination attempt." I touched my throat and swallowed hard. "Not even if it kills me."

"Whoa," Tiffany said. "That's fucked up."

"It's really fucked up! And I did it to myself, because I was desperate and scared and *stupid*." My voice broke on the last word. I could barely bring myself to meet her eyes, to see the condemnation there. Or worse, the pity.

But when I did, she looked confused instead. "Um, okay," she said. "Desperate, maybe, we've all been there. But I haven't known you five minutes, and *I* know you're not stupid." She poked me in the sternum, not gently. "And as for scared... You held off a dark wizard attack tonight, long enough for me to get there. You faced down three of Blood Moon's top fighters this morning. No idea what you did this afternoon, but I'm sure it was epic."

I'd been threatening Marjorie Kelly with exposure while Hannah rifled through her husband's study.

Actually, when you thought about it, it had been kind of an eventful day.

I sniffed. "I was scared the whole time."

"Sure," she conceded. "But you did it." She poked me again. "So, like, buck up, or whatever. You and Oona have a plan to deal with the thing you can't tell me about, and tomorrow's another day." She grinned at me, her teeth just a little too sharp in the yellow light of the subway entrance lamp. "The way I look at it, if you're still breathing, you're winning."

I stepped back before she could poke me a third time. She was right. We had a plan, and we were going to pull it off. We *were* going to stop Callahan Construction and the Kellys and their whole gross conspiracy. "Thank you," I said.

"No problem."

"And, um, please don't tell anyone else about the oath."

She mimed locking her lips and throwing away the key, and winked at me. "All part of the service from your friendly neighborhood alpha." Her head came up as if she'd heard something, and her eyes flashed yellow. "Okay, you good? I have to run three blocks downtown."

"I'm good," I said, and headed down the stairs, Robert Luhrens's other-else pulsing inside mine and questions about this strange see-inside ability swirling through my head.

I was pretty far from good. But I was still breathing.

Chapter Sixteen

All things considered, I should have had a terrible night's rest. Instead, I woke feeling energetic and optimistic—at least, until the scrap of Robert Luhrens woke up too. His other-else was as suspicious and angry as a feral cat, snarling and twisting inside me.

"Stop that," I muttered. "I don't like it either. It was his fault for trying to trap me."

Robert's other-else wasn't noticeably appeased by this argument. It felt a bit like metaphysical indigestion, like a lump of something hard and hot was nestled right under my breastbone. I'd been vaguely hoping it would fade overnight, but clearly I was going to have to do something drastic to get rid of it.

I might even have to work out how to give it *back*, although I didn't want to be within a mile of its owner ever again. My own other-else stirred and wrapped around it sleepily while I dressed and combed my hair. I'd packed an old duffel bag with things I thought might be useful for the evening, trying not to think about how dangerous this whole situation was. Warding off a human supremacist group and a dark wizard with old gardening gloves and a heavy-duty flashlight didn't seem very practical, but it was what I was doing.

When I came downstairs, Mom was at the dining table, reading the paper on her tablet while she drank what was probably her third coffee of the morning. "Did you hear about this march downtown?" she asked.

"What march?"

"A Humans First rally." She gave her tablet a disapproving look. "These idiots give the rest of us a bad name."

I poured coffee into my travel mug and kissed her cheek. I needed to figure out how to properly express my gratitude for the charm—without revealing that it was currently a lump of charred wood and twisted metal. Well, that was a tomorrow problem. "Don't worry, Mom. I know it's not all humans."

"Well, I should hope not," she huffed. "Is it going to be another long day, honey? Only I was hoping we could eat out tonight."

"Sorry," I said, sticking my head in the fridge so that I wouldn't have to look at her. "I'll be late again. Really late, actually—there's an event on tonight. Oona said I can crash with her if I'm too tired to get home safe."

"They're keeping you *that* late? I hope they're paying you what you're worth. Non-profit doesn't mean they should be underpaying their employees."

According to everything I'd heard about non-profits, that was often exactly what it meant, but I made a noise of agreement and poured almond milk into my mug. "Did you sleep well?" I asked.

"Night sweats again. Perimenopause is a bitch, Charlie. Note that down somewhere."

"Noted."

"I'd tell you not to get old, but the alternative is worse."

I thought of how close I'd been to the alternative last night, and had to tamp down a shudder.

"What's that for?" she asked, nodding at my duffel.

"Oh. Change of clothes for tonight."

"Ooh-la-la. Your black dress?"

"Mm," I said, hoping that would pass for a yes. My mother trusted me, so I tried to limit the lies. "Can I open this blueberry yogurt?"

"Yes. And your young man is waiting outside."

I dropped the tub of yogurt on the kitchen floor. "Mom!"

"I invited him in for a coffee while he waited, and he said 'no thank you, ma'am,' which I thought was charming."

"Mom, you could have told me earlier!" I grabbed paper towels and tried to scoop up the yogurt, succeeding only in smearing it over the wooden floor. "And what do you mean, you invited him in? He could have been a vampire!"

"I think you would have told me if he were a vampire." Mom's eyes twinkled at me over her tablet. She looked completely innocent. I wasn't fooled. She'd probably used that tablet to do a complete social media investigation of Anton before she even opened the door.

Oh hell, Mr. Salamanca from across the street was going to be out and watering his border perennials any moment. The neighborhood watch group chat was probably pinging as we spoke.

The alien other-else responded to my social unease by going into high alert. It didn't seem able to *do* anything, but I didn't like the savage impulse to crush and tear anything it viewed as a threat. I'd had the shameful thought that maybe this scrap of Luhrens would give my own magic a boost, but now I was relieved that wasn't the case. I didn't want power from this source.

Mom had apparently had enough fun. She put the tablet down and went to the sink, wetting down a cloth. "I'll take care of that, Charlie. You don't want to be late."

"I can do it," I said, in the face of all the evidence. The floor now looked like a Rothko in lavender and cream.

"Go!"

There was no arguing with that tone. I grabbed my bag and went.

At the last moment, I darted back to hug Mom. "I love you," I said.

"Likewise," she said, frowning at the floor.

I headed out, hoping that wasn't the last thing I ever said to her.

***

Anton had a loaner—a clunky station wagon emblazoned with a grimy logo—that I figured he'd picked up from work. I hadn't quite figured out how to tell him that Oona and I had been attacked, but he solved that problem for me by immediately asking if I was okay with such intensity that it was clear Oona had already filled him in.

"Mostly," I said. "A few metaphysical aftereffects, maybe." Robert's other-else grumbled inside me.

"And after you'd already dealt with the pack," he said, and gently took both of my hands in his, inspecting the scrapes on my palms.

Unfortunately, the gesture kind of reminded me that the scrapes existed, and I winced.

"Sorry," he said.

"I've had worse from middle school dodgeball," I said.

He didn't smile. "I should have told Bev no and made sure you and Oona got you home."

"Not your fault." I tugged gently and he got the hint, releasing me immediately. His frown didn't clear when he started the motor. I concentrated on getting my seatbelt fastened, which took more effort than I thought was ideal.

The drive into work was quiet, at least inside the car. I tried to make conversation a few times, but Anton was deep in thought. The only thing I got out of him was that Bev had taken him to see, not Tiffany, but Tiffany's great-aunt, the former pack alpha. She was apparently the one who'd taken exception to Tiffany's adventure with the handrail.

"It was scary," he said. "This tiny little woman, sitting in a chair covered in blankets. There were two guys there with her, I think maybe her sons? They acted like they were terrified of her." He brooded a moment more. "Even Bev was careful," he added.

"I would have been scared too," I said. Anyone Bev Thornton was wary around wasn't someone I wanted to provoke.

"I apologized like a million times, and she eventually was like, 'I didn't actually *order* anyone to destroy your car, I just asked if anyone was going to do anything about this insult to the pack.'"

"Will no one rid me of this turbulent priest?" I murmured.

Anton might not have known the reference, but he nodded at the tone. "Yeah, pretty much. So I apologized a million more times, and then her sons took me out back and I tuned up her Cadillac. And then she fed me until I couldn't eat another bite and told me to get a haircut. After that I went back to the rec center just in case you were still there, and walked in on Oona and Blake making out on the reception desk. As if my day hadn't been bad enough."

I laughed, and he gave me a sidelong smile, which dropped almost immediately. "And Oona told me what had happened then. Are you *really* okay?"

"I will be," I said, ignoring the churning in my gut. "I just want to get this over with." Surely Robert Luhrens wouldn't care about me, once his job was over? Callahan Construction had paid for wards against the park, and presumably paid him extra to take care of me, the person running around with all this dangerous knowledge in her head. They couldn't know about the suppressors, or the little group that had gathered around me, but they had to be nervous that I'd tell *someone* and make it stick.

Once the park problem had been settled, Callahan wouldn't have any reason to invest further. They wouldn't pay Luhrens anymore, and he wouldn't have any reason to come after me. Surely someone that greed-motivated wouldn't waste his time settling grudges for nothing.

Surely.

"Tonight," Anton promised. "Stop the park, save Bev, and keep your job."

"That's the plan," I said. "God. I hope it works."

***

Of all the days I'd spent at the Thirteenth Avenue Rec Center—all four of them—this one felt like the longest.

Bev was around all day, so Hannah, Oona and I were limited to hurried whispers and meaningful eye contact. The one piece of good news Hannah managed to pass on was that the construction site was clear. Apart from a security guard, Callahan Construction had packed up and left. That meant they'd finished everything they meant to do to the park before the opening, which wasn't entirely good news, but at least we wouldn't have to account for a bunch of people in hi-vis.

It was Sam's day off, so he'd join us after hours. Anton loitered in the storeroom, ostensibly building some shelves, but really avoiding both Bev and any werewolves who might not have heard yet that the vendetta was over. He still didn't actually work here, but no one seemed to find this strange. Even the clients paid barely any attention to the occasional bangs and curse words escaping from the doors.

Felantheril wafted in at noon and airily announced she was ordering lunch for everyone, apparently because she'd heard that was what bosses did. I'd brought a bagel from home, but gratefully ate two slices of pepperoni pizza instead. Oona talked me through the newsletter system—the rec center had nearly a dozen mailing lists for different demographics, and woe betide the hapless peon who sent the kids' sports updates to the bingo fanatics.

Zenith the succubus turned up to run another heels class in the afternoon. As promised, her effect on me wasn't as strong as our first encounter, but I still got a jolt when her fingers brushed against mine.

She jerked her hand back and blinked at me.

I blinked back.

"Oh, *Anton*," she said, with a kind of affectionate dismay, and sauntered down the corridor to the dance studio.

I put that in the ever-growing pile of things to worry about later, and went back to social media stalking at the reception desktop computer.

Surprising no one, Robert Luhrens didn't exist, at least under that name, but we were still calling him that for convenience. After Oona's vision, Hannah and Oona had kind of skimped on the due diligence for the other candidates. His resume was pretty slick, but it didn't stand up to in-depth scrutiny. I tried some reverse image searching on his headshot. Unfortunately, there was no exact match, so he hadn't put this particular photo online anywhere. And there were an awful lot of smug, dark-haired, white finance dudes in this city.

Thomme called just before sunset, and Oona put the call downstairs to the reception desk phone.

"Just wanted to let you know that catering is good to go," Thomme said cheerily. "Have you considered decorations?"

Oh, right. In addition to making it impossible for Callahan Construction to open *their* proposed park, I also had to make sure that Lady Seraphine had *her* park opening.

"Is a big ribbon okay?" I didn't know where I'd find one, but you could get anything in this town.

Thomme coughed. "Lady Seraphine has previously indicated that she finds ribbon-cutting to be a touch... déclassé."

"So giant novelty scissors are right out, then?"

Thomme had a nice laugh. I wondered if they'd laughed with Ian Kelly while they lay in that hotel room. I was glad Anton and Oona had talked me out of blackmail, but I still felt some guilt that I'd seen pictures of Thomme that weren't for public consumption.

And what on earth had drawn them to Ian Kelly in the first place?

"Perhaps some ferns on a plinth? Greenery is always good. Although I suppose the park will provide plenty of that."

I scribbled a note. "I'll see what I can do."

"I'm sure you have it all in hand," Thomme said, with what I thought was probably false confidence. It was kind of them to say it, though. "Well, Charlie, I bet you also have ten thousand things to do, so I'll— Oh? Yes, of course. Charlie, Raphael wants a quick word."

I braced, and reminded myself not to lie.

Raphael's voice was almost too much for the phone. "Hello," he said, and I absolutely did not shiver.

"Hello."

There was a pause. If I hadn't known better, I'd think that he was nervous. "I hope things are going well at the rec center?"

Hm. "I think they're going okay, given the circumstances." There, that was true enough.

"I'm pleased to hear it." Another pause. A curly-haired woman came in, tying a red belt around her white martial arts uniform, and waved her season pass at me. I waved back and gave her a thumbs up.

"Did you see the recent mayoral campaign announcement?" Raphael asked.

My spine stiffened involuntarily. "I did."

"I wasn't sure if you kept up with local politics."

"Not as much as I should, but I did see that. You mean Ian Kelly, right?"

"Correct."

Two kids came in. One had a season pass, but the other hovered by the desk, looking at me expectantly.

"We're a little busy here, Raphael," I said.

"Of course. I just thought you should know that the park opening is very *special* to Lady Seraphine."

Crap, crap, crap. "Thank you for telling me," I said. "I'm doing everything in my power to make sure it goes smoothly."

He let out a relieved sound. "Good. Actually, I was wondering if afterwards—"

"I have to go, I'm sorry," I said, and put the phone back in the cradle.

Oh, damn. I'd lied about being sorry.

Hannah came down two hours before closing and shooed me off the desk for a break. I walked up carefully, hugging the wall.

That missing railing was a real hazard. Maybe one of us should have suggested Anton fix that instead of whatever he was doing in the storage room.

Except that he was avoiding Bev. We were all avoiding Bev. Hannah had spent most of the day in the conference room, pleading that she needed to be left alone to work on a grant application, and Oona had put her headphones on and claimed intense worry over the clothes swap categories.

I walked into the office and realized our luck had run out. Bev was sitting on the edge of her desk, arms folded, and Oona was standing in front of her, looking like a guilty schoolgirl.

"So," Bev said, her voice level. "Tell me about this dark wizard attack."

Chapter Seventeen

I glanced wide-eyed at Oona, who looked just as stunned as I did.

Bev rolled her eyes. "Did it not occur to either of you that word might get back to me?"

"We didn't want to worry you," Oona said. "He ran away."

"Uh-huh." Bev beckoned me closer and pointed to another chair. I sat. "And this geas you're both under?"

Tiffany must have told her. Well, it made sense—she thought of the rec center as being on her turf, and despite Felantheril's title, Bev was the real power here.

"We can't tell you," Oona said.

Bev grunted. "Charlie? You in some sort of trouble?"

I laughed.

I couldn't help it. I was in so *many* sorts of trouble that the question seemed ridiculous. For a moment, I thought about laying it all out for her. Bev Thornton had solved problems like this for decades before I was born. She could probably take care of a mauvais wizard without disturbing her stiff grey curls, stopping halfway through for a cigarette break.

Well, Bev, I got this job under false pretenses, swore an oath to your boss—who's High Fae, by the way, did you know? Because no one else seems to—discovered a human supremacist group is creating a monstrosity in the lot next door, was made responsible for the success of the park opening when I also need to smash the park to bits, unsuccessfully threatened a woman whose husband is making a mayoral run, barely survived a run-in with an Eighth Class mauvais wizard who has a master he's scared of and, oh yeah, I accidentally tore off a bit of his magical essence and now it's inside me. My job, freedom of will, and life are on the line. I don't know—would you say that's some sort of trouble?

I slapped my hands over my mouth, as if I could cram the laughter back in.

"It's okay," Bev said, with surprising gentleness. "Can you write it down for me? Writing's sometimes easier."

I could tell her everything, right now. The temptation was so strong. Oona had predicted Bev's death if I wasn't there—but I could still go along *with* Bev, right? Maybe I could just hang around in the back, while she dealt with the night watchman and heroically dismantled whatever artifact was holding the wards in place.

Oona had gone so white she was faintly greenish, her lips pressed into a thin line, but I didn't think she'd stop me from spilling the beans. I'd nearly died last night. I didn't know Oona very well, but I was sure she wouldn't straight up trade my life for Bev's.

"No," I said. "I can't write it down. Don't worry, Bev. We're taking care of it."

Oona sagged so violently with relief that I was worried she'd fall out of her chair. "Blake's helping us," she volunteered.

Bev's eyes sharpened. "Is he?" she said. It sounded more like a statement than a question, but Oona rallied in response.

"Yes. Actually, he's being really sweet about it."

"Yeah, Anton told me about that," I said, partly to distract Bev, and partly because it was hilarious. Oona blushed.

Bev pushed away from her desk. "All right. I suppose Blake's a competent enough magician. But any more trouble, and I'll be taking a personal interest, you understand?"

"Yes, Bev," we chorused. The unintentional echo made us both giggle, and Bev rolled her eyes.

"No more hiring people under thirty," she muttered. "I'm getting out of this place. You two are closing up. Anton can make sure you both get home." She pointed at me. "Make sure he knows he's not working here permanently. Today was a one-off. Next week he goes back to night school."

"I don't have any say in what Anton does," I said, startled.

Bev raised both eyebrows. I shifted my weight. Oona was valiantly trying not to catch my eye, probably because that would set us both off again.

"Good night," Bev said finally, and headed for the door, her giant purse dragging on her shoulder, and her limp catching at her steps. Under the harsh fluorescent lights she looked like a tired old woman.

I opened my mouth when the door closed behind her, but Oona shook her head and theatrically held up her hand, fingers spread wide. She counted a slow five beat, folding down each finger.

I heard the delayed thud of sensible shoes on the stairs. It was pure projection, but I thought the door at the foot of the stairwell closed with a particularly annoyed bang.

"Okay," Oona said quietly. "We're in the clear."

"Did you see her listening?"

"No. I could feel her death getting more likely while she tried to make you talk. And then you said no, and the probability lessened, but not quite back to where it had been." Oona smiled, with an effort. "On the other hand, I don't need to be an oracle to know that Bev will listen at doors if she thinks someone's keeping secrets."

"You can actually feel the probabilities changing?"

Oona's smile looked more genuine now. "Like an election-night dial? No, nothing that precise. More like a shift in the temperature, when a cloud goes over the sun."

"How does it—" I stopped, aghast at myself. It was unforgivably rude to ask about someone's power like that, especially when you'd met less than a week ago.

Oona didn't look offended, though. She looked thoughtful instead. "How does it work? I'll tell you, if you tell me about yours."

"I don't have much to tell," I said. "You probably know more about wizards than I do."

"Your knack, I mean. For guessing people's power."

"Oh, that. I told you, I just feel it. It's handy sometimes, but it's nothing special."

Oona got up, checked that the door was closed, and said, out loud, "Hannah, if you're here, we could use some privacy."

"She's downstairs, on the desk."

"Right," Oona said, and sat down again. "Charlie, do you remember being tested as a kid?"

"Sure, in first grade. There was a magician with a pretty pink crystal, and when I touched the crystal it hummed a little bit and glowed. Faintly," I added ruefully. "The testing wizard had to pull the drapes to make sure it wasn't just a trick of the light. Then she said I was a Magician First Class, congratulations, and gave me a letter to take home. Seemed pretty standard to me."

"It was," Oona said.

"So I figured feeling power levels was normal wizard stuff, if she was doing it."

"Yeah, no," Oona said. "That's *not* standard. That pretty pink crystal was a powerful artifact enchanted by a full Circle of Twelve. That was what was actually doing the testing. The wizard was just there to carry it around."

I stared at her. "What?"

"I've known Blake since he was thirteen," Oona said. "His mom and dad are Seventh and Eighth Class, and he's Tenth, and none of them would be able to figure out someone's place on the Abbot-Grace scale by sitting beside them. Blake probably *could* cast a diagnostic spell on his own, but he'd have to put some real effort into it. And he'd be able to sense that Tiffany's a werewolf and Felantheril's fae, but you do even better than that, with more subtle magics. Most people think I'm human, but you knew I wasn't right away. You figured out Anton was a half-demon through a military-grade suppressor. That's *not* normal, Charlie."

"Are you saying that my weird knack is actually an unimaginably rare talent that's only been concealed by my total incompetence in every other sphere of wizardry?" I said.

I was trying to make it a joke, but Oona locked eyes with me, deadly serious.

"Yes," she said. "That's exactly what I'm saying."

I stared at her.

"The crystal thing is a trade secret, by the way," she added. "I only know about it because Blake's mom is on the North American Certification Board, and she's complained about how draining it is to create them. Even most wizards think the testing wizard is casting a proprietary diagnostic spell, and the crystal's just there to amplify it. If you'd spent any time at a magical academy, or even much time around other magicians, you'd have already worked out you could do something they couldn't."

"There were other magicians at Columbia," I said defensively. "There were two in my senior seminar!"

"Did you ever talk to them about this?"

"I don't usually *talk* about it. It's like smelling someone's deodorant. You don't go up to them and say, 'Hey, is that Axe Scarlet Tempest?' I really embarrassed a girl in high school by outing her as a half-demon and now I keep my mouth shut."

"Good. I'd keep doing that."

Hannah had left Mr. Scruffles at home that day. None of us had asked her why, but we all knew that she didn't want him anywhere near the danger zone if our adventure went wrong. It was a shame. I could have really used the comfort of giving a furry, slightly smelly dog a good petting.

Instead, I sat there like a lump while Oona, apparently determined to be fair, explained how her own power worked. Her magic was constantly gathering unconscious clues from her physical and metaphysical environment, which was why most of her visions involved people she knew or knew of, instead of total strangers. Whenever her power had sucked up enough data to reach some kind of crucial probability threshold, it interpreted the information as best it could and sprang a vision on her. Vision might not have been the appropriate word—nine times out of ten she just "had a feeling", and most of the remaining occasions involved more sound and smell than sight.

It was all pretty interesting, and at any other time I would have followed up with more questions, but now I nodded and said, "Yeah, that makes sense. We receive most of our mundane sensory input from our eyes, so your magic is finding other ways to express itself through other routes."

"That's the theory," Oona said. "It's not that useful, and it's definitely not that comforting when it's telling me not to get in the empty subway car. I *know* there's a reason that car is empty.

I don't actually need to smell the shit to know I should avoid it. But my visions send me the stench anyway."

"Ew," I said, with feeling.

Oona's desk phone rang then, and she answered it, while I picked at my no-longer-perfectly manicured nails. I'd spent a lot of time as a kid daydreaming that I'd suddenly develop some super awesome power and people would realize I was *much* more impressive than an ordinary First Class. But learning what I'd always thought of as a reliable little extra was actually a big deal diagnostic talent didn't feel nearly as wonderful as I'd imagined.

Especially as Oona seemed to think I shouldn't let anyone know about it.

"Charlie," Oona said patiently, her eyebrows raised in a way that indicated it wasn't the first time she'd said it. "Hannah wants you to go downstairs and take over the desk. She says she needs to leave at her normal time, so if anyone's watching they think we're just going about the routine."

"What's routine around here?" I asked.

Oona's eyes glinted. "I'll tell you when I figure it out."

***

Oona and I dutifully followed what routine we had. We saw out the last of our clients. We checked the bathrooms for stragglers or anyone who might have fallen asleep on the toilet. (This had apparently happened more than once.) We turned off most of the lights and closed and locked the doors—though from the inside. A few minutes later, Hannah drifted back in through the wall. Sam, who I had vaguely figured might climb in from the roof, politely knocked on the back door.

The little rec center crew gathered upstairs, and Hannah crisply outlined the plan of attack she'd come up with instead of the promised grant application.

Blake was going to join us at 10 p.m. He'd mute the park wards, put the night watchman to sleep, and throw a look-away spell over the area, so no one noticed us at work. It sounded like a lot of simultaneous, powerful magic to me, but Oona seemed confident he could manage it.

Blake doing the heavy magical lifting did mean that Oona and I would be starting the physical hard work. Armed with the tools Anton had secured for us, we'd dig a hole in the salt circle, which would let Hannah and Anton inside. Then Anton would take off his suppressor and use his demon strength and a sledgehammer to start destroying the work on the cross-shaped pavement. Sam thought that if he broke enough of one section, it would no longer be a sufficient deterrent to vampires.

During the Anton-uses-demon-strength-without-a-suppressor part, Hannah had tactfully placed me as far as she could from the fountain. I didn't mind, because I also didn't want a repeat of the public make-out session. Oona and I were supposed to be digging out the yarrow and carting it off-site. It was destined for Ravn's auto shop, where Anton could put it with the rest of the hazardous material the garage produced. Our best guess was that the plants would lose most of their efficacy when they were uprooted, but we didn't want to leave it lying around, either.

With the cross broken and Sam's strength added to the mix, we could destroy the rest of the silver-salted pavements and dig out the fae-repelling rowan trees. And hopefully take care of anything else I hadn't noticed in my one hasty inspection of the site.

If we were really lucky, Blake would also be able to find and destroy the artifact that was holding the wards in place and break that. Otherwise, they were going to pop right back up the second he stopped concentrating on his mute spell.

If Blake could destroy the artifact, we'd be able to tell other people about the whole stupid mess; people like Raphael and Tiffany, who had resources we didn't. Hell, we'd be able to tell Lady Seraphine, though I might want a stiff drink before I tried.

I wasn't pinning much hope on the possibility. Robert Luhrens was a terrible person, but he was a very good wizard. My bet was that the ward artifact was hidden in layers of illusion, and we wouldn't be able to identify it even if we were right on top of it. Our best chance would be if it got destroyed while we were breaking everything else.

I'd been worried about how Sam would manage all the silver, but he'd apparently borrowed some enchanted gloves from a friend, which should provide some protection.

"I won't be comfortable," he admitted. "But I'm not as silver-sensitive as some vampires, and it's not like I expect to be that comfortable anyway."

I thought of my brief visit to the park, the way it had felt to recognize the hatred built into its bones, and shivered.

Our plan was reckless and messy, but Hannah was behaving as if she thought it would work. That was vastly reassuring.

Unfortunately, I wasn't optimistic about what the park was going to look like afterwards. The bad things would be gone, but we'd be effectively wrecking the place to do it. Oona said that Blake might be able to cast an illusion of a lovely green space that would last through the opening, but I thought she said it with more hope than confidence.

"I, um, I went to a garden center today," Sam volunteered. "I wasn't sure about what kind of soil it is or anything, so I asked them to recommend me some sturdy flowers and bushes that look nice, supernatural approved." He pulled a folded printout from his pocket and handed it to me. "They'll be delivered first thing tomorrow. I know it's not the same as having walkways and railings, but at least we can have some plants in there."

I spread the paper out on my knee. He'd ordered peonies and daylilies and dozens of marigolds. For shrubs, he'd gone with a bunch of dwarf viburnums, with some lilacs and azaleas added for variation.

"Are they all right?" he asked.

I swallowed the urge to cry, but my voice was still husky when I said, "They're amazing, Sam. Thank you." It was also something I could genuinely help with. Summer and spring breaks with Grandmother Cross meant that I had a lot of transplant experience.

"And you said the kids' playground equipment didn't look that bad," Oona said.

"I didn't get that good a look at it," I admitted. "But I think it was mostly, you know, plastic play equipment. Slides, a climbing thing, wood chips to soften falls. They wouldn't have been able to alter much without adding structural problems. I figured they were counting on everything else to keep the scary supernaturals away from their children." I folded the garden center printout and slid it into my pocket, like the precious thing it was. "Wow. With this, I might even keep my job."

"You better," Oona said indignantly. "After everything you're doing for her, Lady Seraphine should throw you a parade."

"How much do I owe you for the plants, Sam?" I rubbed my forehead. "I'll, uh, have to ask you to wait until my first check, I'm sorry." Or maybe my second or third. Azaleas didn't come cheap.

Hannah frowned. "We can probably find room in the budget somewhere."

Sam looked at me and then glanced away. "Don't worry about it."

"I can't let you—"

"You have no obligation and no debt," he said, his voice quiet and intense. "I was— I have some money put away. I don't spend it often. I'm glad to spend it on this."

Oona looked as curious as I was. Anton looked blank.

Hannah... looked neutral. *Too* neutral. Whatever Sam was referring to, she knew about it. Now that I thought about it, fading into invisibility when she wasn't concentrating probably led to a lot of overhearing awkward situations. Or maybe, considering how easily she'd found those photos, she was as big a snoop as a certain ghostly journalist I knew.

I really should introduce Hannah to Tilly. Ghosts with jobs were unusual enough that they'd already have one thing in common.

It was just after 8 p.m., and we had to wait until 10—Oona had explained that Blake had an after-work function he just couldn't get out of. I caught Hannah's rolled eyes and Anton's quickly suppressed snort and wondered if he'd actually tried. I hadn't even met the guy, and I'd already formed a poor impression of him.

Still, his magic was going to do all the heavy lifting tonight. I'd try to keep an open mind, for my own sake as much as Oona's.

The closer we got to the appointed time, the quieter the rec center became, and the tighter my stomach felt. It didn't help that Robert's other-else was behaving like an angry cat in a carrier, yowling at me every couple of minutes. Oona went to make tea, and Anton followed her into the kitchen, where they got into a quiet, intense argument. I unsuccessfully tried to eavesdrop on them, and Hannah caught me in the act and sent me downstairs to take a look in the storage room instead.

I went in, duly chastened, and immediately forgot about the tension in my stomach. Even the foreign other-else subsided a little.

I'd been in the storage room a few times; it was a dim, crowded space full of sporting equipment, tools, plastic tubs crammed with seasonal decorations and various miscellanea. Oona seemed to have a photographic memory for where every-thing was located within it, but she never had time to organize the contents properly, and the two rickety metal shelves weren't nearly enough storage.

When Anton had said he was "working on some shelving", I'd expected flatpack shelves put together with an allen key, which would have been a huge improvement. Instead, he'd neatly arranged the tubs and boxes on beautiful wooden shelves, clearly custom-made, but assembled inside the room. The wood was golden-brown, almost glowing with polished wax, and held together with wooden pegs and very few screws. Some of the upright facings had been carved with straight and wavy lines. Others had more elaborate carving, with apples and pomegran-ates nesting among curling acanthus leaves. I spotted a tiny weasel peeking over the tight curve of a leaf and laughed out loud, touching the pointy face with the tip of my finger.

"Do you like them?" Anton asked, and I turned around to beam at him.

"I *love* them. Did you make all this? It must have taken months!"

"Rafn and Jafr helped with the carving, and Bjorn helped me get it all here." He pointed at one of the far corners. "It's been sitting there for a few weeks now. Bev kept chasing me away before I could put them up."

Now that he said it, I vaguely recalled a pile of something covered in a dust sheet.

"Anton, these are gorgeous," I said. "These shelves belong in someone's house, not tucked away here where no one will see them."

He shook his head. "It's only a prototype, for proof of concept." He came up alongside me and pointed at one of the pomegranates, just a little lopsided. "See? Clumsy work."

I would never have noticed if he hadn't pointed it out. "What's the proof of concept for?"

"I want to make like, kind of upscale flatpack stuff. Cheaper than custom-made, but good quality, and with some added touches that make them beautiful and interesting." He sighed. "The problem is scale."

I had no idea how business worked and my biggest exposure to the side-hustle had been my dorm-mate Simone's Etsy store to sell the little animals she crocheted furiously before finals. But Anton was standing very close to me, smelling pleasantly of pine wood and wax, with a tang of good, honest sweat underneath. I turned and looped my arms around his neck, and his solid hands rose to my hips, his heat radiating through my cheap black polyester slacks to the skin beneath.

"Hey," he said. It was almost a question.

"Hey, there. I keep thinking, I don't really know you at all."

His hands moved as if to fall away, and I tightened my grip, pulling him a little closer. His eyelashes were thick and long, brushing his cheeks like startled moths as he blinked at me.

I smiled. "No, I mean... I don't know you yet. But I think I'd like to. You make beautiful things, and you care about people, and you're a damn good kisser."

He blushed, going dark red to the roots of his black hair. This did not make him less appealing.

"I'd like that too," he said. "I mean… I already heard this rumor we were dating."

"What? That's crazy," I said, and kissed him.

I meant it to be just a soft press of lips to seal the deal, but his hands tightened on my hips, and my lips opened in surprise, which he took as an invitation, and then it turned out it *was* an invitation, because I melted into him. There was none of that irresistible pull, the incubus power that had turned my brain off like a light switch. I was fully present, as self-aware and in control as I'd be if I was kissing any other guy.

But I was kissing *this* guy, this guy who wanted me to be safe but didn't want to blackmail people for things he thought they shouldn't be ashamed of, this guy who was trying his best to keep his old savior alive, this man who had abilities he couldn't trust and power he couldn't rely on, just like me…

I pulled back a little, settling back onto my heels. Anton leaned his forehead against mine. "Wow," he whispered, and the word vibrated against my skin.

We stayed there a moment, holding each other and breathing.

Hannah poked her head through the door, but for once I didn't feel startled or embarrassed. Standing in Anton's arms felt entirely natural.

Hannah didn't comment on our embrace. "It's time," she said. "Ready to go?"

Chapter Eighteen

I t was time. It was well past time.

And Blake wasn't here.

I'd changed from my last office-appropriate outfit (I had no idea what I was going to wear tomorrow, but that was very much a *tomorrow* problem) into my sturdiest chore clothes, which featured paint-spattered denim, a long-sleeved flannel, and my grossest sneakers. Anton was wearing his garage overalls, Sam had black jeans and a black polo shirt, Hannah was wearing her usual clothes, because any dirt would slide off the second she walked through a wall, and Oona was wearing designer yoga pants and a cute cropped hoodie.

I was thinking about everybody's outfit to avoid thinking about the part where it was nearly 10:30 p.m. and Blake wasn't here.

Oona stared at her phone as if she could will a response to her texts into existence.

"You'd better call him," Hannah said.

"He hates calls. I'm sure he'll see the notifications soon."

"It's been twenty minutes since you texted, Oona."

Oona made a face, but tapped the button, turning slightly away from us.

I waited, fidgeting with my heavy-duty gardening gloves, tucked into my belt. A patch of former mud flaked off and drifted onto the floor.

"Hey, babe," Oona said, her voice just a little too bright and perky. "I know, I'm sorry. But I was just wondering, are you on your way? Because it's half an hour past— Right, it's just you haven't been answering my texts." She paused. "Yeah, no, I get it. Of course. No, I do. I appreciate that." She grimaced. "It's just that the timing on this is pretty— *Tomorrow?*"

Her shoulders straightened. "No, Blake, it has to be tonight. Uh-huh. Yeah. Okay, how *much* later?" She pulled the phone away from her ear and glared at it, then put it back to her mouth. "Yes, I realize your time is important too. I was actually attacked last night, remember? Well, could you act like you do? Good. Yeah, fine. See you then. Okay. Fine."

She stabbed the phone with a slender finger and turned back to us. "He's on his way," she said, through clenched teeth. "ETA about forty minutes. And after this is done, we are *so* broken up."

"Again," Anton mumbled. Sam elbowed him in the ribs.

"Good for you," Hannah said. "All right, we'll need to adjust the schedule a little, but I think we can still—"

My other-else erupted like a volcano in my heart.

I doubled over, trying not to pass out from the pain. Through the haze of agony, I could hear Oona's startled yip and Anton's alarmed shout, but it was Sam who got to me before I could fall, his supernaturally strong hands lowering me gently to the ground.

"What's wrong?" Hannah's voice said. She sounded calm, but I could feel the urgency in the question.

The pain ebbed, like a terrible cramp passing, and I gasped. It wasn't my other-else at all. It was that scrap of Robert's other-else that had felt that awful, rupturing tear. My own other-else had been caught up in the blow, but now it was valiantly trying to suppress the pain.

Robert's other-else wasn't just hurting. It was bewildered, unable to understand why its wizard was trying to make it do something it just couldn't. It was like a broken ankle he was trying to walk on. I focused on that, pushed in, and then along that torn connection to Robert himself, who was dealing with his own discomfort, and— Oh.

"He's next door," I said, and straightened up. "Robert Luhrens, or whatever his name is. He's at the park *right now* and he's getting ready to do something to the wards."

"Blake's on his way," Oona said urgently.

"He'll be too late!" I staggered towards the door, hot, jagged rocks colliding in my stomach, and after a moment Anton caught up and helped me move.

"Where are we going?"

"The fence," I said, gritting my teeth.

Robert didn't seem to be aware of me, not the same way I was of him. We were connected, but it was the part of his other-else inside me that was reflecting his feelings. He was still tired from last night, furious about what I'd done to him, and resentful that his mentor had read him the riot act that evening.

I gritted my teeth and pushed for more detail. It felt as if I were slowly boring a spike into my own skull, but Robert's thoughts swirled up into mine, all of them sulky and mean.

His master hadn't been angry with him for trying to kill someone, but because it had been a private job, not under her orders. Then he'd nearly been caught, and by a werewolf, at that. After his mentor had finished verbally skinning him, she'd sent him to the construction site to fine-tune the wards, so that they'd turn away everyone except her and him until they were ready to spring the trap on Lady Seraphine. No more general exception for magicians and humans—there was no need, not now those unevolved humans had done their part, and it was clearly the loophole that redheaded magician girl had exploited...

I pulled back and gasped with the release of that hideous pressure in my head. Anton was taking most of my weight, and I hadn't been paying attention to anything external, but we were somehow at the fence, the others clustered around us. I was confused about Robert being sent to kill me by a private party, not Callahan, but there were more urgent matters at hand.

"I've got to get inside," I said.

Anton's grip tightened on me. "Are you kidding? That guy tried to kill you yesterday!"

"He's fucking with the wards," I said urgently. "We're all going to forget about the park as soon as he's done."

"What's wrong with the park?" Tiffany's voice said behind us.

I straightened up and turned to her. She was standing a few feet away, regarding us all with a quizzical expression.

"It's a metaphysical time bomb," I said. "And it's about to go off. We *have* to get inside."

"Huh," Tiffany said, and regarded the fence. She was frowning, and for a moment, I wondered if she could resist the wards through sheer willpower. She certainly had determination to burn.

But her eyes glazed over in that familiar way, and she shrugged jerkily. "Okay, well, have a good night," she said, and started wandering down the block.

Despair almost overwhelmed me then. What could I do against a powerful mauvais wizard, alone? Even the tugging at my throat, my oath reminding me that the park was something

I had to *work really hard* on, couldn't provide enough momentum.

Curiously enough, it was that little piece of Robert, bewildered and hurting and *angry*, that gave me enough courage to start climbing the fence.

I wasn't very good at it. Anton got his hands under my foot and gave me a boost. "Dig through the salt," he said urgently, as I pulled myself up and over, the round bar at the top digging into my stomach. I balanced there for a second, wondering if I should say something to him, maybe pass on some final words to my mom... and then my hands slipped and I half-tumbled, half-slid down the other side, landing on my feet more or less by accident.

I stood there for a moment, knowing that there wasn't nearly enough time for me to dig through the salt circle, that I had to stop Robert now. Was I really doing this? I wasn't a hero or a martyr. I was a recent college graduate with a tiny bit of magical power, and a knack for figuring out people's power levels that was apparently a lot weirder than I'd thought it was.

But I was all the neighborhood had. So yeah, I was doing this.

I took a couple of steps forwards, and then, with a rustle and a thump, Oona appeared over the fence and landed behind me.

She did it a lot more gracefully than I had.

"What?" she whispered. "Did you think I was going to let you go *alone*?"

I grinned at her, dizzy with relief, but there was no time to express how happy I was about the back-up.

"You do the salt circle, I'll handle the magician," I whispered.

She nodded, produced a trowel from the pocket of her adorable hoodie and started digging.

I set off, my ears straining for the sounds of an alarm, letting the other-else draw me towards Robert. He was laying down some sort of circle, carefully scribing the runes. It was taking more effort than he expected, and he was frustrated about that. How long was he going to be working with reduced power? God, it was nearly as bad as being Fourth Class again. Stupid werewolf chick, stupid redhead who'd gotten the job he should have walked into, and hadn't his master had something to say about *that*.

I pulled the curtain across my window into his consciousness again. It was getting easier, if no more pleasant, to take peeks at him and keep moving. He was in the center of the park, by the fountain, because it had the most space to inscribe the circle.

My eyes had adjusted, well enough that I could make out shadows and shapes in the dimness. Except in a blackout, New York is never completely dark. I kept to the shadows, walking as quickly as I dared, crouching over out of some half-formed idea that it would be more stealthy.

"How long will this take?" a man asked, and I paused. Oh, *fuck*. In all the panic, I'd completely forgotten about the night watchman.

Robert felt another surge of irritation at the interruption. "As long as it does," he said, and I heard his voice oddly doubled. "You'll know when it happens," he added, with a touch of malice. "Have you got it? Good. Put it there."

My heartbeat got even faster. They were talking about the artifact; they had to be. Okay, then. I'd been thinking I could rush Robert before he knew I was there, maybe knock him down and start hitting until Oona broke the circle and Anton arrived. No matter how talented a wizard you are, it's hard to concentrate on a spell when someone's trying their best to break your nose.

But I couldn't take on two of them. I'd concentrate on the artifact instead, because if I broke that, their plans were ruined. No matter what they did to me afterwards.

I couldn't think about that, or the fear would freeze me. I clenched my fists, held my other-else close, and charged.

There weren't two men. There were three: Robert; the night watchman in black jeans and a dark blue jacket emblazoned with SECURITY; and my old friend site manager Dave. They all swung towards me, but it felt like they were moving underwater. Adrenaline has a kind of magic all its own; time dilated around me, my motions smooth and sure.

Dave was holding something the size of a shoebox in both hands. I didn't really know how to fight, so I didn't waste time trying to kick or punch it free. I just threw my whole body-weight at him, aiming vaguely for his arms.

The shoebox—it *was* a shoebox—dropped to the silver-salted concrete.

Dave had staggered, but not fallen, and he seized me in a bear-hug, trapping my arms by my sides. I felt more than saw the night watchman reaching for his belt, and Robert was trying to untangle himself from the circle spell, probably so that he could do something really nasty.

I didn't care. Triumph singing through my veins, I reared back, lifted both feet off the ground, and stamped down on the box as hard as I could.

My feet tore through cardboard, hit something hard and un-yielding, and skidded off it. If not for Dave's accidental support, I would have fallen. As it was, he hauled me away. I got a final, desperate kick in, and succeeded only in bruising my toes.

Dave yanked me further back and shifted his grip to my arms. He did something that forced me to my knees, arms wrenched up behind me, shoulders already aching with the strain. My hair was coming out of my braid, falling limp around my face. The sound of my panting was harsh in my ears, and the adrenaline rush had fallen away to a shuddering, cold reaction.

I'd failed.

Robert had divested himself from the circle spell and was striding towards me. I flinched as he grabbed a fistful of my hair and wrenched my face up. "Is that *it*?" he asked.

I glared at him.

"Like, really, smash the artifact? That was the best you could come up with?" He went over to the box and pulled something free of the torn cardboard and stalked back, holding it up so I could see. "How were you gonna smash this, bitch?"

It was an uneven chunk of rock, about the size of my two fists. Even in the dim light, I could make out the striated layers and the polished metal runes that had been set in it. Serpentine, his other-else informed me. His mentor had worked over it until it was brimming with her power, and then Robert had done the inscription under her supervision, each rune carved and then filled with enchanted silver laced with the blood of magicians and humans. And then it had been handed over and hidden, because Callahan Construction didn't trust their hired magical guns.

"Were you going to use Galacki's Geological Deconstruction?" Robert asked me. "Or a splinter spell—I wish you had, that would have bounced right back in your face. Basic fire summoning wouldn't work, but Ling's Crucible might have at least melted off the silver." He laughed. "What am I saying? You don't even know what those *are*."

He was half-right. I had no idea what spells he was talking about. But his other-else was busily filling in the blanks, helpfully laying out matrices and power grids that spun through my dizzied brain and vanished before I could study them. It wouldn't have been useful anyway; even a brief glance showed me that all of those spells required much more natural power than I could summon at the best of times.

I was not having the best of times.

But my brain had started working again, and my hope was that I could *delay,* until Oona could bring help. How far down was that damn salt circle buried?

"So you tried to break it with your *feet,*" Robert said, and shook his head, smiling. "Useless."

I spat at his feet and he jumped backwards in disgust. "At least I didn't carve out my humanity," I said. "I wasn't so pathetically desperate for more power that I toadied to a dark wizard and *begged* to be her next makeover project."

His eyes narrowed and he grabbed my chin, fingers crawling painfully over my jaw. "Shut up," he suggested.

"And you couldn't even do that right," I said, forcing the words through my teeth. "Someone's in trouble." I lilted the words, like a grade-school tattle-tale, and he used his grip to shake my head, hard. Pain shot up my neck and I gasped.

He looked satisfied, then the malice turned into a thoughtful expression I liked even less. "How do you know about my master?" he asked.

I rolled my eyes, because if he thought I was just going to give him that information—and then my body went up in flames.

I'd thought the searing agony of Robert trying to use the piece of other-else he didn't have any more was the worst pain I'd ever felt. But that, after the initial shock, had been bearable. I'd been able to think and even to move. This much pain made it impossible to do either. It radiated first from his fingers on my skin, but in a flash my entire world was agony. Pain blazed across every nerve, blotted out all existence, all memory, until I came back to myself, face down on the ground, crumpled and sobbing at Robert's feet. I'd torn myself free from Dave's grip with my convulsions, and my shoulders felt weird, swollen and floppy at the same time. My scraped palms were bleeding again.

The flames had been imaginary, my body's frantic interpretation of what had been done to me. I wasn't even singed. But I'd do almost anything to stop him from repeating the spell. I'd tell him anything he wanted to know. I'd die, and be happy to die, if it meant I never had to feel like that again.

Robert's other-else was whimpering inside me, and my own was begging for me to put it to use, to try a shield or protection spell that might stop the torture from repeating. Robert's other-else timidly suggested a structure that a First Class might be able to handle, a simple lattice that prevented skin-to-skin contact. I forced my fingers to move and drew four lines on the ground, tracing each one with my other-else.

Robert, looking smug, reached out to grab my chin again… and his fingers slid off. My one in four successful spell-rate had come through this time.

"Fuck you," I gasped, through my own snot and tears. "I'm not telling you shit."

Dave grabbed my arms again. He could do that through my flannel; the spell *only* prevented skin touching my skin. It couldn't save me from being manhandled, or someone hitting me with something. It wouldn't stop a bullet, blade, nail gun or blowtorch. If Robert thought about it for two seconds, he could come up with a lot of ways to torture me that would be just as effective.

But he couldn't touch my skin, and he needed to for that particular spell. And even that minor obstacle was infuriating for him.

"It doesn't matter," he said, recovering his composure with visible effort. He glanced at the night watchman, who had his gun out, held at his side. "Kill her."

"Wait," Dave said sharply. "She might have brought help. You'd better check, Wayne."

"Take care of her first," Robert said, jerking his chin towards me.

"She's taken care of," Dave said. He shook my arms to demonstrate, and I gasped as my shoulders wrenched. "We don't need to go overboard."

"She's a witch," Robert said. "I thought you hated all of us, yes? No need to be so tenderhearted."

"You said it yourself, she's not much of a witch. And we're not your body disposal squad. Finish your spell, and then it's not an issue anymore."

Robert scowled. "Then I'll do it myself."

"You need to save your power—"

"Fuck you!" Robert said. "You don't give me orders! You don't know shit about power! Get back, or you'll go with her!"

After a hesitation so brief I might have imagined it, Dave let me go and stepped back. I collapsed, barely catching myself on my aching forearms. Robert pointed at me, and I could *see* the mauvais magic gathering around his finger, feel the electrical crackle in the air of the lightning he was going to call down on me. My life narrowed to microseconds.

Robert Luhrens was smiling.

And Bev Thornton stepped from the shadows and clubbed him in the back of the head with a length of two by four.

He went down like a sack of potatoes.

Bev was already turning towards the night watchman, hurling the wood at his gun arm, straight as a spear. His arm swung wide, the gun flying from his grip, and then she was on him, limbs moving efficiently, no wasted effort.

I didn't waste time being ecstatic that I was alive or fretting that Bev was here after all, the one place she definitely should not be. I crawled towards the serpentine stone lying in the middle of the circle, my arms barely working and my feet scrabbling to find purchase on the pavement.

The gun shot sounded like a car backfiring right in my eardrum, *way* louder than guns sounded on TV. I heard a breathy grunt, but didn't dare look around to see who was hit. The serpentine was inches away from my outstretched hand. With a final heave, I surged forward and got my bleeding palm on it.

Robert's other-else recognized the magic here. It had helped lay it down, so proud to be of service to its master. The ward patterns lit up to my metaphysical eyes, a careful tracing of intersecting energies. Every time someone from the excluded groups came near, it suggested they look away and wander off, either gently or with more firmness, depending on how much power they could bring to resist it. But before the ward could do that, it had to identify each person who came in range; that was why the silver was mixed with blood. The ward needed to recognize the nature and substance of power, the source and flavor of each person's abilities.

Oh. That was *easy*. I *knew* how to do that.

My blood was smeared on the stone's surface, and my other-else flowed into the artifact along the runic pathways, lighting up nodes like stars in a constellation map. Here was Anton, a banked fire of yearning, and there was Sam, with a hunger he kept well-hidden, even from himself, and Oona, a shifting, shimmering prism of multiple possibilities. I felt Hannah, a drifting presence tethered to the world by what she loved, and

Robert, who, even unconscious, was a roiling oil slick of dark power. Faintly, on the borders of the ward's reach, I could feel Tiffany's joyous ferocity. She was still hanging around, puzzled by her own disinterest in the park, when normally she wanted to know everything that went down in her neighborhood.

And I felt the three humans in here with me.

I'd thought I'd been identifying humans through a *lack* of inherent magic, but that wasn't it. They had their own aura, more subtle than the flare of magicians or the bright strength of a werewolf, but still there. Humanity felt like a bass note sounding so deep the ear couldn't pick it out under the melody, but grounding every other note of the music. Wayne was dazed and Dave was afraid and Bev was pure determination, layers of will so deep that I almost missed the life force bleeding away from her.

I didn't have the power to unbind these wards. But the artifact *did.* The runework had been Robert's, but the serpentine stone itself had been prepared by his master, which was the only way even an Eighth Class had been able to put together wards this strong. I caught the tiniest glimpse of her power, shimmering off the stone like the moon reflecting sunlight, and flinched away. The stone was anxious about that. It assured me that it was happy to be handled, and would be happy to help, provided I didn't attempt to violate its core function. Its goal was to protect this place, and the keep-away spell had been one way to do that.

I told it there could be a different way.

The stone warmed under my hand, curious. I tried to show it what I meant, imagining wards that would keep the park safe for everyone who entered. A place as protected as the subway, but aboveground, in light and air, with growing things and flowing water. What if the artifact could make everyone welcome here?

The artifact mulled it over for a moment and decided that sounded nice. The runes flowed of their own accord into new shapes I didn't recognize, but *felt* right, turning unbreachable walls into gates flung wide open.

"Thank you," I said out loud, the word slurring from my mouth. "Good work." I was floating in a golden pool of warm light, as happy here as I'd been miserable in Robert's torture spell. The neighborhood was waking, all those little stars of consciousness stirring. I could feel Tiffany's outrage as her head came up, scenting blood, feel Baz's bar full of customers realize something was up down the block, feel a blazing sun of wizardry come out of the shielded subway and bolt towards us, knowing Oona was in danger.

Now we just had to make sure these new wards stayed safe. The stone would be delighted to do that too. I gently pushed down on the chunk of serpentine and it sank into and through the pavement with no resistance, as easy as breathing. My palm was flat against the concrete, but my other-else followed the stone down, deeper and deeper, through the dirt and soil and soft rock beneath, until it nestled in the bedrock holding us all up. Here the serpentine artifact would protect this space until the world shook apart; I'd made this small piece of it safe forever.

My other-else floated up and into me and I came back to reality.

It wasn't great.

Robert Luhrens had vanished while I was in my golden haze, probably teleporting to safety again. His other-else was a small, sad lump inside me. Wayne the night watchman was down, and so was Bev. Even from here I could make out the dark stain on her white blouse, spreading across her abdomen. She was still conscious, and I think she must have had a charm that had stopped her from going into shock, but that was about the best that could be said about that situation.

Dave was standing over her, holding the gun she'd knocked out of Wayne's hand, breathing hard.

"That's Bev Thornton," I croaked, and he startled, twisting to look at me. "*The* Bev Thornton? Saved New York's kids from that vampire councilor, remember? You don't want to be the one who killed her, Dave."

He stared at me, then at her. "She's dying anyway," he said, harsh and helpless at the same time.

"Put the gun down," I suggested, and the wards reinforced the suggestion. The serpentine wouldn't let him actually pull the trigger, but he might hurt himself trying, and I just couldn't see the point. I was tired, so incredibly tired, and Bev was bleeding on the ground.

Dave bent down to put the gun on the ground and then backed away from it a few steps, looking freaked out.

I got myself to hands and knees and doggedly started the crawl to Bev, but I wasn't even halfway there before Oona appeared and threw herself down at Bev's side. She was absolutely filthy, and I found out later that she'd had to dig down nearly two feet with her little trowel; she'd hit the salt layer just as I'd repositioned the wards. Anton was hot on her heels, and he wavered a moment before he zeroed in on Dave, murder in his eyes.

"Don't," I said. "Don't, Anton. He can't hurt anyone here. And neither can you."

He wavered again, and then went to his knees and gathered me up into his lap, all of that incredible demonic strength vibrating with the need to hold me. He'd taken his suppressor off, ready to fight, but he didn't want me just now; he wanted to *protect* me, with a burning need as strong as his lust had been yesterday. And he made me want that too, so I snuggled into his arms, when I might have otherwise sent him to help Bev.

Fortunately, the others were there. Hannah had made herself completely solid, hands pressing over the wound while she spoke quietly to Bev, and Oona was speaking to emergency dispatch on her phone, the forced calm in her voice a contrast to the tears rolling down her dirty face.

"I've got this, babe," a man said. His calm voice was totally at odds with the roiling emotion I'd felt race towards us a few moments before. But it was definitely the same man, with the blaze of power that announced a Tenth Class wizard. I couldn't see him as clearly as when I'd been communing with the stone, but I still had my knack, and this couldn't be anyone but Blake.

I'd been imagining someone tall and imposing, but in fact he was a short man, with delicate features and straight black hair, a touch longer than business standard at the sides and back. He looked a little like Oona, actually, tan where she was pale, but with similar high cheekbones and full mouth. But while her mouth was made for smiling, his seemed more inclined to sulks. He bent over Bev and did something that was both beneficial and incredibly aggressive, like he was *commanding* her to heal. Bev gasped and sat up, batting at his arms, and he let the smashed bullet drop from his hands to tinkle on the concrete, then smiled at Oona.

She didn't smile back.

"Okay," he said, brushing off his hands and standing up. "What's next?"

"I've got the list," Hannah said. "If we're sure Bev's okay?"

"I'm fine," Bev said, her voice like gravel. "Check on the kid."

"I'm all right," I said, going boneless with relief in Anton's arms. "You're alive. Oona nailed it. I was here, and now you're going to live."

After that, things went a bit hazy. Blake healed my sprained shoulders and bleeding hands, but I'm not sure if that was before or after he started breaking apart the concrete with a series of precise, tightly controlled explosive spells. Deep beneath us, the serpentine murmured over the violence of those spells, but decided they weren't aimed at another being, and could be permitted. Sam turned up after that, and then Tiffany came charging into the park with what felt like half the pack, and Hannah had to bring her up to speed.

"What are you even doing here?" I asked Bev. "We tried to stop you from coming."

"Kid, you're going to need to learn how to sneak a lot better." She snorted. "Though I'll admit the birthday thing threw me off."

Tiffany gathered her pack and started a series of sharp, crisp orders.

The werewolves stayed away from the silver-dusted paths, but took care of the fae-repelling trees and flowers, and dug up the rest of the salt circle. Sam started work on the concrete, and then more people started coming in; a few goblins and humans from the bar, a pair of nixen who purified the aconite-tainted water in the fountain, and the bridge troll I'd seen the other day, who tore the rest of the concrete out of the paths. Zenith the succubus arrived with her boyfriend Mark, an older man with a terrible combover and permanent frown lines. He was Ninth Class, and didn't seem happy about Blake being there. I got the feeling he wasn't used to being outranked. But he found some subtle, malicious spellwork Blake had missed, and started pulling that apart while the goblins clambered over the playground equipment, checking for any hidden surprises.

The ambulance Oona had called arrived; they loaded Wayne into it, and Dave went with him, looking more than a little confused about how the night had turned out. Bev went home too, claiming more explanations could wait for the morning. Blake had a tense conversation with Oona, and then left, looking genuinely upset. I hoped he felt bad—he'd saved the day for Bev, true, but if he hadn't been playing stupid power games, she wouldn't have needed saving.

Bjorn and Jafr showed up from the garage with a pick-up truck they loaded with all the concrete and metal scrap. They drove off to the special waste disposal site under Manhattan Bridge. It wasn't going to be open at that time of the morning, but they didn't seem to think that was a problem.

Thomme arrived a couple of hours before dawn, wearing a tight sequined mini-dress and the highest platform heels I'd seen outside a strip club; they'd been clubbing downtown and had missed most of the excitement. I think it was they who called Raphael, who arrived shortly afterwards. He looked a little less business-perfect than usual in jeans and a polo shirt, his unstyled blond hair falling into his eyes.

I grinned at him from my park bench. Anton had deposited me there a few hours ago, when his incubus spark had suddenly noticed that I was all healed up and could probably survive a vigorous make-out session. He'd only just got the suppressor back on in time, and hurried off to help Tiffany break things, with red cheeks and an awkward gait. Everyone had wanted to send me home, or at least back to the rec center to rest, but I was staying. I had to see this through. I needed to see the park made the haven it should have been from the start.

Raphael stood there for a moment, looking down at me. "Well," he said finally. "It seems that setting you to oversee the park project was an even better decision than I'd initially thought."

"Oh, fuck you," I said, with enormous cheerfulness. There was a teetering moment while he decided whether to be offended or amused, and then he laughed, and sat beside me.

"What did you do to this place?" he asked. "I haven't eaten yet tonight; I should have to be exerting some self-control among all these warm bodies. But my hunger disappeared the second I stepped over the border."

I blinked at him, and he shrugged back. "That's the nature of my condition. I *do* exert self-control, of course. I have for centuries. However, at the moment, I don't feel the need to do so, and I should."

I told him what I'd done. There wasn't much point in keeping it secret that I'd done *something*. Blake had worked out that I must have reworked the ward artifact, and had been unflatteringly shocked that I'd been capable of anything that powerful and delicate. I'd told him the truth, mostly; that I'd desperately improvised my way through it, and the stone had *wanted* to help, providing all the actual power. I kept my knack, and Robert's scrap of other-else, to myself.

I didn't tell him that the wards were permanent, either. A permanent ward was ridiculous, the stuff of myth and legend. All wards wore away, or died with their creators.

This one wouldn't. I was sure of it. But I couldn't say so without seeming delusional or *way* more powerful than I had any right to be.

"Do you think the park will meet Lady S's standards?" I said, looking around doubtfully. We could put new plants in, but the paths were basically mud by now, and the viewing platform was being dismantled as we watched. The fountain statue of Joan of Arc was still there, because we hadn't known what to do with it. Her horse was trampling a dragon while she stabbed it with a spear, which was both more of a St. George thing, and definitely not something the historic Joan had ever done.

The dragon had vampire fangs. You could never accuse Only Humans of being *subtle*.

"I'll make sure she approves," Raphael said.

I relaxed a little, my shoulder leaning into his. "Thank you."

"You're most welcome."

Hannah was striding towards me, Oona trailing behind her. "You and Oona need rest," she said bluntly. "We're almost done with the demolition, and I'll supervise the planting when the delivery arrives."

"I want to see it done," I said, and Hannah shook her head.

"You have *work* tomorrow," she said. "The opening isn't until four p.m., and I'm declaring the rec center closed tomorrow morning. Go home, sleep, and be back here by two."

"Sensible," Raphael murmured.

"What the hell is going on here?" someone demanded, and we all turned to regard a red-faced man in a business suit, clutching a plastic folder stuffed with files. "This is a Callahan Construction project you're vandalizing!"

"And your connection to Callahan?" Raphael asked politely.

"I'm their lawyer, asshole! You're about to face the mother of all lawsuits!"

"Ah," Raphael said. "Mine, I think. Be well, Charlie." He caught my hand before I could react, raised it to his lips, and kissed the knuckles, a quick, dry brush of lips. Then he stood up. "Raphael Bergsen, Esquire. First, let's discuss the alleged contract your clients have with mine..."

I stared at his back as he hustled the man away, then blinked down at my hand.

"Ooh," Oona said. "Somebody likes you."

"Whatever," I muttered, which wasn't eloquent, but was definitely the best I could muster. "Let's grab our stuff and go. Still okay to crash at yours?"

"Absolutely." Oona looked ruefully down her body. She'd wiped her face clean at some point, but her clothes were a lost cause. "But I get first call on the shower."

We ambled back to the rec center, neither of us saying much. I felt emptied out but clean, the strange, giddy clarity that comes after a desperate all-nighter, once you've handed the paper in. Pass or fail, it wasn't in my hands anymore.

I did frown as we stepped over the threshold. "The building wards have finally given up," I reported. There wasn't a trace of them left.

"Oof, expensive. We can tell Felantheril tomorrow." Oona shuffled over to the reception desk. ""I'll make a sign for the door saying we're opening late. Can you grab my bag from upstairs?"

"Sure." I headed to the stairwell and clambered up, so tired I had to actively make myself climb each step.

Robert Luhrens was waiting for me in the office.

Chapter Nineteen

The only warning I got was from his other-else, screaming a frantic alarm. I ducked, and an honest-to-God enormous *sword* whistled over my head, his invisibility spell shredding as he swung.

He overbalanced, then got the sword back under control, grinning at me. There was blood on his teeth and dirt on his face, and he looked completely deranged.

"What is *wrong* with you?" I screamed, so frustrated that I nearly forgot to be afraid. I jumped away from the next swing. "You're beaten! *Be* beaten!"

"Never," he said, and tried a thrust. I was less successful twisting away from that, and I felt the edge snag on my shirt, slicing through fabric and just scraping the skin below.

I saw Bev's supply closet broken open behind him, which is where he must have gotten the sword. If I survived, I might have to talk to her about that. Destroying the wards on Bev's supply closet would have taken more effort than the building wards, but he'd still got in and armed himself.

The only good thing was that he'd obviously completely exhausted his magic for now, the last of it going into that invisibility spell. He had to rely on murdering me by mundane means. This was going to be difficult for him, not least because he clearly wasn't a swordsman.

But equally, I couldn't evade him forever. I was too tired and I'd made too many demands on my adrenaline supply, and if he managed to stick me with the pointy end, I'd be just as dead as if a professional did it. I watched his eyes, watched the tip of the sword, and as he shifted his weight and readied himself to swing again, I ran for it, bolting for the door behind me and the stairs down.

"Run, Oona!" I yelled. She was already poking her head into the stairwell to see what the noise was about, and she yelped and got out of the way as I came thundering down the steps.

Robert came after me.

If you've never run headlong down a steep flight of stairs while a mad wizard tries to slice at you with four feet of sharp metal, I can't recommend it. I was halfway down when his other-else shrieked again and I sat down abruptly on the steps with a thump that knocked the air out of me.

The blade buried itself in the wall. I twisted around, thinking maybe I could rush him while it was stuck, but he tugged it free, eyes shining with malice, and swung it back for another go.

The weight of the sword pulled him to the right. He staggered, tried to regain his balance, dropped the sword, grabbed for the hand rail that *wasn't there* and fell straight off the edge of the stairs, nearly a full story down to the concrete floor below.

He made an odd gurgling sound, his limbs jerked, and he went limp.

Oona and I looked at him, then at each other. His other-else hiccupped inside me.

"I think... he's still alive?" I said.

"Ugh," Oona said, and dialed 911. "I'm going to start getting a reputation with dispatch."

"We're going to have to talk to the *cops*," I said, and glared at Robert's limp body. "You fucking asshole. I'm *never* getting to bed tonight."

***

The cops were surprisingly nice about it. Perhaps it was the part where Oona and I were both pretty banged up, or perhaps it was the part where a scary blond vampire lawyer with political ties insisted that they leave questioning until "my clients have had a chance to rest, officer—you certainly wouldn't want this case falling apart in court because witness testimony had been extracted under duress." Oona and I both handed over our contact details and promised that we'd talk to the police when they wanted us or when Robert woke up, whichever came first.

Then we went back to her loft, two blocks south of the rec center, and I think I passed out before I was even fully horizontal on her pull-out sofa.

I woke up around noon to soft singing in the kitchen, as Oona finished the last of a stack of sour cream blueberry pancakes and handed them to me on a funky patterned plate, with a fork.

"My favorite," I said, and dug in.

She winked at me. "I know."

"Did you look into the future and see what kind of breakfast I liked best?"

"I think you might have been dreaming about pancakes," she said. "I'm not an oneiromancer, but the way I see things is close enough, if someone's sleeping near me. My subconscious takes it in, along with everything else, and throws me a vision. I woke smelling blueberry batter and knew what you'd most like to eat this morning."

"Well, these are amazing," I said, and forked another mouthful in to emphasize the fact. In the morning light, her home was gorgeous, a lovely little loft on the sixth floor of her building, two blocks south of the rec center. I'd have asked if there were any apartments coming up for rent, but it was obvious I could never afford to live there. It was small—this was still Manhattan, after all—but the high ceilings made it feel more spacious than it was, and she'd decorated with a lot of high-fashion prints and green glass ornaments.

"I love your home," I said.

"Thanks. Hey, Charlie?"

"Yeah?"

"Did your knack have something to do with how you fixed the wards?"

I put my fork down. "I think so."

Oona let out a controlled exhale. "Maybe don't tell anyone else that?"

"No," I agreed. "I don't think I will."

I was already going to attract some curiosity when the news about the park wards spread. I didn't want people to look any more closely at me, especially because I *wasn't* a secretly powerful magician, cunning and proud, who'd been hiding this whole time. I was exactly who I'd always been, and I'd just been lucky enough to be in the right place at the right moment, with an admittedly useful affinity for the task at hand.

If I was proud of anything, I was proud of that; that I'd made myself be there in time to do some good.

"Okay," I said. "Next problem. What am I going to wear to work? I brought fresh underwear. Do you think I can just get away with wearing yesterday's outfit again?"

Oona beamed at me. "That's not a problem. It's an *opportunity.*"

We walked to work together, Oona in a pale green shift dress with puffy sleeves, and me in a borrowed peach dress that went oddly well with my hair. On Oona, the dress probably gave the impression of floating around her in an ethereal cloud the color of sunset. On me, the fit was tighter, the hem was higher, and I had to wear my own shoes, black ballet-style slip-ons that really didn't match. It was still by far the nicest outfit I'd worn that week.

It was another bright spring day, like the first time I'd come down Thirteenth Avenue to the rec center, not even a week ago, on the sixtieth anniversary of the Cataclysm. At the time, I'd thought I was desperate, taking a shot at a job interview so that I could maybe move out of the suburbs. Well, I'd gotten that, and a whole lot more besides. I glanced at Oona. Not all of it was bad.

"What's that face for?" she asked.

"I just realized I'm going to have to start apartment-hunting," I said. "Do you know of anyone with a spare closet they could squeeze me into?" Oona's was probably big enough, but living with your workmate was definitely a bad idea.

"Put a note up on the community board," she suggested. "There are some decent places in the neighborhood."

For some reason, maybe something to do with the wizard who'd tried to kill me three times, I was a bit reluctant to enter the stairwell. Oona went first, which was kind of her, but when she gasped I was right behind her, defenses up.

There was a new railing on the stairs. It was beautiful dark wood, gleaming under the light, and just by looking at it I could tell it would feel wonderful under my hand, smooth and warm as I mounted the steps.

"Anton?" I asked, and then realized that it couldn't have been. Anton could have carved us a hand rail and attached it with metal brackets, but this one wasn't a straight line running up; it was a curved and twisting thing that looked as if it had grown right out of the steps.

"Felantheril," Bev said behind us. "Keep moving, ladies."

We went up, and I braced for a scolding, but she only nodded at both of us and said "Thanks," a bit gruffly as she went past us to her desk.

Oona's eyes were as big as I'd ever seen. I felt my cheeks go on fire.

"Next time, you *tell* me," Bev added, sounding much more like herself. "You did well with what you had, but I could have organized you a stronger team."

"Oona said you might try to stop it yourself, and die," I said. "Or that you wouldn't let me help, when I needed to."

She stared at me as if I'd developed two heads and started speaking Sanskrit from both of them. "Of course I'd take your help," she said. "Did you think I did any of it *alone*?"

I opened my mouth and closed it again. I *had* thought she'd done it alone, and from my glance at Oona, she was thinking the exact same thing.

"The stories..." I said tentatively. But I was already thinking about that last Bev story, the one where she'd called in so many favors and made so many deals that the councilman couldn't stop her. I'd known she had a network. Why hadn't I thought that she'd had a team?

Bev snorted and shook her head. "People love lone hero stories," she said. "They'll try to push you into one, if they can. But there's no such thing. We get the work done *together*." She glared at us for a moment, to make sure the message had gone in, and then turned her computer on, ignoring us completely while she played online poker. *Work* was clearly a relative term.

Unfortunately, I couldn't *not* work. The oath wouldn't let me. But we had no clients today, so for the next couple of hours, I checked the calendar and made promo graphics for each event coming up—Oona could use them or not, and it was nice, low-stakes stuff. There wasn't anything left for me to do on the park opening; Thomme had sent me an email telling me that everything was taken care of, courtesy of Lady S's office, since I'd already "contributed significantly to the success of the event."

I walked over to look at it anyway.

The park seemed smaller in the daylight. Last night it had been a shifting mass of shadows and danger, but now, with the fences taken down and the last of the scrap taken away, it was just a patch of green on the corner of the block, maybe a bit bigger than the footprint of my mom's yard in New Rochelle.

The muddy paths had been filled in with clean white gravel. I had no idea where that had come from, but it looked a lot better than dirt. Thomme's crew had put up tables and arranged red, white and blue balloon stands on either side of the fountain. Someone had diplomatically filed down the dragon's fangs, so Joan was now slaying a perfectly ordinary member of *Draco draconis*. The statue might piss off environmentalists, because most species of dragon were critically endangered, but at least it wasn't an anti-vampire statement anymore.

The biggest surprise was the new plants. They hadn't just been transplanted. They were flourishing, the peonies and daylilies in lavish bloom, the marigolds bursting with bright color. I blinked at the lilac and azalea bushes, which were taller and much bushier than I'd expected from garden center transplants, and then stared at the trees lining the back two walls of the lot. No, I wasn't imagining it. Those were cherry trees.

They weren't saplings. They were fully twice my height and covered in fresh green leaves, as if they'd bloomed the week before.

"Your boss did that," Tiffany said. She was lounging along one of the wooden benches, her combat-booted feet dangling off the edge, looking totally out of place and completely at home at the same time.

"Huh?"

"The trees. Felantheril walked in this morning while we were doing the planting, looked upset, and told everybody to get out and close their eyes. When we opened them, boom, all the flowers were in beds and there were full-grown trees." She yawned, exposing sharp teeth, and swung herself upright. "I guess she's useful for *something*. The Blood Moon pack officially owes you one, by the way."

She said it as casually as I might offer to pay for someone's coffee, but a favor from a pack leader wasn't casual at all. Tiffany had just officially placed herself and her pack in my debt.

"I didn't do anything for the pack," I said, more startled than pleased.

"Sure you did." She gestured at the playground. "Do you know what it would be like, if you were a kid, and you saw this, but you couldn't play on it? Couldn't even run along the paths or splash in the fountain? Summer's coming. This place is gonna get a lot of use." She gave me a level look. "We try to keep our children safe, always. But there are things we can't protect them from, a hundred thousand ways the world's gonna try to cut out their hearts. You saved them from this one."

"Okay, but... you'd already saved my life before that. Call us even."

She shook her head. Various piercings jingled. "That was me doing my job," she said, sounding very definite. "Gotta protect your territory to keep it."

I looked at the park, fresh and clean and safe forever. "I was just doing my job, too." For the first time in hours, I felt the oath at my throat. Right then, it didn't feel like a collar, choking off my air. It felt like a silk scarf, laid lightly across the skin.

It could still strangle me, of course, but it was being a lot nicer about the reminder.

"Yeah, okay," Tiffany said, and shoved up off the bench.

"Thanks for not telling anyone about the oath," I said, trying to make it sound like an assumption instead of a request.

Tiffany hesitated. "I won't," she said. "But like I said, you have a favor."

I frowned for a moment, trying to work out how the Blood Moon pack could possibly help me with an oath that I'd made to a High Fae—and then I did work it out, and jerked away from her.

If a fae holding your oath refuses to let you go, there's one sure way to break that bond. Tiffany had, in her casual, totally terrifying way, just told me that she'd be willing to kill Felantheril to set me free. She probably didn't *want* to—no matter how annoying Tiffany personally found Felantheril, her death would be bound to set off all sorts of repercussions in the neighborhood—but she was letting me know that if I asked, she'd try.

"No," I said, my mouth backing the decision my body had already made for me, recoiling in horror from the idea.

Tiffany nodded, and I didn't think I was imagining the relief in her eyes. "Okay. Well, if there's anything else you can think of to address that, and we can help..."

"I'll let you know," I said. Maybe there would be something. Other people had broken faesworn oaths, through trickery or clever interpretation of the wording. I hadn't really had the time or peace to go looking for answers, but I would soon.

"See you around," Tiffany said.

"You're not staying for the opening?"

She snorted. "I *was* here for the opening. You opened the park. All that fangy bitch is going to do is smile for the cameras and announce her mayoral run."

"You don't think she'd be a good mayor?"

"I think that if you give a vampire the tiniest fingernail scrap of power, they try to take the whole hand."

"Says the Blood Moon pack leader."

"Yeah," Tiffany said, her eyes flashing gold. "So I should know, shouldn't I?" She gave me a final nod and walked away.

I looked at the trees again, feeling that silk scarf across my collarbones.

"Charlie," Thomme called, and I headed over to where they were standing by the tables. Today Thomme was wearing a sort of parody of an 80s suit, a mini-skirt over black lace tights, and a huge blazer-cape thing with enormous shoulders that stood out so far from their body that the rest of the blazer just hung down, and their arms came out of two slits in the front, not the sleeves. Both the skirt and the blazer were made of the same black-and-pink pinstripe material, and they'd accessorized with huge gold ear drops and a chain belt.

Last night I'd seen Thomme pull a yew sapling out of the ground with their bare hands, but now they looked as fresh as if they'd spent the last three days at a spa and hired other people to touch grass for them.

"Are we ready to go?" they asked. "Only the press will start arriving soon."

"Sure thing," I said, and pulled on my final reserves of energy. "Let's do this."

***

The opening went fine.

Honestly, Thomme had everything well under control. I wasn't sure they actually needed the rec center crew there, but they seemed determined to make sure we were a part of the event anyway. Anton and Hannah were put on guarding-the-food duty, Bev was keeping an eye on everyone who'd showed up without an invitation, and Oona and I showed people the way to the bathrooms in the rec center. We all clapped while Lady Seraphine d'Arc made a speech about how much she and her illustrious ancestress both cared about protecting their communities, and then modestly announced the mayoral bid everyone knew was coming.

I'd been half-wondering if the Kellys had something planned, one last-minute wrench to throw in the gears. I wouldn't have put it past Marjorie for a second. But the speech concluded, and the press were permitted twenty minutes for questions, and nothing had gone wrong yet.

Most of the questions seemed designed for the smooth, funny, humble-yet-self-promoting answers Seraphine gave, and I was guessing Thomme had called in some favors with their friends in the press gallery.

I saw a ghostly hand shoot up from the middle of the pack, a bracelet of amber beads shining, and Seraphine nodded and said "Tilly?"

Letting her pose a question was the best move, because Tilly Bernbach was the longest-serving journalist in the city; other reporters followed where she led. Also, as I had reason to know, Tilly could be incredibly persistent. But I don't think I imagined Seraphine bracing herself just the tiniest bit.

"Any comment on the rumors that Callahan Construction is a front for Only Humans?" Tilly asked.

"You're the first one to mention that to me," Seraphine said, without skipping a beat. "I'm just delighted that the Thirteenth Avenue Community Rec Center, with the support of the d'Arc Foundation, was able to offer such a safe and welcoming place to the whole neighborhood."

"Follow-up," Tilly said, tommy-gun fast. "What's your take on Ian Kelly?"

You could have bounced diamonds off Seraphine's smile. "Like my fellow New Yorkers, I honor Mr. Kelly's work on the behalf of the defenseless in the terrible times that followed the Cataclysm. But New York is no longer defenseless. It is time for a new approach to city politics. We don't need to live in the past, but forge a future for *all* New Yorkers to prosper in our city." She gestured at the space around her, a wide sweep of her arm. The implication was as clear as her perfect skin. The park was an example of her munificence, an oasis of comfort and safety—and also the first step in her mission to make the whole city just as wonderful.

"She's taking all the credit," Oona muttered indignantly.

"Let her," I said. I won't pretend I wasn't a bit disgruntled about it, but it would draw a handy veil over my own role in the proceedings. "The people who matter know, anyway."

Tilly and a few other journalists had their hands up, but Thomme stepped up to the mic and directed everyone over to the refreshment tables instead. Journalists like free food as much as anyone, and Thomme's caterers were laying out trays of mini sliders, crudité platters, tiny blinis topped with your choice of smoked salmon or the carrot-based vegan version, and a lot more. There was a rush for the tables, and some people started wandering around the park, taking selfies and making videos, and occasionally asking Oona and I where the bathrooms might be.

In between bathroom requests, I listened to the serpentine, humming in its bedrock home, happy that so many people were using the space it protected.

Oona nudged my shoulder and coughed. "Cutie at three o'clock, checking you out," she whispered.

I looked, expecting to see Anton, but instead it was an even more familiar figure lurking at the edge of the park, wearing jeans, hiking boots and a flannel shirt. I'd recognize that silhouette anywhere.

"Laurence?" I said in disbelief, and his head came up, werewolf hearing picking his name out of the hubbub. Then we were moving towards each other, the crowds melting away between us. When I got close enough I launched myself at him, hugging him so hard he made a pretend-strangled noise—pretend, because he was approximately eighteen times stronger than me.

"When did you get back?" I demanded.

"Last night," he said. The breeze was ruffling his curly brown hair, which had gotten a little longer than the last time I'd seen him at Thanksgiving. I could swear he'd gotten even broader, too; he spent most of his free time hiking and the rest in the kind of gym that caters to supernaturals who can deadlift 300 pounds as easily as I'd pick up a book. But he looked exactly the same otherwise—still my familiar, nerdy Laurence with his sharp, observant eyes. "I wanted to surprise you."

"I'm surprised," I assured him. "How long are you staying?"

"Indefinitely," he said, and his smile widened. "I got a job."

"Here?" I said. "In the city?" Laurence had been studying ecology and magical zoology at Evergreen State College, way on the other side of the continent. I'd been more or less expecting him to disappear into the wilderness as soon as he graduated.

"Here. You're looking at the newest Halswell Green Society Ecological Specialist. They're putting me on a cryptozoological survey of Riverside Park."

"You'll be right next door!"

"Yep."

Anton was wandering over from the food tables, looking inquisitive. "Laurence, here's someone I want you to meet," I said, and held out my hand to Anton, who slipped his arm around my waist instead. I smiled up at him before turning back to Laurence. "Laurence, this is Anton. Anton, this is Laurence, my best friend since middle school. Our parents are next-door neighbors. He's coming to work in the city!"

"Hey, man," Anton said, and thrust out his hand.

"Hi," Laurence said, and shook it gravely. He frowned over Anton's shoulder. "Is that statue depicting a *Draco draconis*?"

I looked around for Oona, wanting to introduce her too, and saw her just a few feet away. She was staring at the three of us, her eyes glowing silver.

"What did you see?" I asked when she came towards us.

Laurence looked politely baffled, but Anton's attention sharpened.

Oona shrugged. "Nothing definite," she said, and then giggled for no reason I could see. "Charlie, we'd better get back to the rec center. Thomme says we're not needed here any more, and we've got to start organizing the donations for tomorrow."

"The clothes swap!" I said. "Right, I'm on it." I turned back to the guys, who were giving each other cautious, measuring looks. "See you two later."

"Sure thing, babe," Anton said. "Want a ride home after work?"

"I can do that," Laurence told him. "Got my truck parked on 96th, and we're going to the same place."

Anton looked earnest. "It's great of you to offer, man, but you'll probably want to get back out to New Rochelle earlier. Charlie works late."

"I don't mind," Laurence said. "It'll give me a chance to explore the neighborhood."

"We can sort it out later," I said. "Oona, what do you think about combining all the kids' clothes on one rack? There aren't many kid vampires or ghosts."

"Good call!" Oona said. "I don't think we've got a lot of werewolf clothes yet either, but I asked Tiffany to pass the word, and she thinks people will bring more tomorrow, so we'll need at least one spare rack anyway."

It was actually nice to be getting back to work.

Chapter Twenty

L ater, after we'd sorted through eight huge bags of donated clothing and hung them on the wheeled racks Oona had wheedled from neighborhood clothing stores, Oona and I went upstairs to take a break, and at least in my case, do some research.

Oona looked over my shoulder at my computer screen. "What are you reading?"

"Employment law," I said, and got up to grab some pages from the ancient printer.

"Why?"

"Uh... personal interest." I circled a few paragraphs with pink highlighter. "Is Felantheril in her office?"

"She can't authorize bonuses," Oona warned me. "Not that you don't deserve one for last night, but there's no budget line for them."

"It's something else," I said, and went before she could ask me what.

Felantheril *was* in her office, humming something to herself. I sat down in the chair in front of her desk without being invited.

"I've been thinking about my oath," I said.

"Have you?" Felantheril said vaguely. "That's nice."

"Most fae could have released me from my oath, if they wanted to," I said. "Because I didn't specify a time limit, but I also didn't say I'd work really hard forever. You could say, Charlie, you worked *really hard* on fixing the park problem, and I'd be free."

"You did work really hard on the park problem," Felantheril agreed, and I caught my breath.

But the oath hadn't released. When I felt for it, that silken scarf was still there, wrapped around my neck. Well, I'd reasoned that it wouldn't be that easy. Disappointing, but expected.

Felantheril sighed. "I am truly sorry." And that had to be true, because High Fae couldn't lie.

So she genuinely wanted to let me go, but couldn't. I fell back to the next part of my decision tree.

"In that case, I have to think that *you're* under some kind of binding. One where you're bound to another entity, and you have to interpret any oaths to *you* under the strictest possible terms." Which meant I wasn't just bonded to Felantheril, but through her, to whoever held her leash.

It was Robert Luhrens who had given me the idea, him and his mysterious mentor. I'd been right inside his head, and he'd never once thought her name or pictured her face. Something had prevented him from doing so, the same way Felantheril seemed unable to speak about why she couldn't let me go.

Felantheril was sitting very still, but her eyes were lighting up. "I imagine that any such binding would make it nearly impossible for the bound one to speak of it," she said. "To prevent the provision of explanation, or a request for assistance."

Now we were getting somewhere. "And if someone were to release the original bound one from the original binding, might it then allow them to grant freedom to anyone bound to them?" I asked.

Felantheril opened her mouth, but no words came out. She shrugged at me helplessly. But that, in itself, was a kind of answer.

I changed tack. "All right. Would you agree that I'm your employee?"

"Certainly."

"So actually, you *need* to tell me if there's anything I *can* do to get free. I know that in Faerie I'd just be your oathsworn servant, but here I'm your employee, and you're my boss, and that means you have a duty of care towards my physical and mental health, which is endangered by my oath." I pointed towards the relevant part of the printout, highlighted in pink. "And under the Faerie Accords Act, which you have ipso facto agreed to by residing in the iron world, you are hereby enjoined to make all reasonable efforts to assist me in breaking the bond."

Her eyes lightened. "Ooh. An interesting point."

"Well?"

She took a deep breath, opened her mouth, and gagged on air. She tried again and shook her head, grimacing.

My other-else was calm, but Robert's was going nuts. It was much better aligned to mauvais workings, and it could sense an old, malign magic, lazily stirring. My skin prickled.

"I need a pen," Felantheril said, her voice oddly breathy, and I offered her the printout and the highlighter I'd used on it. She clenched the pink plastic in her hand and touched the tip to the paper.

She was trying to write something. I could see her slender wrist shaking with the effort. But the pen didn't move.

I glanced at her face, and saw her eyes narrowed in unfamiliar effort, her teeth set in her lip. She set her jaw, and bit down hard. Dark green blood flowed down her chin.

"Stop," I said, alarmed. "You *really* can't tell me. I get it."

"I should be able to," she said, looking wild-eyed. "Oh, it was such a good solution. I wish I'd thought of it myself." I handed her a tissue, and she looked at it blankly.

I mimed mopping my chin, and she followed suit, looking at the blood she dabbed away with mild interest. "Better not leave any of that lying around," she murmured, and found a lighter and ashtray to set the green-stained tissue on fire.

Smoke rose. Felantheril's burning blood smelled like ripe apples and crisp nights. I fell into the warmth of wool wrapped around my neck, the taste of pumpkin spice lattes and tea spiked with bourbon, the crackle of firewood and the sound of crunching leaves under foot.

I pulled my mind out of the synesthetic haze.

Felantheril was looking at me steadily. Whatever bound her was far more carefully considered than my hastily spoken vow. She couldn't tell me who had bound her, or even confirm that she was bound, much less what I could do to get her—and myself—released from the bond. She'd left everyone believing she was a dryad, a low-ranking client fae from the Spring or Summer Courts.

But my weird knack had told me she was High Fae. And now her blood had told me which Court she belonged to.

It was probably the best clue she could give me. It wasn't much to work with.

But it was a place to start.

***

Mom was happy to see me and even happier to hear that Laurence was back; he'd driven me home and we'd talked the whole time about his new job and how fun it was going to be to be able to meet up for lunch and go to events together. We agreed that we'd look for apartments together too, once we both had some idea of what we could afford.

I kept a few things about my own recent experiences back; I wasn't going to keep secrets from Laurence forever, but I wanted to think about what to say, when.

After dinner, I settled in to do some research. Felantheril was powerful enough that she must have ranked highly within the Autumn Court. I was betting that she'd been exiled, and that it had something to do with whatever bond was holding her in the iron world—and also wouldn't let her release *me*.

Mom knocked on my door while I was deep in a comparative sociological analysis of the Faerie Courts that had been written by a human who'd actually visited them all, and left unscathed. He didn't have a lot to say about the Autumn Court that I hadn't already vaguely known, but I was taking meticulous notes anyway. At some point, my Columbia library log-in was going to stop working and I'd lose access to the journals database, so I had to get down what I could.

What I really needed was a family tree of the High Court, especially one detailed enough that I could trace any broken-off branches, but it was becoming increasingly clear that the reason the author *had* left the Realms unscathed was because he'd never been curious—or foolish—enough to ask that kind of question.

"Yeah?" I asked, in response to the knock.

"There's someone here to see you," Mom said. Her voice sounded stiff, and I tensed, but Robert's other-else didn't sense anything malicious. Still, I got up right away, and went downstairs.

Mom tried to escort me to the front door.

"I've got this," I said.

Marjorie Kelly was waiting on the porch, in another perfect shift dress, a light cardigan thrown over her shoulders for the evening chill. She was wearing court shoes and carrying a little purse, and if she'd had any magical talent at all, the glare she directed at me would have seared me to the bone.

I didn't have any right to be upset that she'd followed me to my home, because I'd gone to hers, but I was upset all the same. I stepped outside, closed the door behind me, and said, "What do you want?"

"It's a matter of what we both want," she said, tight-lipped, and reached into her tiny purse. I tensed again, but she pulled out an envelope, not a weapon.

A tattered, very familiar envelope, that held very familiar photographs.

I stared at it, then at her. "Where did you get those?"

"Oh, please," Marjorie said. "Don't play games with me. You're not that good at it. Anyone who knew what they were doing would have sent me their copies, not the originals. But I assume you weren't stupid enough not to *make* copies, so here's how this is going to go." Her voice was clipped and precise, as if she was using tongs to pick up something nasty. "You won't show anyone else these supposed pictures of my husband with that *disgusting* degenerate, and I won't indulge in any more... unusual tactics. Do we have a deal?"

It genuinely took me a second to realize what she was talking about, or rather talking around, but when I caught up, I gaped at her. "*You* hired Robert!" I blurted. "It wasn't part of his contract with Callahan. You hired him to kill me!"

"I don't know what you're talking about," Marjorie said, while her cold eyes signaled *Yes, I did, and I'd do it again*. She shoved the envelope back in her purse. The last time I'd seen them, they'd been locked in Hannah's desk. *Someone* had sent them to her, and she'd naturally assumed it was me, the woman who'd confronted her at her home.

The woman she'd tried to have killed.

"I didn't—" I said, and then shut my mouth. I wouldn't gain anything by telling Marjorie I wasn't the one blackmailing her. She wouldn't believe me. And if she did, I might just become an easy target again.

"Let's have a clean campaign. I think, on the whole, that would be better for the city. Don't you?" She held her hand out for me to shake, and I took it reflexively.

She used the grip to pull me close, her lips going to my ear. "If you ever fuck with me or my husband again, you will regret it for the rest of your very short life, you hell-bound witch," she said, a whisper just louder than a breath, and then she shoved me back. "My regards to your mother, Charlie," she said, much louder. "Good night."

I watched her walk down the front path to her waiting town car, her back ramrod straight, entirely human and incredibly dangerous. My heartbeat was thundering in my ears. Whatever she said, that woman meant me harm.

But I'd survived so far.

And I wasn't done yet.

About the Author

Karen Healey lives in New Zealand and writes cozy fantasy romance, science fiction, and young adult fiction. Kate Healey, who looks suspiciously similar, lives in New Zealand and writes spicy contemporary romance and urban fantasy.

Karen is an Aurealis and Sir Julius Vogel Award winner and has been a finalist for the ALA Morris Award, the New Zealand Book Award for Children and Young Adults, and the Andre Norton Award. Kate hasn't won anything yet, but give her time.

They both drink far too much coffee.

Sign up for my newsletter at http://thathealeygirl.com . You'll get the first news on new books, weird research rabbit-holes, frequent rambling on living a creative life, and occasional freebies! If you're interested in even more bonus content (and early reader copies!) check out my Patreon at http://patreon.com/thathealeygirl !

Acknowledgements

The Sparks and Recreation universe began with a setting that jumped into my brain and insisted I write it when I really didn't have time. I tried to turn it into a table-top role-playing game campaign instead. This wasn't an *entirely* successful avoidance strategy.

So I will start with massive thanks to Erin, Mads, Rebecca, and Chloe for expanding the world of Thirteenth Avenue and graciously giving me full control of their original player-characters to my own nefarious ends, to Magpie Games for creating *Urban Shadows*, a very good ttrpg about hidden magic and dark agendas that I shamelessly hacked into unintended shapes, and to Rev, Kim, Megan, Jake, and Tass of the CritShow for their excellent and inspirational *Urban Shadows* run.

I am, as ever, delighted to be working with Robyn Fleming, my development editor. Thank you for talking me through suppressors and listening while I painstakingly delineated the difference between magicians and wizards. I am newly grateful for the line editing and proofreading work of Adie Hart, and for Melanie Reese's stellar cover design. Thank you to Ellen, Delia, Libba and Barry for hosting me in NYC on various occasions and to Emily and Tara for giving location specific feedback. (Further, my apologies to Ellen and Delia for plopping another avenue in front of the river. I did leave you the park.)

Books are for readers. Thank you to everyone who reads and reviews and tells their friends and requests from the library and makes this whole writing thing both gratifying and possible. I also want to thank my hairstylist, Tash, who is responsible for probably sixty percent of the compliments I receive, and may actually be a curls wizard.

This book was made possible with the assistance of many Kickstarter backers and my lovely Patreon members. If you would like to join my Patreon at http://patreon.com/thatheal eygirl, you too can support my work *and* get early reader copies, a place in the acknowledgements, and bonus content! Special thanks go to Allie, Villephox, Rachel Halpern, Miriam Faye and SK Gaski for their support. You're all real ones.

Second Chance Charms

R ead on for an extract from the next book in the Sparks and Recreation series!

***

It started one Friday evening in early June when my boss handed me a creamy envelope made of some gorgeous thick parchment. On it was written *Charlie Cross* in calligraphy so ornate it took me a second to recognize my own name.

Oona, who was standing beside me at the reception desk, squeaked in excitement. When I glanced at her, her eyes had that silvery shimmer that indicated a vision, so I was guessing she already knew what was inside.

"Open it," Felantheril said.

The oath I'd accidentally made her a few weeks ago tightened around my throat, and I raised my eyebrows at her. We'd recently had a private discussion about her making commands in the workplace. I'd sworn to *work really hard*, and it meant I couldn't disobey even the most trivial instruction without the threat of dire consequences. Felantheril wanted my help to escape her own binding obligations. In return, I'd asked her to stop ordering me around.

"Please," she amended, making it a request, not a demand, and the invisible collar on my neck loosened again. I slipped my fingernail under the wax seal on the back and popped it open, shaking out the envelope's contents.

They were much more prosaic than the presentation. There were a paycheck and a payslip, explaining the deductions that had been taken from the original, pitifully small number to make it even smaller. And there was also a confirmation of employment letter. It had probably been typed by Hannah, who was our operating officer, but it was signed with Felantheril's looping, flourishing signature, in which I could just about make out an F and a t if I squinted.

I was no longer on trial. I was officially a full-time employee of the Thirteenth Avenue Community Recreation Center. The oath tingled against my collarbones and settled again.

"Yay!" Oona said, and hugged me.

I hugged back, more relieved than I'd thought I would be. "Um, I'm not sure what to do with this?" I said, flourishing the check.

"That's just for show," Felantheril told me. "Your salary will be paid electronically, by Hannah. Or maybe Sam?" She waved that away. The functionality of the payroll system was clearly beneath her notice. "Nevertheless, I thought you might enjoy the ceremony. Things are so much more *important* on paper, don't you feel?"

"Are we going to do this for all new people from now on?" Oona asked.

"Alas, it might be some time before we can welcome anyone new," Felantheril said. "The cost of the new wards alone... no,

I think Charlie might have to be an exception." Her leaf-green eyes widened at me.

I had my suspicions about those eyes. Felantheril's eyes and greenish hair and dedication to her plants all declared that she was a dryad, and therefore a lower-ranked fae of the Spring or Summer Court. I happened to know that she was High Fae, and a member of the Autumn Court, and tightly constrained from revealing either. She could only give me clues through hints and misdirection, and I had no way of checking if I was interpreting them correctly.

I looked at the signature again. It really was impossible to read, but surely it was too long to be "Felantheril". I folded everything back into the envelope, and took another look at the wax seal while I was doing it. It was red and gold wax, impressed with some sort of crest. The seal stamp had wobbled at the last minute, as if the person applying it hadn't been able to make a clean impression. A shield shape, and within it a smudged outline that could be a tree, or a cloud, or a Rorschach blot... I put the envelope in my pocket to look at later.

"Thank you," I told Felantheril. "This does feel important."

She beamed. "Lovely! Well, I'm off. You two girls have a wonderful evening." And she was out the door, waving an airy hand. We still had three hours left in the rec center day, but that was for peons like Oona and I, not the rec center director.

Oona turned to me. "We need to celebrate!"

"Anton and I were going to grab dinner after work."

"Well, of course Anton's coming too!" Her phone was in her hands, her thumbs blurring over the screen. "I'm texting Blake."

"Um," I said. I liked Oona a lot, but I wasn't nearly so keen on her on-again/off-again boyfriend. When Blake wasn't patronizing me from his lofty Wizard Tenth Class heights, he was trying to get me to tell him how I, a mere magician, and First

Class at that, had managed to twist some really nasty magic in the park next door into a ward that welcomed and protected everyone in the space. You couldn't hurt anyone in that park, including yourself. The usual scrapes and bruises from the kids playground just didn't happen.

I'd told him I didn't know, and I was sticking to that story, but the more time I spent around him, the thinner it got.

I was trying to come up with a way to say no, or maybe invite Oona to dinner *without* Blake. We were going to Vanessa's for dumplings; maybe once he heard that he wouldn't want to come.

"Fable at ten?" Oona asked, beaming at me, and I wavered. I loved dancing. I hadn't gone clubbing for a couple of months, what with finals and the job hunt and the long hours at the rec center, and I *missed* it. And Fable was my favorite club.

"There's a cover on Fridays," I said, and looked ruefully at my paycheck. "I'm not sure I should-"

"Oh, Blake will cover it," Oona said readily. "He'll get us a table."

I just barely managed to stop my jaw from dropping. I'd been to Fable maybe a dozen times since I turned twenty-one, and I'd never once dreamed of table service. The fees for those *started* at a thousand dollars.

Oona read my face. "I know, it's weird. But that's honestly pocket change to him."

"I don't think I've ever asked about his job," I said weakly.

"Research and Development at Dee Tech. Lab wizardry, mostly. He's working on mass teleportation at the moment."

Safe, repeatable mass teleportation was one of the holy grails of research wizards. If Blake could crack that, he'd be a billionaire overnight.

"Sure," I said. "Fable at ten. I'll let Anton know."

Oona beamed at me. "We'll have a great time!" she promised. Unfortunately, that wasn't a prophecy.

***

Oona had been totally correct that Blake would pay for everything. He'd casually tipped the bouncer a hundred as we walked past the queue, given the hostess another hundred as she ushered us to our seats, and asked for her to set up tequila shots. The hostess didn't tell him how much that was going to cost, and he didn't seem to care.

My mouth stinging with lime juice and salt, I hit the dance floor with Oona and Anton.

My boyfriend—and after only a couple of weeks, that still felt weird to say—would be hot no matter what he was wearing. Normally, he was a T-shirt and jeans kind of guy. But tonight, in respect to Fable's dress code, he'd gone a step further, and turned up in a short-sleeved black button-down and black pants. The button-down had a subtle glimmer to it, like a gold thread had been woven into the black, and it made his olive skin glow, his dark eyes deepen.

I wiggled against him, a quick hip shimmy that turned into a grind. Anton gasped, then spun me out so that I turned to Oona, who was tearing up the floor in her metallic mini.

I took the hint Anton and moved into Oona's space, shifting to incorporate her waving arms and off-beat hip movement. Even viewed through the lens of friendship, she wasn't a great dancer. But she was cute as a button and enthusiastic as hell, and that made up for a lot.

It didn't quite make up for not being being able to grind on my boyfriend, but those were the breaks.

Anton was part-demon, with a slate of powers from his incubus grandfather that he couldn't really control. The increased strength and toughness didn't worry him, and neither did his ability to hide unseen in shadows. But his pull, the power that made an incubus an incubus, had emerged suddenly when he was fifteen. It was an irresistible temptation. The enthralled person wouldn't be able to think of anything but Anton, of wanting to be with him, of wanting to touch him and kiss him and adore him.

The stereotypes about fifteen-year-old boys would have Anton punching the air and high-fiving anyone in range. In reality, he'd been terrified. The pull had flared up almost at random. It was worse for people he was attracted to. And his government-issued suppressor charm had only damped down the effect of his power.

Now, Anton had a proper, military-grade suppressor and wasn't in any danger of losing control unless he put it aside, but he was still understandably wary of the whole sex thing.

We were taking it slow. And while I respected and understood Anton's choices, I also really wanted to rip that shirt off and have my wicked way with him. Of course, he'd need to wear his suppressor. But I wanted him wearing *only* the suppressor.

For now, though, I let myself slip into the rhythm. My body went loose, my red hair swaying, my hips shifting to the beat. There hadn't been time for me to get home between closing and our booking, so Oona had taken me back to her place and dressed me from her expansive closet. I was half a foot taller than she was, so my pants were the same black slacks I'd worn to work. To be honest, I'd worn them dancing before, and they were a little too tight to be work-appropriate, but my other choices were limited and no one at the rec center had said anything yet. My top was actually a stretchy black thing that had been another minidress. The dress had a cut-out detail that went from my cleavage to my right collarbone. On Oona, the cut-out had probably been a classy peek at the assets. On me, the cut-out stretched further and showed a lot more.

The dance floor was filling up as more people got past the bouncers. I closed my eyes and let my magic expand into the space.

My other-else was the additional sense that made me a magician and not a baseline human. That, and liking Oona, were probably the only things Blake and I had in common. I'd recently discovered my ability to figure out what flavor of magic somebody was, and how powerful they were wasn't just a fun knack and the only reliable thing I could do with my magic, but a rare skill. Like, unheard of rare. And until I knew more about what was going on with that, I wasn't going to spread the word.

But that didn't mean I couldn't enjoy it. With my other-else sampling the air, I could taste the presence of everyone around me on a metaphysical level. I could feel Oona's shimmery seer power and Anton's half-demon heat—muted by his suppressor, but still warm on my back. Two werewolf girls wriggled through the crowd, and their strength straightened my shoulders. A pack of pixies were swooping overhead, and my fingers borrowed the bright sparkle of their movement. A trio of vampires had staked out one of the other tables, their hunger sated for the night, their desire lazy and heavy-lidded. And underneath it all, the deep bass note of humans, which the wards in the park had taught me to recognize.

I was surrounded, physically and metaphysically, my other-else thrilling in delighted recognition of the crowd. My world expanded into a varied, beautiful haze of sensation.

"Hey," Anton said in my ear, and I spun to face him, my arms looping around his neck. This time, I kept my hips out of the danger zone.

"Hey," I said, and he kissed me.

It was a soft brush of lips, with the merest touch of tongue. I melted against him, my body humming with the sensation. But I stepped back before I could give into the temptation to push for more, and saw the wry gratitude in his smile.

"You two are *adorable*," Oona shouted. She was sort of hopping from side to side, her hands wiggling around her knees. I looked at her to respond, and saw the exact moment her face fell.

Even from the dance floor I'd been able to feel the blaze of Tenth Class power that was Blake sitting at our table. Now, as Oona slowed and stopped, I also recognized the group of bright, but lesser lights walking through the club to join him. Five wizards, each Sixth Class or above.

"What's wrong?"

"I didn't know Blake had invited his friends," she said, and then obviously rallied. "I mean, he paid for the table, so I guess... and Messina's here, she's nice."

I turned to inspect the new wizards. Two men in button-down shirts and slacks, two women in bodycon dresses with strategic cut-outs, one person whose gender presentation wasn't clear, all of them glowing with good health and great hair and the kind of dental work that comes with a six figure salary. "Which one's Messina?"

"The younger woman, the brunette." It was hard to tell in the club, but I thought her voice went flat. "The older blonde is Jacqui."

Jacqui was Eighth Class, the highest ranking there next to Blake. She slid into the booth beside him and adjusted his collar, tossing her pale hair back.

"Okay, so we hate Jacqui," I said.

I wouldn't have been surprised if Oona defended her, however half-heartedly, but instead she nodded. "Jacqui is *not* a good person," she said.

Blake said something to the blonde, then scanned the crowd, spotting Oona and waving her over. He probably didn't care if Anton and I came back, but the friend code of conduct was clear. We tagged along.

"You all know Oona," Blake said, and held out his hand to her. "Move over, Jacqui." After a brief hesitation, Jacqui did, and Oona snuggled into Blake's side. "And that's Anton and Charlie. She's a Magician First Class." Anton, as a non-magician, apparently didn't rate a status check.

I waved. "Hi."

The others introduced themselves, politely enough, and my other-else automatically sorted them, matching names to power levels. Ren, Jameson, and Messina were Sixth Class. Karl was Seventh Class.

"Jacqui Deakin, Seventh Class," the blonde said, and held out her hand, an insincere smile plastered across her face.

My instincts went on immediate high alert. She *wasn't* Seventh Class. She was definitely Eighth, and there was only one reason she'd lie about it—her colleagues all thought she was Seventh, and they thought that because that's what her paperwork said. She'd gone mauvais.

Not fully mauvais—she'd only cut out a little of her empathy, enough to raise her a single Class level. It was still an ominous precedent. Whatever she'd lost the ability to care about, she'd never be able to care about it again.

For now, I smiled with equal insincerity and shook her hand.

And that was when my own special connection to a mauvais wizard woke up.

I had a scrap of someone else's other-else living inside me. Not even the police had been able to discover his real name, so we'd been calling him Robert Luhrens, the name he'd given the rec center. Luhrens was currently in a coma in a magical prison ward, after attempting to murder me three times. I'd picked up the piece of his other-else during the first attempt. Luhren's other-else was paranoid, and scornful of whatever it considered lesser enchantments (ie, everything I could do), but it did know a lot about malign magic, and it seemed to like me, in the same way a feral cat might show some affection towards a food provider.

Lately, I'd been calling it Bob.

Bob did *not* like Jacqui. The second my hand touched her skin, he was suggesting various ways I could bind her to my will or neutralize her as a threat, all of them completely horrible and way out of my power class.

No, I said, my internal voice firm. I didn't typically "speak" to my own other-else—that would be like speaking to my foot, or my tongue—but Bob responded better to verbalized instruction.

I got the other-else version of a sigh, and then a list of spells that a Magician First Class could maybe pull off. I could tie her shoelaces together, or telekinetically pull out her chair as she sat down...

Her shoes don't have laces and we're in a booth, I told him. *Calm down. She's not a threat.*

Bob disagreed, but he subsided into a muttering presence at the back of my skull. I let Jacqui's hand go, and turned to the group. "Nice to meet you all," I said brightly. "Do you all work with Blake?"

They did, and boy, were they happy to talk about it. The conversation became shop talk almost immediately, jargon and in-jokes flying across the table faster than the beat. Ren and Jameson got into an argument about something that had happened in a lab two years ago, and Karl spilled the tequila salt on the table and started drawing spellwork in it, loudly proclaiming how wrong they both were.

Anton huffed a breath, and I felt it warm on the back of my neck. "We could be eating dumplings right now," he murmured.

I patted his thigh, so conveniently pressed against mine and felt the hard muscle there twitch under my hand. "Give it another thirty minutes?"

I couldn't really regret coming out tonight. I was still buzzing from that moment of ecstatic gestalt on the dance floor, which had been worth any amount of snotty, work-obsessed wizards. But I *was* sorry Anton wasn't having a good time.

Messina, the brunette across the table, looked like she'd also been cut out of the conversation. I made eye contact, and she smiled at me hopefully. She was younger than the other wizards, with a round face and an impressive rack, barely contained by the stretchy fabric of her dress.

"How long have you been at Dee Tech?" I asked.

"Only six months," she said, which explained why she wasn't keeping up with the in-jokes. Blake's friends seemed like exactly the kind of people who'd throw a newbie in to sink or swim. "I'm learning so much, though! My job before that was in the city hall archives, and database spellwork is *so* boring. I mean, I'm still doing a lot of filing, but the documentation is much more interesting at Dee."

The closest I could manage to proper archival spellwork was a charm to alphabetize my citations, but I nodded in sympathy.

"You and Oona work together, right? What's the rec center like?"

I shouldn't have been so surprised that she'd asked me a question, and even seemed interested in the answer, but my expectations had been low. "Oh, it's great. Long hours, but great company, and the work is really interesting. Lots of variety."

"That sounds really fun."

"We're always looking for volunteers," I said. "Our Magic for Beginners tutor had to leave last week"—because she'd been teaching under the influence, but no need to mention that—"and we've only got an interim tutor for a few weeks to tide us over. You could stop by and check us out."

"Oh," Messina said, her eyes going wide and faintly hunted. "I didn't... I mean, work keeps me pretty busy..."

I grinned at her. "I'm just teasing. I don't really expect you to give up your time for a woman you've just met."

"Right, of course not."

"Unless you are interested, in which case I'm deadly serious."

She took a moment to check my face, and then laughed.

"So I told them, if you want Tenth Class results, you need to fund Tenth Class equipment," Blake shouted over the music. The table roared with laughter. Ren slapped him on the back, and Jacqui gave him a melting look.

He wasn't trying to impress them, though. He was watching Oona, who smiled peacably up at him and caught his hand in hers.

God, why were shitty men always into the nicest women? I didn't doubt that Blake genuinely loved Oona. A few weeks ago, I'd felt the hurricane force of his fear and shame when his careless pettiness had accidentally exposed her to real danger.

But if love couldn't make him *stop* being careless and petty, was it worth it?

Unfortunately, he was Oona's choice, and I couldn't make it for her. I chatted with Messina instead, who it turned out had taken a lot of History electives along with her data science degree at the Sycamore Institute of Magical Technology. We were in happy agreement over whether Henry VIII had been a wizard (no) and whether his fifth wife Katherine Parr had fae ancestry (yes). Anton seemed content to sit beside me, occasionally moving his fingers on my thigh in time with the beat.

Messina and I swapped socials, and I took the opportunity to check the time. Nearly midnight. I had to be at the rec center from 11 a.m. and I thought we'd spent enough time at the club not to be rude. I leaned into Anton.

"Do you want to get out of here?" I asked. "We could grab a slice on the way home."

"Yes," he said, and then glanced at the heaving floor. "Do you want to go out there again first?"

I weakened. "One last dance?"

He grinned at me. "You go ahead."

I stood up. "I'm heading to the floor," I said over the music, to no one in particular.

Messina stood too, tugging the hem of her dress down. Her platform heels were high, but she moved easily in them. "I'll come with you," she said happily. I gave Oona an inquiring look, but she shook her head, snuggled happily against Blake's side.

Oh well. Messina was a good dance partner. Her generous curves drew attention, and we were soon surrounded by an admiring crowd, including one of the vampires I'd spotted before. But apparently Messina wasn't to his tastes. He waited for one track to slide into another, slightly slower one, and slid in beside me. "You're the most beautiful woman I've seen in centuries," he said, flashing his fangs as he smiled.

I laughed. "Please. I'm not even close to the most beautiful woman in this club."

"My tastes are more refined than those of mortal blood," he crooned, which probably just meant he had a thing for red-heads. He was lying about the "in centuries" thing too—he looked to be in his mid-thirties, and my other-else had pegged him as being a vampire for less than a decade.

"No, thanks," I said, and turned away. He moved faster, plac-ing himself in my field of vision, trying to catch my eyes with his own. I had one split-second when I recognized what he was trying to do, and yanked my gaze away before he could try to enthrall me. "Hey, asshole!" I said, and stepped back. "Back off!"

"Or what?" he sneered, and shifted close again. Messina was just starting to realize something was wrong, breaking from the circle of her own admirers.

"Or me," a voice said cheerily, and two gnarled, clawed hands gripped the vampire's shoulders tight. "Hello, Charlie lass."

"Erik," I said gratefully. On first glance, my favorite bouncer looked like a short, heavy-set man, prematurely gray, with thick white eyebrows and teeth that had never seen a dentist. On second glance—especially if you were looking at his arms, which were nearly as long as he was tall, and featured huge hands with sharp talons—it was clear he wasn't a human man at all.

Erik was a redcap, a kind of goblin, and the cherry red news-boy cap perched on his head wasn't just a nice contrast note against his bouncer black shirt and slacks. Once, his hat had soaked in the blood of his enemies—who were really the ene-mies of his High Fae liege lord. Erik, like a lot of "lesser fae", had come to New York to get away from the feudal servitude of the

Fae Realms. Now his hat got soaked in the occasional broken nose of a belligerent patron at Fable.

"Time to be on your way," Erik told the vampire, his voice deceptively genial. "And don't be coming back again."

The vampire, proving himself to be stupid as well as an asshole, tore free from Erik's grip. His fangs fully descended, he snarled at the goblin, lunging forward.

This time, Erik caught him by the throat.

The vampire's feet came off the ground. Erik's armspan was long enough that he could hold the vampire completely away from his body. The vampire could only kick and punch at his arm, but he did that with a vicious will. If one of those blows had hit me, I'd need an ambulance. Erik just stood there, calm and unaffected, in the middle of the rapidly clearing dance floor.

Not *completely* clearing, of course. Every New Yorker loves a floor show, so while people were getting out of range, they were also making sure to get a good view. People were even getting up at the tables, craning to see what was going on. More black-clad bouncers were pushing through the crowd.

The DJ didn't stop, though she did turn down the volume. Priorities.

I couldn't be too judgy about it, because even as I got out of range, I'd made sure that I had a front-row seat. I ended up standing beside Messina, whose hands were glowing with a faint radiance.

"Are you okay?" she said urgently.

"I'm fine."

"What happened?"

"He tried to snare me."

Her face went set and hard and the glow around her hands got brighter. Vampire snaring acts a little like Rohypnol on a victim's will, and decent people react with the same disgust to either.

I could feel Anton making his way towards me, hindered by the crowd, and hoped he hadn't taken his suppressor off in the urgency of the moment. The same incubus instincts that made him irresistibly attractive to me without it also made him highly protective. If his powers weren't damped down, he might be driven to attack the vampire who'd tried to harm me, and that would get us both kicked out of my favorite club.

There was a whisper of movement and my other-else pinged just as the other two vampires arrived in the middle of the cleared space. I hadn't seen them come. Unlike my assailant, these two *were* centuries old, with the power to match. That made them pre-Cataclysm, which meant they'd survived the long years before magic came back to the world.

I hoped that also meant they were good at conflict negotiation. Three vampires versus a redcap might just be a fair fight. It would also cause a lot of collateral damage.

Erik turned to face them, still holding their comrade up by the throat. A human would have passed out by now, but vampires don't need to breathe. He went limp anyway, possibly realizing that he might be in more trouble than he thought.

"Did Trevor cause some offense?" one of the vampires asked, her alto voice smooth.

Erik gestured with his free hand at me, but didn't take his eyes off the two of them. "He tried the charming eye on this young lady."

The vampire turned to look at me. She was racehorse lean and muscular, with the calm oval face and high hairline that had been the height of beauty in the Renaissance. "Is this so?"

"Yes," I said, very glad I could be honest. Some vampires—like my kind-of lawyer Raphael—could tell if you were lying.

She made a disappointed noise, and then signaled her partner, who held her arms out for Trevor. "My apologies. We'll leave now."

Erik didn't move.

"He's to stay out of Fable," he said. "And seek no revenge."

"We'll make sure of it."

Erik let the silence stretch.

"My word on it," the vampire said, with an air of resignation, and Erik dropped Trevor into his compatriot's waiting arms. A promise to a lesser fae wasn't quite as life-or-death as the oath I'd made Felantheril, but nobody sensible would break one, and this vampire struck me as the sensible type.

Trevor looked bruised and weak in the other vampire's arms. I refused to feel sorry for him.

The vampires left without another word, Erik moved back to his position by the wall, and the DJ turned the volume back up.

With the crowd thinning out, Anton finally got to me. "Hey," he said, scanning me quickly, then pulling me in for a hug. "All good?"

I breathed out, letting myself consider the question. I wasn't *happy* about the situation, but I did think it had been handled. "Yeah, I'm okay."

Messina hadn't moved. "Isn't anyone going to call the police?" she asked.

Anton and I both looked at her.

"Um, no?" I said.

"But he tried to enthrall you!"

"Yeah, but the cops aren't going to do anything about that." And anything they did do might make things worse, depending on how those particular cops viewed vampires, fae, or magicians, what kind of day they'd had, and if they were mad about something.

"They have to. It's against the law."

"Sure," I said, as kindly as I could. "But, you know, it's taken care of now, so there's really no need. Look, I've got work tomorrow, and I think Anton and I are going to head out. But it was super nice to meet you—I'm serious, drop by the center some time, and Oona and I will show you round."

"I will!" she said, cheering up immediately.

"Charlie? Charlie, that is you!"

A slender, dark-skinned woman had emerged from the crowd, her face tight with concern. After a shamefully long moment, I placed her—Simone d'Aburnay, my former dormmate at Columbia College.

"Hi, Simone. Don't worry, I'm fine."

She frowned. "What?"

"Oh, uh—I thought you were talking about the incident just now?"

"What incident?" She shook her head. "No, but I'm glad to see you. We need your help!" She leaned in close, her eyes glossier than usual, and I caught the alcohol on her breath as her voice became soft and urgent. "It's an emergency."

***

The emergency was a stained dress.

I texted Anton to let him know everything was fine and I'd be a few moments, and then focused on the problem at hand. The unbreakable code of drunk girls in club bathrooms required me to do what I could to fix the issue, but I was only two shots down, and way too sober to treat this emergency with the solemnity Simone obviously thought it deserved.

"It was an entire pitcher of sangria," said Kelsey, the girl in the dress in question. It had previously been lovely, draping her body in a series of intricate white folds that looked fantastic with her smooth brown skin. But she'd obviously tried to rinse it out while she was still wearing it, and now she was wearing a wet, partially transparent dress with a huge, dark red splash stain over the torso. "Who drinks sangria in the club?"

"Don't worry," Simone said, patting her shoulder. "Charlie's a wizard! She can fix it."

"I'm a magician," I said hastily, and shot a glance at Messina, who'd come in with me. She didn't seem the type to get snotty about people mistaking me for the real deal, but you never knew. "Maybe a drycleaner would be a better idea?"

Messina was looking at the dress with an appraising eye. "I don't think drycleaning could fix that."

Kelsey burst into tears.

Simone hugged her fiercely. "No, no, Charlie can help you! She helped me get a chocolate stain out of my favorite jeans!"

"Your vintage Sevens?"

"Yes!"

Kelsey gulped for air. "Those jeans are so cute on you."

"That was a much smaller area," I pointed out.

"Please?" Simone said, fixing her big, dark eyes on my face. "Kelsey borrowed this dress from her roommate."

I blinked. "Did her roommate know?"

"Yes, of course," Kelsey said indignantly.

Messina looked confused. "Just buy her another one."

Kelsey dabbed at her eyes. "Obviously I would but I looked the dress up online and it costs nineteen hundred dollars!"

Okay, well, that was serious. From Messina's face, she didn't understand why it might be a problem, but she at least didn't say it out loud.

An older woman stepped out of the stall and went to wash her hands. "Honey, I've got some tissues in here for you," she said, and fished around in her purse, pressing them into Kelsey's hand. A tall half-demon woman with spectacular, curling horns offered her a breath mint. Bathroom code.

"All right," I said. "No promises, but I'll see what I can do." I had one sometimes-reliable laundry spell that was usually good for removing small stains, but I wasn't sure how it would handle this Jackson Pollock crime scene. I poked Bob, just in case he had a better spell, but he was no help to me; domestic magic wasn't something Robert Luhrens had ever bothered with. I was assuming Messina felt the same way, or perhaps she didn't know she should be helping another woman out. Either way, I didn't really want her judging my efforts from her Sixth Class heights, but there seemed to be no help for it.

I took a deep breath, mentally crossed my fingers, and physically swept my real fingers over the stain. The little rhyme I said with the gesture was really just nonsense syllables, a focus for my other-else to latch onto.

My other-else seemed more enthusiastic than usual. Maybe it was just trying to show off to Bob, who it seemed to regard as a belligerent cousin. It valiantly flowed down my fingers and into the fabric, painstakingly stripping the fibers of their unwanted color and shifting them back to their original, shimmering white. I moved my hand down Kelsey's stomach and across to her hip, not quite making contact, as my magic cleared the stain.

I was just starting to believe that I could actually pull this off when my other-else winced, faltered, and pulled back inside me.

I sighed and stepped back. "Sorry," I said. "That's the best I can do." Most of the stain had gone, but there was still a noticeable splotch at the hip.

Kelsey sniffed, and gave me a watery smile. "Thanks anyway. Maybe the drycleaner can take care of the rest."

"No, we can fix it," Simone said. She wobbled in her heels as she straightened up, which was odd. Simone had double-majored in Biology and Chemistry, and even in our currently awful job market, she'd walked straight into a position at a food science research lab. She worked hard, and she liked to party in moderation, but I'd never seen her messy enough to lose her footing. Her eyes were still bright, with that glossy sheen I'd noticed before.

"We just need some water," she continued, and stumbled over to one of the basins.

"You okay, girl?" Kelsey asked.

"Great!" Simone told her. Her teeth were straight and white and... a little bit sharper than they had been before? "Just need a little bit of water." She held her hand over the faucet.

She didn't turn it on. And yet water began to flow, gushing out of the faucet with such ferocity that the tiny basin overflowed. The woman next to her exclaimed and jumped back as her own faucet exploded. Through the walls next to us, I could hear shouting from the male and gender-neutral bathrooms.

"What the hell?" Messina asked, and then there was an explosive roar and screaming from the stalls.

"Stop it!" I said, staring at Simone. Sodden, yelling women were crowding the small space, and Kelsey wasn't the only one drenched to the skin.

Simone looked at me dreamily. Her eyes, normally dark, had gone bright blue, the color of the ocean on a summer's day. "We only need some water," she assured me.

That was when the sprinklers went off.

Simone fainted. I lunged forward to catch her before she hit the ground, barely managing to keep her head from bouncing off the tiled floor.

Simone and I had known each other for four years. We'd lived on the same floor for two of those years, trading homework help in the humanities and sciences, passing each other in the hallways, grabbing meals and celebrating wins. We weren't besties, but I knew and liked her.

And I knew she was human.

So why, while I knelt on the wet tile with her head in my lap, was my other-else telling me she was fae?

Also by the Author

As Kate Healey

Sparks and Recreation series:
Magician First Class
Second Chance Charms

Olympus Inc. Series:
Penelope Pops the Question.
The Love Labyrinth (standalone novella)

Arc One: The Olympians
#1 *Persephone in Bloom*
#2 *Aphrodite Unbound*
#3 *Hera Takes Charge*

Arc Two: The Trojan Women
#4 *Ask Cassandra*
#5 *Love, Laodice*
#6 *XO, Xena*

As Karen Healey

The Movie Magic Series:

"Taylor Made" (a newsletter freebie, available when you sign up
at http://thathealeygirl.com)
Bespoke & Bespelled
Savory & Supernatural

The Hidden Histories Series (with Robyn Fleming):

The Empress of Timbra
The Spymaster's Apprentice

Young Adult Works:

What We Reach For: Three Stories of Love and Magic
Guardian of the Dead
The Shattering
When We Wake
While We Run